W9-APX-618

WITHDRAWN

FLANNERY

Flannery

LISA MOORE

Groundwood Books
House of Anansi Press
Toronto Berkeley

Published in Canada and the USA in 2016 by Groundwood Books

Groundwood Books / House of Anansi Press
groundwoodbooks.com

We acknowledge for their financial support of our publishing program the Canada
Council for the Arts, the Ontario Arts Council and the Government of Canada.

 Canada Council   Conseil des Arts   ONTARIO ARTS COUNCIL
for the Arts   du Canada   CONSEIL DES ARTS DE L'ONTARIO

With the participation of the Government of Canada   Canadä
Avec la participation du gouvernement du Canada

Library and Archives Canada Cataloguing in Publication
Moore, Lisa Lynne, author
Flannery / Lisa Moore.
Issued in print and electronic formats. ISBN 978-1-55498-076-5 (bound).—
ISBN 978-1-55498-873-0 (epub).—ISBN 978-1-55498-874-7 (mobi)
I. Title.
PS8576.O614444F53 2016   jC813'.54   C2015-904606-8
C2015-904607-6

Jacket illustration by Carey Sookocheff
Design by Michael Solomon

Groundwood Books is committed to protecting our natural environment. As part of our
efforts, the interior of this book is printed on paper that contains 100% post-consumer
recycled fibers, is acid-free and is processed chlorine-free.

Printed and bound in Canada

For the gang from Livingstone —
Emily, Shannon, Eva, Theo and Angel
(and gang associates Rachel, Ben, Max and Jack)

1

————

I'm walking up Long's Hill, hoofing it because I am about to be late for school. Again.

If you're late for school you get an automated phone call. A fake-human voice, faux-friendly and regular-guy-sounding, calls to rat you out.

A child in your household named — and when it says "named," the voice changes. A completely different voice inserts your name right into Regular Guy's sentence.

And the second voice is very disappointed in you. The second voice sounds all blamey and sad and rumbling like a clap of thunder. The voice says FLANNERY.

And after your name it goes back to the first voice.

Regular Guy. Mild-mannered guy, who is just doing his job.

A child in your household named *Flannery* was absent for period one on September 17th. Regular Guy goes on to tell whoever picked up the phone that they better send a note explaining why *Flannery* was absent, or else the child in your household named *Flannery* will be condemned to the bowels of hell from now to eternity.

Yesterday was the third phone call since I started grade twelve, a mere two weeks ago.

I'm always the one to answer the phone. Miranda, my mother, never answers the phone. She hates the phone.

Then I have to write myself a note and forge Miranda's signature because if she does it, she'll write a manifesto about how she doesn't believe in punctuality. She believes punctuality promotes conformity, and high-school kids need more sleep and fewer alarm clocks screaming through their early-morning dreams.

I usually have to write the note the next morning. I am tearing through the house looking for a piece of paper to write the note and then I'm late again.

So this morning I am hoofing it, because otherwise, tomorrow FLANNERY will receive phone call number four.

First period is Entrepreneurship. It's the last elective I need to graduate high school and, frankly, the only one that fits into my schedule.

It's raining in slanting sheets and my jeans are plastered onto my thighs and I'm trying to think of what my unit is going to be. The unit I'm going to produce for 60 percent of my grade in my Entrepreneurship class.

Mr. Payne advised us to think about the sorts of things people don't have already. Things they only realize they want the instant they clamp eyes on them.

You have to create a desire for your product, Mr. Payne said. Where, hitherto, there had been no desire and no need at all. That is the essence, he said, the very soul of being an entrepreneur.

For instance: furry toilet-seat covers, pet rocks, fluorescent-pink feather dusters, avocado scoopers, ice-cube trays molded into starfish, and Christmas sweaters with lights that blink on and off. Mr. Payne had a PowerPoint presentation and he flicked through images of these items.

Next there was an image of a vegetable juicer. Then a yogurt maker and a massage chair with straps and buckles that looked medieval. Then an image of fridge-magnet words so people could make poetry on the front of their fridges while sipping their morning coffees.

All things people got along fine without until they were invented, Mr. Payne said. He closed the lid of the laptop.

That's the sort of thing, Mr. Payne continued, that you should design for your unit. You have to intuit what the world is waiting for, because the desire for new products is insatiable. Make something new or reinvent something old so it appears to be new.

Stuff, he said. Let's make stuff.

Rumor has it that Mr. Payne once invented a grain-sized microchip that could be inserted painlessly between a child's shoulder blades and was sensitive to the biometric changes that occurred whenever the child told a lie. A fluctuation in temperature, quickening of the pulse, dilation of the pupils and sweaty palms. The microchip was said to emit a high-pitched alarm on the parent's key chain when the lie rolled off the tongue.

Apparently it did not take off. But Mr. Payne still has the black hairy eyebrows and gelled helmet hair of a scientific genius.

First I was thinking a waterproof bra. A waterproof bra that actually fits properly. I am a girl with big boobs, and an innovative bra design could revolutionize the lingerie market.

A bra that could offer a girl support.

But a bra might be embarrassing to present in front of the class.

So now I'm thinking a designer toilet plunger. Something with polka dots or stripes.

The design of your typical household plunger never really changes. Everybody has the same plunger. Black rubber bell, wooden handle. Nobody ever really seems to buy them, but everybody has one. Where do they come from?

But maybe there's room for a plunger with pizzazz. After all, the humble plunger has a noble function; it removes stoppages.

That's what they're called: stoppages.

Things that get in the way of the natural flow. Why not celebrate that simple service with a few polka dots?

And there, in the middle of Long's Hill, water wheezing through my Converse sneakers with every step, I experience one of those stoppages. I see Tyrone O'Rourke flying through a red light on his motorcycle. He takes the corner and a huge splash flies up and he's gone.

I feel the stoppage under my ribs.

I picture a polka-dotted plunger with cosmic suck, the big suck clamped onto my chest, right over my heart.

This is how Tyrone makes me feel: *boom, boom, boom.*

I imagine the Angel of Love giving the cosmic plunger a little elbow action. Before you know it: *plop.* My purple, gushing, blood-squirting, shivering heart is sucked way the hell out of my body straight into that rubber receptacle.

The heart ripped, torn, stamped on, minced and mangled, flushed down the crapper. That's what love with Tyrone would be like.

Our mothers gave birth to Tyrone and me a few hours apart in Grace Hospital. That's how they met. They were sharing the hospital's industrial-sized breast pump. No wonder they ended up bonding with each other. They were both single mothers and they rented public housing on opposite sides of the same street.

Tyrone and I ran around in diapers together at Happy Kids daycare. There's a photo of the two of us and Tyrone's mom on the first day of kindergarten, on the school steps. Tyrone has a brand new Transformers knapsack; I have a Dora the Explorer lunchbox. He's holding his mom's hand and looking up at her, but she's got her head turned the other way. She's looking down the street as if something big and important has her attention — maybe a three-car pile-up or a good-looking guy.

But when Tyrone's mom met Tyrone's stepdad, they moved out of downtown and up to an apartment behind the Super 8 with the eighty-foot water slide.

So Tyrone was zoned for Macdonald Drive Junior High then, and I was going to Brother Rice. Things just changed. Tyrone was into basketball for a while, then skateboarding. I got on the school newspaper.

In grade nine everybody at Brother Rice transferred to Holy Heart for high school and in grade ten, everybody from Macdonald Drive transferred to Heart too. And there, on the first day of grade ten, a head taller than everyone else in the sea of students thronging down the corridor, was Tyrone/not Tyrone.

I mean, he had the same big brown eyes as the Tyrone I knew by heart, with the sooty black eyelashes. The same black curly hair — but now it was long, near his jaw. His once-pudgy little cheeks were sharp-angled cheekbones. He had the same gangly lope, but now I had to look up at him.

He was the same Tyrone O'Rourke who made a Tyrannosaurus rex out of Play-Doh in kindergarten when we were supposed to be making farm animals and the teacher peeled it off the palm of his hand and squished it, telling him to start again. A dinosaur is not a farm animal, she said.

Maybe that was the beginning of Tyrone's troubles at school.

He was the same Tyrone who, when we were eight, rode down Long's Hill in a supermarket shopping cart, the whole thing rocking and jittering and then tipping on two wheels, gathering speed as it headed for the harbor until the front left wheel nicked a pothole and we crashed into a parked car. I was flung over the hood, unharmed — except for an everlasting fear of shopping carts.

But Tyrone landed on his feet, also unharmed — with an everlasting fear of absolutely nothing.

This grade-ten Tyrone had the same megawatts of trouble/ glee in his eyes — but this was not the same Tyrone as the eight-year-old who tried to tame the bucking bronco of a shopping cart.

This Tyrone had big shoulders and a jean jacket so faded and worn it seemed like a second skin. This Tyrone made all the girls in the corridor fumble with their binders and flick their hair over their shoulders as he walked by, hoping to get his attention.

This Tyrone was not only very different from the Tyrone I'd played with almost every day from K through six; he was different than every other boy at Holy Heart.

He did not walk in a cloud of nose-lacerating cologne, he was not plagued by pimples and sweat-sock funk, he did not thunder around the basketball court, part of a team of stampeding rhinoceroses, he did not try to disrupt the class in the middle of *all the perfumes of Arabia will not sweeten this little hand.*

In fact, he didn't even show up for class all that often.

Tyrone was not a gronky, sweaty, profane, pretending-to-be-fencepost-stupid, arrogant, loud, math-failing, poetry-hating, eat-a-whole-pizza-by-yourself-in-less-than-five-minutes-and-burp-the-loudest, fart-joke-telling, buy-a-40-ouncer-off-a-taxi-driver-and-get-drunk-at-parties-and-puke-all-over-somebody's-carpet, typical high-school person of the male persuasion.

Tyrone had become an artist.

A graffiti artist.

An outlaw.

His tags and murals are all over St. John's and there have been letters in the paper. The cops have even come out with a statement. They'll stop at nothing to find SprayPig — that's Tyrone's tag.

He smells of fresh air and sometimes, faintly, of pot. He can pick up any sort of musical instrument and play a riff on "American Pie" or "Stairway to Heaven" or "Hot Cross Buns."

He owns a motorcycle. The rumor is he took it apart on a garage floor and lovingly polished each nut and bolt and put it back together.

That first morning of grade ten, Tyrone O'Rourke's face lit up when he saw me.

He was the same Tyrone who had chased me around Bannerman Park with water balloons the year I got my sneakers that flashed red lights, and the same Tyrone who dressed as an astronaut for Halloween in grade three, with silver spray-painted cereal boxes on his shoulders and a section of hose from his mom's dryer glued onto his hockey helmet and a backpack of "oxygen." He was the same Tyrone who made potions of dirt and mustard and vinegar from the packets we'd saved from Ches's fish and chips — potions we mixed in old spaghetti sauce jars, hoping they would work like gasoline if we poured them over the pedals of our tricycles to make them go faster.

He was one-and-the-same Tyrone of yore, but when Jenny Clarke walked past and asked him if he wanted some of her chocolate bar and he said yes — and she folded back the foil and held it up to his mouth and he took a nibble, looking her straight in the eyes, and chocolate crumbs tumbled off his beautiful plump bottom lip and onto the collar of his jean jacket and Jenny pressed her index finger onto one of those crumbs and then put the tip of her finger in her mouth and turned and walked away with all of her long hair swinging over her shoulders — then he was not the same Tyrone at all.

Boom.

Boom, boom.

2

The morning buzzer for my first class, Introduction to
Entrepreneurship, rips through the school. Allie Jones sees me
beating it down the hall and at the last second tries to slam the
door in my face. I stomp my foot between the door and the
frame and try to squeeze my body in while she leans against
the door on the other side, trying to squash me.

Then Allie steps away from the door and I almost fall into
the classroom.

Sorry, Allie says. I didn't see you.

Mr. Payne is looking out the window and digging around in
his shirt pocket with two fingers. He doesn't notice me sneaking in late. I slide into my desk behind Amber Mackey. Amber
is my best friend and has big beautiful swimmer's shoulders.

All the better to hide behind, my dear.

Mr. Payne draws a silver laser pen out of his shirt pocket.
This is a new teaching aid for him. He loves gadgets. Mr. Payne
clicks the tip of the laser pen and a sharp purple line slices
through the air over our heads, and at the back of the class, a
frenetic violet dot jiggles over the wall.

Now then, he says. Everybody, quiet please.

Everybody grudgingly turns it down to a low murmur.

I have a few announcements about the Youth Entrepreneurial Fair, Mr. Payne says. We have secured several booths at the Glacier in Mount Pearl. As you know, every high school in the province will be competing. Traditionally, Holy Heart takes the gold. I know it seems like the school year has just started, but Christmas will be upon us before you know it. The Entrepreneurial Fair is the crowning achievement in your graduating year. The media always attends.

The murmuring ratchets up several notches until people are talking and laughing. Allie Jones is taking a selfie while she puts on lipstick. Elaine Power is scribbling notes. Chad Yates-O'Neill is rolling a basketball over the length of his outstretched arm, onto his shoulder, behind his head and down the other arm. Then he bounces it off the back of Allie's head.

Mr. Payne, Allie whines.

There will be lights, there will be cameras, there will be action, says Mr. Payne. Chad, the ball, please. Businesses near and far pay close attention to the winners, people.

Chad unslouches himself out of the desk and dribbles the ball to the front of the class. He passes it a few times under each knee and then he rolls it to the corner of the room and returns to his desk.

In the past, our winners have been offered top-paying summer jobs the day they graduate, says Mr. Payne. He strolls down the aisle and confiscates Allie's phone.

But sir, she says.

After class, Miss Jones. We've even had interest from Toronto. This brings me to my next point. I've noticed some of you people dragging your heels, deciding on what to make for your units. So I have decided to put you into pairs. Business partners.

Everybody goes instantly silent.

He waves the tip of the laser pen in little circles. And then he points it directly at Mark Galway.

An angry violet dot vibrates like a mad hornet over Mark Galway's right eyebrow. Mark's eyebrow twitches.

Mark is the grandson of one of the richest people in Newfoundland, and maybe even Canada and quite possibly all of North America — Mr. Fred Galway, the communications mogul.

Mr. Galway owns all the radio frequency bandwidth available in Newfoundland. He started one of the first television stations here, back in the seventies. It's rumored that he himself was Captain Newfoundland, the superhero who appeared after midnight on NTV back in the nineties, dressed in a hooded cape and a face mask with the map of Newfoundland drawn on it. His cape fluttered into a background of zooming comets and blasts of disco-funk. A deep voice intoned that the captain was *the Spirit of Newfoundland who lives in the hearts of all of us.* You can still see it on YouTube.

This means that Mark is the spawn of Captain Newfoundland, and of course he's planning to make some kind of radio thing for his unit at the Glacier.

The laser dot is jiggling all over Mark's face.

Mr. Payne says, You.

Mark Galway looks quickly over one shoulder, and then the other. The violet dot zips over to his ear, and then it reappears on his cheek. It finally settles on the tip of his nose.

Me, sir? For a split second Mark Galway's eyes cross.

Yes, you, Mr. Payne says. Galway.

I prefer to work alone.

No man is an island, Galway, except maybe Captain Newfoundland. You're not Captain Newfoundland, are you, Galway?

I don't want a partner, Mr. Payne, sir.

Nevertheless, a partner you shall have, Mr. Galway. You are going to be partners with ...

Mr. Payne wiggles the laser pen around. The sharp beam of light slices through several necks in the front row. The tiny dot zips up to the ceiling and down again and zings from one end of the room to the other.

Where's Tyrone? I whisper to Amber. His desk is empty.

Il n'est pas ici, Amber says. *Quelle surprise!*

Amber and I took French last semester.

Mr. Payne is gently prodding the air with the laser pen, sort of in my direction. I duck down behind Amber. The laser beam skims over us and lands on Elaine Power's giant dangling dragon earring. The tiny violet dot hits the teensy chip of red glass in the dragon's eye and I swear the thing winks.

Mr. Payne says, And you, Miss Power, will be Mark Galway's business partner.

But Mr. Payne, why can't I choose my own partner? Elaine asks. Elaine Power despises Mark Galway.

Elaine has a nose ring and wears the same black T-shirt, held together with safety pins, every single day. Her nails are long and black and her lipstick is black and her eyeliner is black and she often has a little sprinkle of blue-black glitter on her cheekbones.

She wears black evening gloves up to her elbows with the fingers cut out. Sometimes, over her T-shirt, she has a lace-up black thing that has been spray-painted gold and has big plastic jewels all over it. It sort of looks like a corset, with a ruffled black lace collar like Henry VIII. On her legs, black fishnet stockings with holes and red-and-black-striped leg warmers. One red Converse sneaker, one black. She has shaved half her head and dyed the other half very black and wears it teased up and stiff with hairspray (though she is always ranting about how Holy Heart should be a scent-free environment!).

Elaine is a mathlete and consults with professors at the university at lunchtime. Or, to be more precise, they consult with her. In her younger years she won an international spelling bee. But then she announced over the PA that spelling is a form of imperialism. She had seen the ugly face of spelling up close, she said, and it was a shackle she had chosen to throw off.

None of us understood a word but we applauded like crazy and the secretary took over the mike with a hiss of static and crackle and announced something about the bus schedule.

All we know is that Elaine is the smartest student in the entire history of the school. That's why she's allowed to wear whatever she likes. The rest of us have to adhere to dress codes. No baseball caps for the boys; no bra straps or midriffs showing for the girls. Elaine has shown the rest of us how to rebel by wearing her bra outside her shirt.

And she's already developed her project and taken it out for a test drive. An app that disseminates electronic petitions around the world in a matter of seconds. The petitions are designed to save a different endangered butterfly every month. Elaine has contacts in twenty-seven countries who translate the petitions simultaneously into twenty-seven different languages, and, as a test, last week she organized a protest to save British farmland butterflies, focusing on the common blue butterfly, which has been endangered but is now projected to make a comeback, partly because of Elaine.

Never mind that Elaine's app isn't really a product you can sell, which is the main requirement of the assignment. Mr. Payne suggested Elaine think of ways to *monetize* her product. Elaine just raised one of her very black drawn-on eyebrows at him.

I wouldn't think of trying to make money off the endangered, she told him.

And I won't think of giving you a passing grade, Mr. Payne said. Elaine slitted her eyes at him.

Mark Galway, on the other hand, would monetize his own grandmother if he could and comes to school in his granddad's Hummer.

I do not need a partner, says Elaine.

It's no good being smart if you can't cooperate with your fellow students, Mr. Payne says.

Would you say that to a boy? Elaine asks. I want to do this alone.

That's too bad, Miss Power. You are now partners with Mark Galway.

Please, Mr. Payne, sir, Elaine says.

But Mr. Payne has moved on. The laser dot is flying all over the place.

You, Mr. Payne says. He has pointed to Gary Bowen.

Uh-oh, whispers Amber. She sits up as tall as she can.

Okay, wait. Let me explain Amber, because this is not her best moment. Amber has puffy black circles around her eyes from her swimming goggles getting suctioned onto her eye sockets, and she smells like chlorine and has to be nudged awake every five minutes or she'll be snoring her head off.

But there's a clip on YouTube from a swim meet in the UK last year.

Amber comes out of a dressing room onto the white poolside and stops to glance around at the crowd. The walls of the pool deck are draped with flags from all over the world. She is dressed in red and white sweats with a big maple leaf on the back of her jacket. She's wearing her goggles and red cap. For the briefest moment, her fingers flutter all over her swimming cap. Fingers flapping fast over her ears like hummingbird wings.

It's just for a brief moment, but if you're her best friend, you know what it means, this finger-flapping thing. Nerves. She has been working toward this race for her whole life.

She raises one arm high over her head. Reaching up on her tiptoes. She waves at the crowd. You can see a lot of little Canadian flags waving back from a big patch of the crowd in the bleachers. I know she's looking for her father, Sean.

Sean is the one who drives her to all those practices at five in the morning. He's the one who paces the side of the pool day after day with the stopwatch. He's the one shouting, Move, go, keep going, yes, yes, Amber, yes!

Amber's mom is an alcoholic. Actually, her father is an alcoholic too, but he's been dry for sixteen years.

In the video, the camera pans over all the swimmers as they slip out of their sweats. The American girl scratches her chin. The Japanese girl holds her arms down at her sides and shakes her hands out. Amber's fingers flutter over her swimming cap once more.

They step up onto the blocks. *On your mark.* The buzzer. They fly off the blocks. I mean they really fly. Then they are underwater. They don't look human. They are too fast for humans. They aren't machines either. What are they?

They are silver arrows they are eels they are licorice they are Lycra they are muscle they are will and will not and want to be and winning, for the first few seconds they are all winning and winning and winning and they are can't and must and will never and don't.

Amber watches the video over and over, looking for a lost second. Somewhere she lost a beat. A measure of time tiny as the head of a pin. She makes me watch it too.

The video has 120,000 views and I swear most of them are Amber and me.

She placed second. Amber did not win as she had promised her father she would. She did not win as she had promised her school she would. She did not win as she had promised her country she would. She did not win as she had planned to do ever since she was a baby and her father took her to a pond and let her kick and splash and eventually put her face in the water to rely on those instincts from the Triassic Period when we gave up our gills for feet and swam out of the ocean up onto land, those instincts that tell you when to hold your breath.

The Japanese girl won. The Japanese girl beat Amber by less than a second.

You should see that Japanese girl's smile. It's worth watching the video 120,000 times, just for that smile. But there's a better moment coming.

Wait for it, wait.

There's Amber. She explodes up out of the water, a big splash of bubbles and froth around her waist. It is my belief that in that moment she still thinks she has won. There's a roaring crowd and clapping and the coaches pouring out onto the pool deck and reporters with cameras and flashes, and the digital boards with the times.

She sees from the boards that she is less than a second behind the Japanese girl. She turns toward the Japanese girl.

And here it is.

Amber reaching over the lane divider to hug the Japanese girl. Amber's face in the camera and it's sincere.

A sincere smile.

That's Amber.

She's goes straight back at the training. In the pool at five every morning except Sunday. They're allowed to sleep in until seven a.m. on Sundays.

Then she comes to school and conks out at her desk.

If a teacher says her name, her head jerks up, and she snorts like a horse and rattles out one of the maybe ten answers she has memorized for just such an occasion.

Answers like: Photosynthesis, sir.

Or: The area equals half the base times the height, miss.

Or: A character trait that brings sorrow or ruin to the protagonist.

Or: The assassination of Archduke Franz Ferdinand.

Or: An imaginary line drawn around the earth equally distant from both poles.

By using this technique she averages a correct answer about one-third of the time. She rattles it out and her head droops again and she's gently snoring.

Swimming is all she's ever wanted or thought about.

Until Gary Bowen.

Suddenly, Amber is all, Swimming? Who cares!

Okay, I'm exaggerating. She still cares about swimming, but boy, is she distracted.

It was spin-the-bottle at Jordan Murphy's, just after the first week of school. We were in Jordan Murphy's rec room with the pool table and the velvet paint-by-numbers of a rearing stallion that Jordan's mom had done (also a crying clown and a frozen river with a stone bridge and a laminated 1,000-piece puzzle of the Mona Lisa).

Gary had snuck in five beers right under Jordan's mom's nose. Each bottle in his knapsack was covered in two black sweatsocks so they wouldn't clink. There was pizza and Kanye West and then everybody got in a circle. Gary finished his beer and leaned into the circle and put the bottle down in the middle. For a while everybody pretended to ignore it. Then Gary gave the bottle a good hard spin.

It spun around on the tiles and when it stopped, it was pointing at Amber.

A few drops of beer had spun out of the mouth of the bottle, and my sock got wet. Everybody went, Oooohhhhh, Amber.

Amber was sitting absolutely still. A blush started in her neck and went all the way up her face to her hairline, *swoosh*. Her hand went up to the side of her head to do the hummingbird flutter, but she just smoothed her hair back and then tucked her hands under her legs so they'd stay still.

A couple of the guys started chanting, *Gar-y, Gar-y, Gar-y.*

Jordan put his thumb and finger in the corners of his lips and whistled so loud that it tickled the inside of my ear.

Moira Kennedy put her legs out straight in front of her, leaned back on her elbows and made her heels drum on the floor, just the way we all used to do at Happy Kids when Miss Stephanie said we were taking a journey in a rainstorm through a tropical rainforest.

Brittany Halliday put her legs out too and Brittany Bishop did the same thing, and then all the girls were doing it. And all the guys were whistling.

When the noise reached its highest pitch, Gary Bowen shuffled across the circle on his hands and knees to where Amber was sitting. He put his hands on her shoulders and leaned in and kissed her on the lips.

Everything stopped.

The boys stopped chanting.

The whistling stopped.

The tropical rainstorm stopped all at once, except for Moira Kennedy, who slowly tapped one foot, just like we also used to do in Happy Kids, so it sounded like a single drop of rain, falling from leaf to leaf to leaf after the storm.

They were still kissing. They kissed in utter silence. They kissed with their tongues. They forgot they were in a circle with people watching them. They forgot the laminated puzzle of Mona Lisa who was gazing down on them and it was hard to say what she thought of it. They kissed until Jordan Murphy wrecked the moment by yelling, Get a room, man.

Since that kiss Amber has been addled and dopey. Everything you say to her, you have to say twice. She came first last week at a provincial meet, the one that determines who gets to go to the Nationals. But she lost a few seconds from her best time and didn't seem to care. And she hasn't mentioned the Nationals since. She's constantly swirling the tip of her pinkie in a little pot of cotton-candy lip gloss. You can see the hard plastic circle of the lip-gloss lid pressed into the very tight back pocket of her jeans, like a charm.

Mr. Payne says, And Gary Bowen's partner will be . . .

The little violet dot from the laser pen hesitates here and there. For a moment it lingers on Tiffany Murphy's face. It rests on Tiffany's chin.

Not Tiffany Murphy, Amber whispers. Please not Tiffany Murphy.

But the dot moves on to John Mercer. John gets the dot right in the eye and he has to dig at his eye socket with his knuckle. The dot zips away before it permanently blinds him.

Finally, the little violet dot sits smack dab in the middle of Amber's lips. There's a direct line from Mr. Payne's laser pen to Amber's lips, as if she's a fish he's about to reel in.

I think it's you, I whisper. But the dot from Mr. Payne's laser pen slides off Amber's mouth. The dot skips over the aisle between the desks and lands right on Gus Wong's Adam's apple.

Gus, says Mr. Payne. You and Gary ...

Amber suddenly flings herself across the aisle into the path of the violet laser dot. She throws herself on top of Gus Wong's desk as the tiny violet dot hits her cheek.

Ms. Mackey, please, says Mr. Payne.

Sorry, sir, Amber says. I dropped my pencil. And, sure enough, she had somehow managed to fling her pencil onto Gus's desk. She picks it up and wiggles it at Mr. Payne.

Sorry about that. It flew right out of my hand, sir.

Okay, said Mr. Payne. Now, let's see. Gary Bowen and Amber Mackey will be partners.

Amber turns to me, and there's that smile again.

The classroom door creaks open and in slinks a boy, black curly mussed-up hair, big brown eyes, lanky (okay, skinny), tall, and the beautiful, worn jean jacket stitched with a patch on the back that says *ARMS ARE FOR HUGGING*, and on the collar, a button with a marijuana leaf, and a tiny Santa Claus pin with a little string and if you pull it, the red plastic nose lights up, and on the back, a patch with *The Clash* cut out of a T-shirt and embroidered on with green silk embroidery thread and jagged little stitches.

A jacket I have lovingly memorized every square inch of.

The boy lopes down the aisle and pours himself into the empty desk.

All heads turn in his direction.

Mr. Payne says, Ah, look who has graced us with his presence!

Tyrone O'Rourke has arrived.

Mr. Payne, without warning, snaps off his laser pen and

drops it in his shirt pocket. He picks up a clipboard and consults. It seems he has paired everyone already, and the dancing laser pen was only for show.

He reads down the list in a flat monotone. Finally he gets to me. Flannery Malone, you will be partners with Tyrone O'Rourke.

It seems like a fortune-cookie message, a marriage vow. I half expect Mr. Payne to ask if anyone present sees any reason why these two people should not be joined together, and if so, speak now or forever hold their peace.

Tyrone glances back at me and lifts his pencil to his temple and gives it a tip, like an army salute. He wiggles his eyebrows. I'm pretty sure a couple of girls in the back groan with disappointment.

Boom. Boom, boom, boom, boom.

Okay class, says Mr. Payne. You'll need to have submitted a proposal for the unit you're going to sell by September 30th. The revised proposal, incorporating my feedback, will be due October 14th. You'll be docked two percent for every day you're late. I simply suggest not being late at all. Off you go.

The buzzer goes and we head down the corridor to the stairwell and Tyrone is on the staircase above me and he leans over the rail and says, Flan, I know what we should do for our unit.

He's being pushed through the door by the waves of students charging to their next classes.

I've got a brilliant idea, he calls out.

But then he's out the door and by the time I get up the stairs to math class, which he's also supposed to be in, he's disappeared.

3

———

When we were in grade one we had to do a project called *All About Me*. We had to write about what we looked like, what we wanted to become, our secrets, our families, our favorite foods, our favorite animals — each topic on a separate page, with a blank space on top for a crayon drawing. Each kid's project went in a duotang with our grade-one school photo glued onto the cover.

My printing went outside the lines and bunched up and slanted like the losing team in a tug of war. When the teacher complained to Miranda that my writing didn't fit between the lines, Miranda said, Make the lines bigger.

My crayon drawings, however, were masterpieces. They were violently emotional. I loved that all the crayons had names printed on the sides. The names were either very dramatic (Banana Mania, Laser Lemon, Cerulean Blue, Atomic Tangerine) or mysteriously plain (Medium Red).

It was during the process of creating *All About Me* that I first noticed I didn't have a father.

I mean, I knew I didn't have one, of course. But it was the first time I noticed that almost everybody else *did*.

On the page that was supposed to be about my father I ended up writing about some guy named Phil, who lived in the house attached to ours for two months and who owned a Doberman.

The Doberman barked and gnashed his teeth against the living-room window and slathered ropes of saliva from his pink-and-black spotted jowls every time someone walked down the sidewalk.

Once Phil gave me a bubble wand. It made giant wobbling bubbles as big as my head that would burst with a cloud of mist. The bubble wand seemed to qualify Phil for page 6 in my duotang, the page about *Dad*.

The Doberman is also featured on the My Favorite Animal page, a portrait in Turquoise Blue and Crimson crayon, with the studs on his dog collar scrawled with my most prized and never-cracked crayon: Silver.

Phil moved out two days after he gave me the bubble wand and we never saw him again.

If I had to write *All About Me* now, complete with crayon illustrations, what would it contain?

Name: Flannery Malone
What I Look Like:
1) Freckles (Burnt Sienna)
2) Pale skin (Silver)
3) Green eyes (Sea Green) ...
4) ... with little hazel flecks shooting through the green (Raw Sienna)
5) Limp, whip-straight orange hair to my shoulders (Sunglow)
6) 5'6" on tiptoes
7) Skinny, except for my boobs, which are, I think we can say, big.

Secrets: I've had the school glockenspiel hidden under
my bed since I quit band in grade five. I quit because
I couldn't do the glockenspiel justice and the teacher
was threatening me with the triangle.

It took me so long to return the glockenspiel that after a
while I was afraid to return it at all. It lives under my bed, silent
in a glockenspiel coffin, a heavy, velvet-lined box of guilt (a
toss-up between Crimson or Medium Red for the lining).

Other: I am sixteen, currently without a boyfriend, though
I am horribly in love with Tyrone O'Rourke. The very worst
kind of love. Unrequited love.

I am in high school at Holy Heart in St. John's, Newfoundland. I have a driver's permit, level one. I once had a math
tutor who told me that whales have veins big enough for a
person to swim through and many other interesting facts that
did not appear on my math exam but have made me feel awe.

I am a person who likes to feel awe.

I also enjoy making pancakes, often spelling my brother's
name with the batter. Which leads me to...

Family: Miranda (mother), Felix (half-brother) and two
goldfish, Spiky and Smooth.

Miranda (see above) has nearly killed these goldfish many
times, but they are true soldiers. She forgets to feed them
when it's her turn, and feeds them again when it's supposed to
be my turn, and lets their water evaporate until they're almost
beached.

Once Miranda let Smooth bellyflop out of the soup ladle
when she was in the middle of transporting them so she
could clean the bowl. She stood there screaming and waving
her hands around her head yelling, Flannery, do something!
Do something! And I had to pick up poor old Smooth and

practically give him mouth-to-gill resuscitation before plopping him back in the bowl.

Once after a party I found a cigar butt floating on the water. Smooth and Spiky climbed up onto the stogie, one on either end, and stood on their fins attempting the age-old sport of log rolling. They made that cigar roll back and forth with deft slaps of their tails, just like the stubble-faced lumberjacks of yore.

Okay, Spiky and Smooth, they didn't really do that with the stogie. But they did waste a day or two head-butting the soggy cigar from one end of the bowl to the other.

They are a lesson in fortitude and commitment.

Father: I have a single artifact, from the once-upon-a-time love affair between my mother and father. A sole memento in the form of a single chocolate shaped like a heart and wrapped in bright red tinfoil and hidden in a jewelry box under my bed.

Soon after my father left, sailing away from St. John's forever, Miranda discovered she had no contact info on him — that, in fact, she hadn't really caught his last name. And, before I was even born, she had already fallen in love with someone else. And then someone else. And so on.

My father's first name is Xavier. That much she knows. It's a French name. That's why I took French last year — I figured that if I ever meet the guy, it would be nice to say a few words in his mother tongue. Father tongue. *Xavier*. X is the unknown variable in a math equation. If Y equals my mother in her tiara, with her love for fairness and feminism and *joie de vivre*, her inability to pay bills, her blogs and her non-existent domestic skills, and if I am the answer, then Dad must be X, right?

So I like to call him — my father — *X*. In my head, I mean, because of course I don't actually get to talk to him or call him anything because, like I said, Miranda forgot that little thing of asking for his address, or his last name, or blood type, or genetic propensities for disease or special talents or whether he has a strong sense of smell, which I do have, or if he was good at the glockenspiel, or if he loves chocolate, or if there are aunts and uncles or even other children. Brothers and sisters.

What she does remember I can fit in a thimble. 1) He had hazel-green eyes; 2) red curly hair; 3) he was six foot two; 4) he cared about the environment; 5) he laughed a lot and they stayed up until dawn on the fateful night of my conception and they drank and went for a skinny dip in the ocean under the cloak of darkness and shortly after that frigid, primordial-soup dip, I was created.

Otherwise, yeah, no father. Though I have more Mom than most people ever have to contend with.

Favorite Things: I love strobe lights, the smell of cloves and bonfire-roasted marshmallows, the feel of my teeth after they've been cleaned at the dentist (though not the actual trip to the dentist, of course).

I love long baths without anybody banging on the door, or would love those kinds of baths, I'm pretty sure, if I ever experienced one.

As it is, I'm lucky if I'm not sharing my bath with, at the very least, a rubber ducky or a wind-up alligator that wags its tail and snaps its jaws, and maybe a fire truck or two.

I love skating on a pond in the evening, even though I can't skate very well, but I love being dragged around the ice by Amber, me holding one end of a very long scarf and Amber holding the other, that moment when you know it's time to turn around and head for home, when it'll soon be getting dark and all the ice on the trees starts to tinkle in the wind and the moon and the sun are there together and Amber swishes to a stop and sprays snow dust with her shiny blade. She digs her toe pick into the ice and uses it as a pivot and I'm gliding in wide arcs around her and then she lets go of her end of the scarf and the centrifugal force spins me out toward the darkening horizon, and I am flying.

These are a few of my favorite things.

And Tyrone.

Obviously.

4

It's a Thursday evening and Miranda and I are in the mall parking lot. That's as far as we've got.

I've turned the truck off but my mother's fingertips are still pressed against the dash, as they have been the whole way to the mall, as if to keep her from flying through the windshield.

There is no need for you to look as white as a piece of paper, I say.

Have I mentioned, my mother asks, how much I hate shopping?

You don't have to shop. Just wait for me to shop, so I don't have to get the bus back. And you've said yourself that I need the driving practice. You can take your hand off the dash now, by the way. I've turned off the ignition.

I'm just waiting for my heart rate to go back to normal, she says.

So I had to slam on the brakes a few times. How was I supposed to know the guy in front of me was going to stop like that?

The stop sign, Miranda says. Is a good clue. I don't like the mall, have I mentioned that?

You've mentioned, I say.

Have I said that in North America we search for meaning in our lives through conspicuous consumption? We spend, therefore we are. This behavior is akin to spiritual annihilation.

You've said.

Have I told you about how when I was sixteen, not so very long ago, and when I did shop, I went shopping with my girlfriends? It's a thing you're supposed to do with your girlfriends. Not your mother. Have I mentioned that?

Yes, you said, "That's what you have girlfriends for."

Absolutely. That is the job of girlfriends. And I've indicated that I am not a girlfriend. I am your mother. Mothers cannot be girlfriends with their daughters. They are mothers. I mean, maybe later in life, when the mother is an old lady and she has a little cloudy glass with her dentures in it on her bedside table and the daughter has six daughters of her own, maybe then they can be friends. But not when a daughter is only sixteen. When a kid is sixteen, a mother is a mother. I'm sure I've explained this.

This won't take long, Miranda.

I don't want to go in there, Flannery.

We enter the mall, I say. I buy the bathing suit. You sit on a bench or browse in the bookstore. You wander the food court. I come out of the bathing-suit store with my purchase and we exit the mall. Resume our driving lesson. Is that asking too much, Miranda? Can you help me here?

Miranda says, It is unnatural. Have I said that? Mothers and daughters shopping together. Completely unnatural.

It goes on like that. She won't get out of the truck. The thing is, according to Miranda, all single mothers hate the mall. She says malls were invented to make the single mother feel bad. She is *the single mother*. She's still got her seatbelt on and she's viciously scratching her wrist.

See, she says, holding out the reddened wrist for me to examine.

You are not breaking out in hives, I say.

Yes, I am, she says. Look.

Okay, Mom. Fine, I say. I only call her Mom when I'm really annoyed.

She sinks her chin down into the collar of her coat, which is a voluminous faux-leopard-skin number, a true find from the Sally Ann back when she was in art school. (My mother calls all her clothes "numbers.") Right now her shoulders hunch in her leopard-skin number and she's frowning and pouting and her brow is wrinkled up.

Don't do that with your forehead, I say. You'll need Botox.

Miranda begins to hum something under her breath. It might be Nirvana's "Come As You Are."

Look, I say. Do you want me to take Felix swimming while you work out or not? That's why I need the stupid bathing suit. My old one doesn't fit and it has see-through patches from the chlorine. I don't have enough money to get the bus back, and besides, I need the driving practice. If you want, you can stay in the truck. Wait for me in the parking lot.

But I know as I'm saying it that Miranda will never go for that. She hates sitting still, and the only thing worse than the mall is the mall parking lot.

All right, my mother says. You asked for it. She flicks open the glove compartment and rummages around inside. Pulls out her tiara, jams it on her head all askew.

She flings open her door so it bounces back on the hinges, her seatbelt slithering up like a rearing snake. She's out, striding across the parking lot. The red lining of her leopard-skin number flaps around her knees.

Maybe I should have left Miranda out of this after all?

But I'm out of the truck too, running to catch up with her.

I leave her at a booth with a very petite Korean woman who does manicures and has a display of false nails with teensy false gems and paintings of palm trees at sunset and ones that have fluffy kittens.

Miranda's face lights up. Flannery, look. Little masterpieces!

Unlike my mother, I actually love it here at the mall. Some of my fondest memories happened here.

When I was twelve, we all used to catch the bus to the mall and hang out. Miranda thought I was at art class. Miranda did not believe the mall was a healthy, creative environment for girls or young women.

My mother, Miranda Malone, believes that we have a duty in this world to live creatively.

If she only knew how creative we were at the mall!

We bought Krazy Glue at Walmart and glued condoms to the floor. We tied a piece of fishing line to a wallet and hid behind a pillar and whenever someone tried to pick up the wallet, we gave the fishing line a yank. We all squashed into the photo booth and hooked our index fingers into the corners of our smiles and pulled them wide and crossed our eyes. Every third picture, our eyes were closed because of the flash.

We'd go to the food court and drink milkshakes, too weak from laughing to lift the cup off the table, so we'd slouch over instead and lower our lips to the straw, sucking back hard to make very loud straw-in-the-empty-wax-paper-cup noises.

And Christmas. The loud crowded mall at Christmas with big bulbs hanging from the rafters and new leather chairs at the Second Cup and Muzak carols and Chris Moose — the Christmas moose who trots around the mall in his big furry suit, a basket of candy canes dangling off his front hoof. We'd run around playing hide-and-seek, the whole gang of us — Brittany Halliday and Brittany Bishop and Amber and Elaine Power and Jordan and David and everybody. Running from the security guards, who didn't want us loitering. Or, if the security guards were on a break, we'd just give in to being lazy, half-blinded from coming out of a matinee movie, and we'd slink into Sears and squirt perfume samples — we didn't care if they were for men or women — on each other's wrists. Scents with names like Irish Tweed, Truth, Midnight Poison. Spraying until we couldn't smell anything at all.

That is the mall when you don't *have* to actually buy anything. A shopping trip for a bathing suit is an entirely different matter.

Buying a bathing suit is a traumatic event if your boobs are big enough to require the term voluptuous. The whole enterprise is bringing back some not-so-wonderful memories of my childhood visits to the mall. Like coming here with Miranda to buy my first bra.

The saleswoman asked Miranda how old I was. I was eleven.

It's the milk, the saleswoman announced for everyone in the store to hear. Hormones in milk and beef. Children are developing too fast.

I had specifically asked Miranda to not ask for help.

Can I help you with anything, ladies? said the woman.

Oh, yes, please, Miranda cheeped.

The saleswoman had silver hair, a fountain of curls scraped into a big pompom on the top of her head. Her own breasts looked pointy and cone-like, and her eyes, sleet-gray, bore into me. She came at me with the measuring tape that had been dangling around her neck, pulling it taut between her hands, making it snap several times.

Let's see what we're dealing with, she said.

I don't think that will be necessary, I said.

Hands up where I can see 'em, she said. I raised my hands in the air. She leaned in and reached around my back with the tape, drawing me close to her. She brought both ends of the measuring tape together at the midpoint between my two breasts. Then she looked shocked by the information the measuring tape had revealed. She clucked her tongue and shook her head, as if I had grown voluptuous breasts on purpose.

I have to wear my underpants while trying on the bathing suit. And here I am in purple Lycra that looks like a sausage skin, my white cotton underwear hanging down below the bathing suit's high-cut hips and the thin little shoulder straps are as weak as over-boiled spaghetti.

But the next suit, a hot-pink number, is not too bad and it's on sale.

And then I'm out of there with my new suit in a plastic bag, looking for Miranda.

She's not at the manicure booth anymore.

Finally, I see a blur of leopard-skin print in the crowd ahead of me. I elbow into a loose circle of people and there's Miranda in the middle, standing under a huge flat-screen TV. She twirls around on one heel and she's clutching a remote in both hands, her arms out straight, and it's pointing right at me. Then I hear a loud buzzing and something smacks hard against the top of my head, and there, also, is the top of my head on the monstrously big flat screen.

It's a toy helicopter drone with video capacity, whizzing up now through the mall rafters, the images on the screen rocking wildly from side to side, the tops of people's heads, walls tipping, the escalators seeming to swing left and right like hanging bridges. I see the display stack of all the drones in boxes with plastic windows on their fronts reflecting the fluorescent ceiling lights. They are piled very high in two pillars behind Miranda.

The salesman in charge of the display is saying how you can record with your phone and live stream all over the world, even as you shoot.

The drone is zipping down and juddering up and spinning, as Miranda sways the remote above her head and circles her arms and swings it to the left and right in violent sweeps. The video on the flat screen shows people jolted up and down as though in the middle of an earthquake, ducking out of the helicopter's path.

After several twists and pirouettes, the helicopter zooms directly toward Miranda's own face, full speed ahead.

There's Miranda on the screen, laughing, gasping for breath, her wild blonde curls loose all over her shoulders, the big grin with the gap between her two front teeth, and her freckles. Her tiara glittering, shooting out spears of pink and blue light. And then the picture freezes — just Miranda's tiara up there, enlarged, big as an iceberg and she ducks and the drone hits the display pillar behind her and boxes topple all over the floor.

Everyone begins to clap.

Miranda straightens her tiara and gives a little curtsy. She hands the remote back to the salesman, who is bent down, picking up the pieces of the smashed helicopter. The little engine cuts in and out, buzzing and choking and finally going quiet.

That was so much fun, Miranda says as she strides out of the mall. And I managed to get a picture of the tiara up there on the screen, did you see that? Did you get your bathing suit?

Miranda calls the tiara her thinking cap. She wears it every-where. My mother has agreed to take part in a conceptual art project. She has to wear the tiara for at least a little while, every single day for a year and take photographs of herself in different locations. Six women from six different continents are taking part in the project, each woman wearing a tiara every day for a year and taking a daily photograph.

Miranda read about the project in the back of a feminist magazine that they sell at the health food store and applied to be the subject from North America.

Miranda was chosen, she says, because of her feminist ideals and because she is a single mother and for her talents as an artist, her ambition and creativity and her commitment to the environment and because, I have suggested, nobody else applied from North America.

They don't have anybody from Antarctica, though I also suggested they probably could have found a talented, ambitious, pro-environment feminist penguin if they'd looked hard enough.

We're hurrying to the down escalator — it's almost six-thirty, time to pick Felix up from his karate class — and there are a bunch of people in front of us and Miranda is grilling me, sort of loudly, about the bathing suit. How much did it cost, and did I get one I liked with lots of support, and she hopes it doesn't have underwire because she's heard that causes breast cancer, and just when I wish she would stop saying the word *breast* so loudly in public, I catch a glimpse of a certain jean jacket with a Clash patch sewn on the back, riding the up escalator. My heart does a leap like the gazelles flying through the plains of Mongolia that I watched on YouTube last night when I was supposed to be doing math.

I almost shout out to Tyrone — we *have* to talk about our unit for the Entrepreneurship project. The proposal is due at the end of September and it's already September 19th. I've Facebook-messaged him and tried his phone, but he hasn't answered me back and he hasn't been in class all week.

Then I notice a girl on the step right behind him. The girl is wearing brown suede moccasins and a vintage patchwork suede coat. She's beautiful, with all this tumbling hair, dyed like a parrot, streaks of orange and magenta and pink, and is she or isn't she with Tyrone O'Rourke?

Meanwhile, Tyrone and I are like ships passing in the night. I crane my neck all the way around, and Miranda is going on now about how she's been to plenty of topless beaches where all you needed in the way of a bathing suit was a little bikini bottom which is sensible, because then you get a tan on your breasts, but nude beaches are even better, because then you can tan your buttocks, and I'm trying to see if this beautiful girl is *actually* leaning against Tyrone, which it sort of looks like, and she's chewing gum and blows a giant bubble and Tyrone turns, because she's nudged him with her shoulder to show him the bubble, and without a word but looking straight in her eyes, he pokes his finger into the bubble.

They are together!

And the bubble breaks.

And Miranda says, I mean, men don't have to cover *their* chests.

The bubble drapes the girl's chin and Tyrone turns back and hops off the up escalator. And she hops off and they disappear — into the Avalon Cineplex, it looks like.

I'm surprised to feel my nose tingling. It's the feeling I get just before I feel tears coming. I sniff them away. I am not about to cry in the Avalon Mall.

And why should we cover our breasts, ever? Miranda is saying. I mean, unless we're cold. She is striding through the mall ahead of me, her leopard-skin number swishing around her knees, red lining flashing.

I think we should rebel and let our breasts swing around all over the place, don't you? And let's shake the lead out, Flan. The last time I was late picking up Felix he karate-chopped a tetrapack of apple juice and it squirted all over the place. Sensei Larry was sticking to the gym floor for weeks.

That's when I notice the shopping bag in Miranda's hand.

What is that?

What is what?

Miranda, you didn't.

I just know Felix will love one of these helicopter drones, Flan. I couldn't help myself. And you got a new bathing suit! I can't go home with something for you and nothing for your poor little brother.

Miranda, we needed that money for the rent.

That isn't due for two weeks.

I roll my eyes. And what about my biology textbook? I say. I don't even *want* this bathing suit, Miranda. I only need it so I can help *you*, remember? And Felix already has a ton of remote control cars.

This is not a remote control *car*, Flannery. It's a *helicopter*. Totally different, and it has a video camera.

But you must have emptied the bank account.

Just think of his face when he sees this thing go. And money will come, Flannery. For heaven's sake. Stop being such a party pooper.

5

On Monday our math teacher, Mr. Green, loses it again. Kyle Keating says the answer to number 26 is 35.

An awful silence falls over the class. Mr. Green strides down the aisle between the desks and puts Kyle in a headlock.

Kyle stays very still. Perhaps he's heard those stories that tell you to play dead if attacked by a bear. Mr. Green digs his knuckles into Kyle's head, giving him a noogie. It's supposed to be a playful noogie but Mr. Green is gritting his teeth with the effort of digging his knuckles into Kyle's skull.

Kyle, likely desperate for air, begins to pound his fist against the top of his desk. He may be trying to pound out a more considered answer to the math problem.

Can anybody, anybody at all, help out Mr. Keating? Mr. Green shouts.

It's 34, I say, though in that position, it's not like Kyle can hear me.

Geez, says Mr. Green. He lets Kyle go and gives himself a full body shake. Kyle is deep red and breathing hard. His eyes are watering, his dreadlocks mashed on one side. Actually, he looks kind of cute.

A girl, Mr. Green says with a shudder of disgust. A *girl* got the answer, Mr. Keating.

Kyle looks at all of us, wondering who his savior was. He touches his throat in an experimental way, as if trying to see if it's still functioning.

A girl! Mr. Green shouts. Mr. Green puts both his hands over his ears and stands for a moment like that, staring at the floor as though a movie's playing there. He whispers to himself all Hamlet-like: A girl, for God's sake!

The buzzer rings and Mr. Green looks up instantly as if nothing has happened.

Okay everybody, Mr. Green says. Good class, good work, good try there, Keating, see you guys tomorrow. And remember, math expands the brain.

He holds his hands up in front of his face, as if they hold a brain, and then very quietly says, *Pow*. He opens his hands, glancing fast to the left and right, as if the brain has exploded all over the classroom and he is watching gray matter drip down the walls.

Mr. Green is a kidder. At least, I hope he's kidding.

Next class: Religions of the World. Ms. Warren wants us to write an essay about our personal spiritual philosophies — the ones we live by.

Kyle Keating says his personal philosophy is existentialism, which means he believes in nothing, and so maybe he should pass in a blank piece of paper. Ms. Warren says he's welcome to do that, and she will give him a big fat nothing for his mark.

My personal spiritual philosophy is a whirling dervish doing a Riverdance in my heart, patent leather shoes beating out a rhythm that goes *Tyrone, Tyrone, Tyrone*.

Today is the sixth day straight Tyrone hasn't been in school. If I hadn't seen him at the mall last week, I'd be worried he'd died in a motorcycle crash or run away to join a cult or a punk band or the circus.

I know I should be furious that he keeps ignoring my messages about our assignment for Entrepreneurship. I should force myself to remember how he looked at that parrot-haired girl on the escalator and forget about him ever loving me back.

But then I find out that the Bursting Boils are reuniting for an all-ages show at the Kirk Community Centre on Friday night. The Bursting Boils were Tyrone's favorite local band before they broke up.

There's no way he won't be there.

On Friday Amber tells me she's going to the concert with Gary, but she'll see me there. I try on every single piece of clothing in my closet and excavate the bottom layer of clothes on my floor and the mountain of clothes piled at the end of my bed, and I take pictures in the mirror of every possible outfit and text them to Amber, but she doesn't text back. Maybe they've scheduled an extra practice at the pool. That's the only time Amber doesn't text back, when she's swimming.

The Kirk is just up the street from my house but I feel weird walking across the parking lot by myself. There's a crowd at the door and I try to blend in with some girls in front of me. They're comparing glow bracelets, waving their arms in the air.

The stars are out and it's dark and the band is already playing and it's packed.

I squish through the double doors and I'm in line to pay my five bucks — the show is a fundraiser for Oxfam — and there's about four people still ahead of me in the lineup when I see Amber.

She's standing on the edge of the stage at the other end of the hall above a mosh pit. People are pogo dancing in the center of the hall. The Bursting Boils are a big deal and there are people from high schools all over the city. People much older than us too, maybe even in their late twenties, and some kids from junior high.

The place is throbbing with punk. Carl Cole, who has a shaved head and a beard to his chest, is gripping the bass like it's a wild rabbit he needs to trap and he's jittering all over the stage trying to keep it from hopping out of his grip. Even from this distance I can see sweat flying off his face. Bubs McCarthy, the lead singer, does a somersault and lands on his feet. The crowd screams.

Kids are lobbing handfuls of cold spaghetti in the air and shaking cans of pop and beer and spraying each other and a bunch of people have brought eggs to throw at the band when they really get going, which is something that used to happen at Bursting Boils concerts in the old days.

Gary is in the mosh pit yelling at Amber, but I can't hear him. Her hands flutter near her ears just for a second.

Gary's pumping his fist at her. He seems to be encouraging her to jump. He's at the outer edge of the mosh pit, trying to muscle his way in, but keeps getting regurgitated by the crowd. Gary won't be anywhere near Amber if she jumps. She could get trampled. What the hell is she doing up there?

Then Amber spreads her arms out to the sides like wings, her fingers still fluttering. She's standing on the very edge of the stage. I jolt forward, ready to run and catch her, but Kyle Keating lurches over the card table and grabs me by the wrist. I hadn't even seen him there.

Hey, he says. Pay up. And thanks for saving me in math class.

I hand him the five bucks and he rolls a rubber stamp across the back of my hand. It says *Grade A Beef* in red ink.

Just then Amber tips forward into the tightly packed mosh.

Her body drops and a yell goes up in the pit. All the bodies in the center bow down, collapsing, a brief implosion like a jellyfish drawing itself together before pulsing forward in the dark. Then the mosh center rises up all at once, and there's Amber's body, floating as though it has no weight at all on the raised hands of the crowd. It seems like she's being passed along on a gazillion fingertips.

Amber's legs wriggle and her arms pull. She's swimming toward the edge of the mosh. She's being passed along and gently lowered at the edge of that tightly packed circle, right in front of Gary. She throws her arms around him and buries her face in his hair and the crowd closes over them.

That's when the sound of sirens tears through the hall, and everybody charges out the exit doors on all sides of the building. There's an ambulance and a fire truck and two cop cars. Ella Sloan has passed out on the lawn outside the hall and the paramedics are loading her onto a stretcher, her arm swinging limply from under a white sheet as they slip her into the back of the ambulance.

I manage to get out before the cops charge in and empty the place and I'm walking down the hill when I hear the slap of running sneakers behind me and the clatter of cans in a knapsack.

There's Tyrone materializing out of the dark, panting hard. The girl with the parrot hair is nowhere in sight.

That was wild, Tyrone says. I egged the cop car.

You didn't, I say. He's still holding the empty egg carton, but he tosses it into the branches of a tree. We're overtaken then by a crowd of girls running down the hill behind us.

Hi, Tyrone, one of them singsongs and they all giggle and run past us and their neon bracelets glow and wink until they turn the corner onto Queens Road.

We should talk about our proposal, Tyrone says, as if the idea has just occurred to him.

For our Entrepreneurship unit, he says. He has stopped in his tracks under a streetlight.

A stoppage.

A police car slows to a crawl beside us. There's an unbroken egg yolk on the tip of its windshield wiper. The car creeps along with us for a moment or two and Tyrone and I start walking, our eyes on the sidewalk in front of us, our fists deep in our pockets.

Then the cop car picks up speed and goes past. The red lights of the fire truck are still riffling through the maple trees up on the big hill of the Kirk parking lot. I'm walking a little ahead, but Tyrone tugs on the cuff of my jacket and then we're standing still. Tyrone has silver glitter in his hair and in his eyelashes and on his cheeks

He really is tall. He's looking down into my eyes. Not just looking, but somehow pouring himself into me. He jerks his chin as if he's calling up my whole being. Whoever I am, he wants to see me right here on the sidewalk, with the crowds pouring out of the Kirk, and all that glitter.

I think we should make potions, he says. Like when we were kids. Remember, we used to make potions in your backyard. These will be a gimmick, like canned fog or pet rocks. People will go crazy for it. Just one sip and bang, you're done. You know what I mean? Gone. Like ready to create the masterpiece of your dreams. Or achieve prosperity. Or become invisible to your enemies. Or a potion for making yourself shrink so you can escape through keyholes when things are bad. Or you fall in love with whoever you happen to set eyes on. I mean it could be just water and food coloring. Jokey, you know. But all profit. That's the part that would have Payne eating out of our hands.

Another crowd of girls are running down the hill from the Kirk and Tyrone looks up and calls out to Lily Parsons.

Hey, Lily, he says. And he turns to watch her walk away.

Hey, Tyrone, she calls without looking back.

A cold breeze rustles up from the harbor. There's a hint of frost in the air. It makes the maple trees swish and jostle over us. It makes a bell of Lily Parsons' skirt as she turns the corner at the bottom of the hill. A bunch of people have fake IDs and they're heading to Distortion. A single yellow leaf drops down near our feet.

I got to go, Tyrone says. He hikes his knapsack up on his shoulder. Again I hear those spray-paint cans. He's obviously going to make graffiti somewhere downtown. His last SprayPig tag was in the paper a few days ago — fluorescent pink and silver, the "S" a big boa constrictor squeezing all the other letters together. There were comments online about it and an editorial. He'd sprayed the Bank of Montreal. People were disgusted.

Think about it, he says. Magic potions. Halfway down the hill he turns and keeps going backwards, still talking.

People will lap it up, he says. We can make a fortune, Flannery. Especially if they start to believe in it.

Then he's gone.

On Monday, Amber and Gary are sitting together in the cafeteria and nobody else is at their table. For some reason I don't even go near. Even though I've eaten lunch with Amber every day since — what, kindergarten? — it's as though they have an invisible force field around them. I stand there with my tray.

Another stoppage.

Finally I make Laura Linegar squish over at the end of a big table with a bunch from the drama club and a few grade tens and the rest are from my homeroom. I've already unwrapped my ham and cheese when I realize I'm sitting across from Elaine Power and Kyle Keating.

Elaine is one of those people who says the word "interestingly" before a lot of her statements. She starts telling Kyle that, interestingly, the adult monarch butterfly lives on nectar from very deep in the flowers.

Kyle wiggles his eyebrows at me and repeats this in a faux-sexy British accent. Nectar from *very* deep in the flower.

And the viceroy butterfly flaps its wings more frequently than the monarch and glides, says Elaine, when it wants to take a rest.

Hey, Flan, just talking about the monarch butterfly, Kyle says. There's a lot of stuff most people just don't know.

Apparently the fundraiser with the Bursting Boils had been Kyle's idea. They'd already raised 1,500 bucks when the cops showed up.

This afternoon I'm heading down to Oxfam with the money, Kyle says. Want to come, Flan?

That's when I notice Tyrone standing in the door of the cafeteria. He's talking to someone. Lily Parsons.

Nah, I say. Thanks, though, Kyle. Got to get started on my Entrepreneurship project.

Started? says Elaine. You mean you haven't *started* yet?

6

Have I mentioned that I love my brother? I do. Or at least I try really hard to. For one thing, Miranda says I have to no matter what. She says we're a family, just the three of us, and we have to be there for each other.

He's six years old, saucy and spoiled rotten. He has broken my bead necklaces just to watch the individual beads ping-ping-ping down the wooden stairs.

Felix yelling, Go for it, beads. Make your escape while you can!

Last summer he sold my Walkman (which was an antique) to some kids down the street for fifty cents. He was clearly breastfed for way too long (until age three and a half, yelling in cafes, *I want breast milk!*) and he had the nerve to come along ten years after me just when I thought for sure I was the center of the universe.

The moment he came home from the hospital, I was demoted from Number One Child to Number One Diaper Changer.

Felix Malone has golden ringlets and the face of a cherub — all rosy cheeks and big blue innocent eyes. But don't let that fool you. This is a boy who got down from his highchair when he was two and a half, picked up a very big glass of orange juice, carefully carrying it all the way across the room without spilling a drop, and then, when I wasn't looking, poured the whole glass down the back of my jeans.

And lately he's been screaming his head off in bank lineups if Miranda says he can't have an ice cream, or else he's lying down on the sidewalk outside Freak Lunchbox kicking his feet and banging his fists on the concrete because she won't let him buy the gumball machine on display in the window.

It was the public tantrums that made Miranda decide he needed to learn about self-discipline. She enrolled him in a Kenpo Karate class that takes place in the Holy Heart auditorium every Thursday evening. I have no idea why Miranda thinks we can afford karate lessons. It's the third week of school and we still haven't been able to buy my biology book, which everybody else has already purchased and which, by the way, is a *required* textbook — if not exactly a potboiler, despite the acclaimed and no doubt compelling chapter on Bunsen-burner safety which I haven't had the pleasure of reading yet.

But I understand why Miranda got the karate lessons when I see Felix racing through the gymnasium door in his little ninja outfit, his rosy face full of joy as he springs into a flying karate kick while yelling *hiiiii-yaaaa*. I can't begrudge him a single thing. Not the karate lessons, not ice cream, not the helicopter drone, not even being born.

On the other hand. Felix has grown fond lately of sneaking up on me at very vulnerable moments wearing steamed-up swimming goggles and a camouflage cap with the head of a cod fish on one side and the tail on the other side. Also a sheriff's badge and a rawhide vest with fringes and a kerchief tied bank-robber style around the lower half of his face. And a checkered tablecloth tied around his shoulders under which he hides a Super Soaker. Even though it's practically October and getting very cold outside and the time for Super Soakers has long since passed.

I will give you an example of the kind of vulnerable moment I mean.

You know when you find yourself in front of a mirror and you try that experiment where you don't blink for as long as you can and you just stare hard into your own eyes?

The room gets dark behind you and your face starts to change. If you stare long enough without blinking, your face wobbles and stretches and it isn't your face anymore.

And maybe you continue to look in the mirror and you begin to wonder, with every atom of your being, if anyone in this whole darned crazy world will ever love you.

And you suddenly imagine yourself dying young.

That is a vulnerable moment.

It is a glance into the abyss. You actually tippy-toe around the abyss of loneliness. Look down. Vertigo. You're dizzy and nauseous and not loved, that's what you are. And, okay, a little self-indulgent, maybe.

But, what if you were to die in some horrific way before true love can find you?

Perhaps you imagine darting out into a busy street to save a toddler from an oncoming bus. Yes, there is a bus. There is a toddler. Cue the violins, slo-mo turn of your head, hair swishing over your shoulder, eyes wide with horror and you start to run. You're running as though through a river of molasses — slow, graceful, beautiful — and you gather up the toddler in your arms and toss her/him/it to the side in time but, alas, too late for you to save yourself.

The bus pile-drives you into tomorrow.

Cut slow-mo; hold the violins.

Oranges and apples burst from your shopping bag and roll downhill. The crowd on the sidewalk screams in terror.

Everything is growing dark. Death has opened its great black maw to swallow you whole. You are prepared to go gently. Goodnight, you think. Goodnight moon, Goodnight bowl of milk, Goodnight cat, Goodnight Tyrone O'Rourke.

But wait! You notice Tyrone O'Rourke, who has been, as divine intervention or sheer coincidence would have it, a passenger on the very bus that has been your doom. He has run to the front of the bus and is smashing his fist against the window. Now, for the first time in your about-to-be-cut-tragically-short life, Tyrone O'Rourke notices you. He finally notices you. Notices your shy beauty, your great spirit ebbing slowly from your half-closed eyes . . .

Tyrone, Tyrone, you whisper. But there is no sound.

He sees you lying on the pavement and thinks of how you have known each other pretty much all your lives. Tyrone is just coming home from hanging at the mall, and he has witnessed the accident and he has had a revelation.

Tyrone O'Rourke loves you.

You're toast, almost. It's curtains. The violins have started up again, they are going crazy right now, those violins. But Tyrone, beating on the glass door of the bus, is screaming, *Let me out, let me out*, perhaps not realizing, in his shock and haste, that the bus door folds *in* and he has to actually step back in order to exit and carry out a successful rescue.

But he does step back, he does, and the doors open with a hiss and there he is on the street, his dark hair all afire with sunlight, tears on his cheeks. Tyrone O'Rourke by your side and about to kiss you, having yelled, *Can't somebody get an ambulance?*

Knowing the end is near, he gathers you into his arms, and in that silent, searching moment, you are forced to nearly burst out of your skin with fright and probably smack your head on the medicine cabinet because of a blast of very authentic-sounding machine-gun fire from a Super Soaker jabbing into your bum.

Felix Malone has been hiding behind the shower curtain the whole time. A stakeout that required the insane patience only a master criminal could summon.

A super-soaker blast and then your jeans are soaking wet. Why you little fink, you stinker, you, you, you. You swing for him. You try to grab the fish tail sticking out of the side of his head but he's out the bathroom door, down the stairs, out the screen door and down the sidewalk and you're left with a fistful of nothing.

This is what you deal with on a regular basis.

7

———

Tyrone O'Rourke is coming over! Here! Today! He's coming over to my house so we can pull the proposal for our Entrepreneurship unit together. I mean, it has to be in on Monday. He said he'd be here by four, so I rushed home after school and I've been trying on every outfit I have, again, and texting pictures to Amber, again, but she hasn't responded, *again*. I sent her a final text — *AMBBBBEEERRRR??????* — but nada. So I go with my jeans and my Ramones T-shirt.

And I start gathering up all the piles of clothes in my bedroom and jamming them into the laundry basket. After about ten minutes I can actually see most of the floorboards. There were a couple of plates under the bed with dried ketchup smeared all over them and an old chip bag that looked like a mouse got at it. Also a broken glass and three dollars in change.

Miranda goes by my room just as I'm putting on some eyeshadow.

You look nice, she says. I tell her Tyrone is coming over and I try to sound casual.

Tyrone O'Rourke? she says.

59

To get our project done, I say. He's my partner in Entrepreneurship. We're going to make potions. His idea.

Like when you were kids! Miranda says.

Yeah, like maybe a love potion or something for prosperity or eternal youth.

Want me to break out those frozen puff pastries? she says. Maybe whip some cream? A little strawberry jam?

I thought you were saving those pastries for your consciousness-raising thing, I say. Your feminist meeting or whatever.

It'd be a nice snack for you and Tyrone, she says. While you work on your project. With the bedroom door open.

I look as shocked as I possibly can.

Of course with the door open, Miranda, I say. It's a school project for gosh sakes. I innocently bat my peacock-blue eyelids at her.

And she's skipping off down the stairs — absurdly humming "Here Comes the Bride" — to dig the frozen pastries out of the freezer. I make my bed and fluff the pillows. I clear off my desk and stuff all the extra papers under the bed. Squirt a little perfume in the air in case everything smells like old chips or the empty pizza box I found in the closet with a few curled-up pepperonis stuck to the cardboard. I decide that when Tyrone arrives I'll put on some music. Last Christmas Miranda gave me a turntable she found at the Sally Ann. It came with three records: Cat Stevens, Beyoncé and Michael Jackson.

I have one of those antique clocks in my room with the numerals on little plastic tabs that flick over every minute. The tabs make a *shish-click* every time they drop down.

At 4:47 I put on Cat Stevens, and the song "Katmandu," for some reason, makes me cry. The line about *strange bewildering skies*. Even just the word *bewildering*. Why does everything have to be so bewildering? Also, the eyeshadow has flaked into my left eye and it's red and irritated.

Miranda appears at the door of my bedroom with a big plate of the pastries.

If you think I'm crying because Tyrone didn't show up, you're sadly mistaken, I tell her.

I didn't think that for a minute, Miranda says.

I'm just worried about our project, which is in danger of being late, and stupid Mr. Payne takes off two percent for every late day and I actually give a damn about my marks, okay?

Absolutely, says Miranda. Have one of these.

I take a pastry and stuff it in my face.

I mean, I'm actually a responsible person, I say.

I know, says Miranda. You blow my mind sometimes.

Yeah, but not too responsible, right? Like, I'm not boring.

Certainly not, says Miranda. She sits down beside me on the bed and starts eating one of the pastries.

I'm capable of rebelling, I say.

Aren't these yummy? she asks.

I mean, I could just, say, forget the stupid Entrepreneurship unit like some people, but then I would fail. And so would Tyrone. That'd show him.

Flannery, you're beautiful. Do you know that? I mean you really are very beautiful. I'm not just saying that because you're my daughter. Although you do have some of my fine features.

And then I am really crying, and also choking on a big gob of whipped cream that went down the wrong pipe.

Hey, I almost forgot what color your bedroom floor was, says Miranda. Then Cat Stevens starts skipping. Miranda pushes herself off the bed and carefully lifts the needle on the turntable and blows away a tiny ball of dust. Then she turns it off.

Listen, girl-child, she says, I'm going to leave these pastries with you. I'm going to go down and see if I can rustle up some real grub for dinner. Why don't you put some time in on your proposal?

I guess, I say. And she closes the door behind her. I sit down at my desk with a pen and paper. And I write like crazy. I've got the whole thing done by 6:17 when Miranda calls out that dinner is ready. I've outlined the whole project. Tyrone and I are going to be manufacturing love potions, eternal youth potions, a potion for prosperity, a potion for divining the future through dreams, and a potion for invisibility.

And when I say *Tyrone*, I mean that at the very end of the proposal I signed his name too.

Even though he didn't do anything.

Even though I put on eyeshadow for him and even though I'm not even worth a text to say he wasn't coming.

Even though girls probably do this kind of thing for Tyrone all the time just because he's handsome and charming and because he makes everybody fall in love with him. Flannery Malone and Tyrone O'Rourke, right there on the cover page of our proposal. I'm pretty sure we'll both get full marks.

On Monday I wait for Amber outside her novel/cinema class. She never did text me back about the outfits, and we didn't talk all weekend, which has to be a first. But the qualifying meet for this year's Nationals is in two weeks so I know she was probably putting in extra swimming time.

Whether she wants to talk about it or not, I know there's a lot of pressure on her for this one. Just because she made the Nationals last year doesn't mean she'll automatically get to go this year. And I know for a fact that the men in her dad's office have formed a betting pool. They have a big of pile money riding on her.

So I decided to leave her be. Though I *was* about to call her once I realized Tyrone wasn't going to show up at four like he said, or at 4:47, or at all.

But something made me change my mind. I knew Amber, and I knew she would definitely be angry with Tyrone for not coming. And she definitely would not be okay with me putting his name on the proposal when he hadn't done any of the work. She might not understand the way his life is. I mean, there were probably plenty of reasons he couldn't show up.

And basically, I want Amber and Tyrone to be friends because they're both going to be in my life forever.

So I decided not to call her. I was in my room on a Saturday night reading *Slaughterhouse Five* and eating popcorn and painting my toenails and the phone was right there on the bedside table and I didn't so much as glance at it.

But when do I *not* call Amber if something has upset me?

So I glanced at the phone. Then I snatched it up and called her.

But she didn't answer. I texted again. She didn't text back.

Sometimes with those swim practices they push her so hard she conks out on the couch as soon as she gets home. Sometimes her parents leave her there all night because they can't wake her up.

So she was probably comatose and snoring her head off and didn't call back. No biggie.

But I'm dying to know what she and Gary are doing for their Entrepreneurship unit. She told me last week it was top secret (though, come on, seriously?) until they handed in their proposal, but that she'd tell me today after her novel/cinema class and I'd be the first, besides Gary, to know.

The classroom door flies open and bangs against the wall and everybody bulges through all at once. But when Amber comes through she's with Melody Martin, who goes out with the drummer in Gary Bowen's band. Melody has her hair dyed pink and she has pink tights and pink patent leather Docs that go up to her knees.

They are both looking at Instagram on Melody's phone. Amber giggles with her hand clamped over her mouth and her eyes open really wide.

Wait, just wait, says Melody. She's flicking through a whack of pictures. They walk a few more steps, their shoulders pressed together because the laughter is making them stumble into each other. They stop again because Melody, apparently, has come to another hilarious picture and they're snorting and doubling over and Amber is doing that fake jaw-drop thing.

Wait until you see this one, Melody says. Are you ready? I'm not sure you're ready for this.

Let me see, let me see, Amber says. And Melody holds the phone out at arm's length, right in front of Amber's face.

Awesome, she says.

Didn't I tell you? says Melody Martin. I told you, didn't I?

Amber, I say.

She looks up, startled.

I realize that I am afraid she will look right through me as if I don't exist. I have never felt anything like this with Amber before. I don't know what kind of expression I have on my face, but it feels accusing and lonely.

I've never seen Amber act that way either, practically falling over with laughter at a dumb picture on somebody's phone. I've never even heard her laugh like that before. It's a new laugh, breathy and full of shivers.

And since when has she been such close friends with Melody Martin? I guess it's because both of their boyfriends are in the same band.

But then there's that Amber smile. She's lit up. Her whole face grinning. She's glad to see me. Really glad.

Oh, Flannery, she says. Look! And she grabs the phone from Melody for me to see. It's a picture of Amber and Melody and Brittany Bishop and Gary Bowen and Jordan and somebody else's feet and somebody's else's arms all piled on a couch together on top of each other, each of them with a beer held up for the picture.

At first I think Amber must have been photoshopped into the picture. She doesn't go to parties with these people. We hardly ever talk to them.

Then I remember trying to text her on Saturday night and she didn't answer.

I can't believe she didn't tell me about the party. She left me out on purpose.

Cool, I say.

Yeah, says Melody. Cool. She takes the phone back and slides it into her back pocket.

See you at the game, Amber, Melody says. And she sashays down the corridor.

What game? I ask.

The basketball game tonight, Amber says.

Because of your new interest in the sport, I say.

I'm interested, yes. In basketball.

But don't you have practice? I say. I sound like Amber's dad. But I thought swimming was why she wasn't answering my texts. Now I realize she's just been ignoring me.

It's a stunning revelation. Although I've seen her do it enough times when her mom calls. She checks the phone to see who it is and then she turns off the ringer and lays it face down and talks just a decibel louder right over the muffled *brrrr* it makes. She behaves as if the phone doesn't exist.

I'm skipping swimming practice, she says.

Now it's my turn to let my jaw drop.

I don't have to practice every single day of my life just because my dad has this pipe dream I'm going to be an Olympic swimmer, she says. And another thing. If I want to go to a party with my boyfriend, I don't have to ask your permission. It was a date, okay? I was invited. I couldn't just invite anyone I wanted to somebody else's house. I thought you'd be happy for me, Flannery. That I was having such a good time.

I wasn't even thinking about that! I say.

I saw the look on your face.

I didn't have any look, I say.

But I know I must have, because my stomach is swirling. She's mad at *me*?

All I know is that I don't want to be in a fight with Amber. We never fight. I don't understand what's happening here, but I don't want her to walk away angry.

So what are you guys doing? For your unit? You and Gary, I say.

Amber hesitates. I can see she's still upset, but she also wants to talk about Gary. She can't help herself.

We're making a music video of his band, she says. We'll sell DVDs and put it on iTunes. I think we can attract the attention of a label if the video is good. I finished the proposal last night while Gary was jamming. I'm kind of proud of it, actually.

And all of a sudden she's smiling again. The Amber smile.

It's going to be so cool, Flannery. Everybody is working on it, and my parents are fronting us the overhead. I want you to help with costumes.

She takes out her phone and flicks through some pictures. There's a list of people working on the production: a videographer, an editor, a sound person — and under costumes, I see my name along with Melody Martin's.

I'm too relieved about being included to be pissed off about not being asked first.

We're thinking of a gangster theme, she says. Black and white, lots of mist, lots of shadows.

Then Amber gets a text.

Oh no, she says. She actually smacks her forehead. Gary is waiting for me. He's *not* going to be happy.

And just like that, she's racing down the corridor, away from me.

Hey, I say. Want to talk after the game?

But she turns the corner and is running down the stairs. She didn't even ask what Tyrone and I have decided to do for our Entrepreneurship thing.

Which is just as well. *Overhead*? That is not a word that made it into my/our Entrepreneurship proposal.

I think of what Tyrone said — *just food coloring and water, all profit* — and I feel a little better.

But then I think, What the heck are we going to put these dazzlingly colorful, profitable creations *in*? I'd forgotten all about packaging!

8

A word about my family's financial situation. Dire. It's a dire situation right now.

The dads — my dad and Felix's dad — have never contributed any child support (in my dad's case, well, he can hardly be held accountable as he doesn't know he's a dad, and in Hank's case, well, he doesn't know he's a dad, either).

Which, well, contributes to the predicament we currently find ourselves in — namely, having to deal with a phone call from Newfoundland Power.

Miranda has not paid the electricity bill. There have been three cut-off notices. The third one says, You have not responded to our previous attempts to contact you. We are sending a field worker into your area to discontinue services.

I watch Miranda fold the third cut-off notice into a fan and bat her eyelashes at me over the top of it.

A field worker sounds kind of intriguing, she says. Do you think he'll be wearing one of those tool belts slung low over his hips? I'm a fool for tool belts.

The third cut-off notice says this: You will see your breath as you stand over the toaster in the morning waiting for your toast to pop.

You know what? the notice says in big red letters. Forget toast. There is no toast. You are toast. We have cut off the electricity. Try burning the kitchen chairs so you can warm your hands over the flames.

Then it says, It's not all bad. Social workers will probably arrive and take your little brother off kicking and screaming to an orphanage. You will never have to share the Oreos with him again. He will be fed to hungry lions.

The third notice says, Have you heard of the dark side of the moon?

Or it says, You know that fairy tale, "The Little Match Girl?" The kid who has to stand outside in sub-zero temperatures lighting one match after another to warm her little hands, and each match holds a memory of, like, a roast chicken or the kid's poor mother who died of consumption under a pile of potato sacks, or some rich guy in a shiny top hat who tossed her a gold coin once, and then she's out of matches and basically turns into a human ice cube. They find her dead in somebody's doorway in the morning. Remember that one? Yeah, well, ditto.

Miranda has never called us accidents. She prefers to call us surprises. My mother loves babies. And she says she loved our fathers.

I know it's true she loved Felix's father, because I know who he is. For a few years before Felix was born, he practically lived with us.

Hank doesn't know he's Felix's dad. And Felix doesn't know it, either. Miranda *pretends* she doesn't know it. We aren't allowed to talk about it.

But I know it. It's something I have to contend with, this knowledge. It feels like a stone tucked under my rib. The trouble is, for a while, maybe I thought of Hank as my dad too.

My father — X — she's happy to talk about. Even though she only knew him that one night before he returned to France and before she noticed her first skipped period. Tra-la.

One thing I may have forgotten to mention: X arrived in St. John's on a sailing vessel made of garbage. Bits of Styrofoam and rubber tires and crushed metal from the dump. He was one of six environmentalists who were circumnavigating the world to protest the practice of selling garbage to developing countries because we have nowhere else to put it.

The kind of garbage people think they want because they watch infomercials at one in the morning where women in leotards strap themselves into big vibrating belts that are supposed to make them lose twenty pounds in two days and only cost $22.99, or the kind of junk we're supposed to invent in our Entrepreneurship class.

There are beaches all over Africa covered with fridge doors and used tampons and Ritz cracker boxes, old shoes, the husks of microwave ovens with the glass smashed out, car batteries leaking neon green juice that would sizzle the eyes out of your head if you even glanced at it, things with a slime of maggots squirming and writhing in the heat, cars crunched and stacked like colorful pancakes — mountains of this stuff dumped on white beaches, mountains that tumble toward the jungles beyond the beach and crawl inland.

This, apparently, enraged my father.

So X and his friends built a boat entirely of garbage. And sailed around the world.

In short, my dad — not exactly Youth Entrepreneur Champion-of-the-Year genetic material.

And then there's my mother. Miranda is an artist, but she makes conceptual art and installations, none of which sell. They aren't *supposed* to sell. Last winter, for instance, she did a series of ice sculptures. Her last piece was a mother polar bear and cub set adrift on an ice pan.

She carved the ice with a chainsaw, chisels and drills, and she polished it with a blowtorch. She wore goggles and a snow-suit, her steel-toed boots. Yanked the pull-cord on the chainsaw and there's a cloud of blue smoke. She touched the chainsaw to the block of ice and a giant fan of ice chips flew into the sky.

I don't know how she could see the shape in the block of ice, but she walked around it and stood back and moved in. She scratched some lines on the surface. Then the saw squealed and ground and ice flew some more and, little by little, the shoulder of a lumbering, downcast momma polar bear emerged, the surface roughed-up like fur, the big head swinging to the side to check for her cub, the doomed little family emerging in the evening light.

Melting is part of the piece. It's a comment on global warming, Miranda said.

The whole piece — two bears on an ice pan — was constructed on logs so it could be rolled out to sea and set adrift. We had a big bonfire the day it was launched. All of Miranda's friends showed up. It felt like half the population of St. John's was there. Amber's mom and dad were there too. Amber and I kept the fire going and helped the little kids roast marshmallows and wieners.

There was an essay about Miranda in *Canadian Art* with lots of pictures, and another one in *Border Crossings* and she heard from galleries across Canada, some of them offering an exhibit. So the piece was a huge success. But of course you couldn't sell a melting polar bear and her cub.

This summer she's doing an installation of sculptures made out of bird corpses covered in oil — it will be a powerful comment on the environmental dangers of the oil industry but not a big money maker, I'm guessing.

Miranda also writes a parenting blog in the hopes that she will garner advertising once she secures a big following. She *was* waitressing and doing shifts at Sunny Horizons, a private company that takes care of babies who are wards of the state. But she had to stay up all night in an apartment behind the mall and the babies were sometimes physically abused and the job made it impossible to really be there for Felix and last year she had to have an ovarian cyst removed and was in hospital for six days and when she got out she felt too weak to work and she applied for welfare.

So that's the situation. We used to be what's called the working poor, but now we're just plain old poor. The fact that Miranda works on her blog every day and volunteers at Eastern Edge Gallery and makes art all the time doesn't seem to qualify as actual work.

So we're welfare. Miranda says sometimes people have to ask for help and there's no shame in that.

But I can see it embarrasses her cashing the check at the supermarket when we get groceries. If she puts the check in the bank, they'll put a hold on it.

It embarrasses the cashiers too. First Miranda will chat with them about the weather, or she'll ask how far into their shift they are, and *then* she brings out her check and her ID and everything goes quiet. Miranda usually tries to get the same cashier, a woman named Cheryl, according to her name tag. Cheryl has Miranda's check in the drawer so fast it's like she's doing a card trick. But Cheryl isn't always working.

The one Miranda doesn't like to get is Tracy, who is not

judgmental about social assistance but very deliberate and often confused.

Tracy lifts her glasses which hang on a string around her neck and puts them on the tip of her nose. She makes a hard little frown and holds the check out at arm's length in one hand and Miranda's driver's license in the other.

Finally, she calls out to the head cashier. By this time there's usually a big lineup behind us. Finally, the head cashier comes over and Tracy lays the check on the little counter and they both really study it. Then the head cashier, whose name tag says Joanne, will pick the check up and look at both sides, and lay it down again and smooth it flat. Then she nods regretfully.

Yes, girl, go ahead, Joanne will say.

What Miranda says about her parenting blog (besides *You'll see, Flan, soon we'll be rolling in advertising dough*) is that parenting is something everybody knows how to do anyway. But there's a lot pressure out there. People need encouragement to listen to themselves.

Innate is one of Miranda's favorite words. She has an *innate* talent for parenting, she says. Look how you turned out, Flannery, she says. You are my finest hour.

As though I myself had nothing to do with it.

She does not allude to Felix Malone during these conversations, because he is not a prime example of good behavior.

So, the blog. Naturally my personal life gets turned into cute, embarrassing little stories for the Internet without regard for my privacy or existence as an actual person with human rights versus Miranda's right to freedom of speech and, as she calls it, "her material."

Her argument generally goes this way: I carried you *inside* me. I have *stretch* marks. I gave up everything for you. Surely that means I can write a few words about the experience.

Felix is flying the helicopter drone around the kitchen. He flicks the remote lever and the drone lowers right in front of my face. The red light is on, so I know he's recording a not very flattering video of me arguing with Miranda. I swat at it with the dish towel.

He zooms the helicopter so it swerves around me and across the kitchen to hover over the phone, which has been ringing for several minutes.

We all know it's Newfoundland Power and I am refusing to answer it.

Answer it, Flannery.

I'm not answering it.

Answer the phone, Flannery.

I'm not lying, Miranda.

Miranda flings out her arm, finger pointing at the phone.

Flannery, answer the phone this instant, she says.

Look, Miranda, I say, I am *not* telling the bill collector that my mother, unfortunately, died in a deep-fat fire just yesterday, leaving two orphan children to mourn.

I'll say it! Felix yells. Let me do it.

The helicopter zooms up over the fridge and hovers over the ringing phone. Miranda is aghast, she says, that I am slavishly and uncritically taking the side of the One Percent, the corporate elite, the faceless power brokers, the freaking *power company* for God's sake, rather than taking the side of the disenfranchised, a.k.a. Miranda.

Your own flesh and blood, she says.

It isn't a joke, Miranda. They're going to cut off the electricity.

So tell them.

The truth is important to me, I say.

The truth is nuanced, she says.

Nuanced? I yell. What's nuanced about faking the death of my mother?

That was a joke, she says.

Oh, ha ha. My mother burned to death, hilarious.

Just tell them I'm not home. Look, at least tell them how unfair the situation is, Flannery. I'm doing my best here and I can't make ends meet. Is that fair? Let's make them uneasy, at least.

I'm not answering the phone, Miranda. It's embarrassing that we can't pay. I find it embarrassing, okay?

She assures me there will be a parenting blog about my betrayal. Then she snatches up the phone. And sure enough it's the Newfoundland Power Company. She listens for a while saying, Mmmhmm, yes. Mmmhmm. I see. Yes. Of course. Mmmhmm.

The helicopter drone has moved across the room and is hovering over the bowl of salad. Tonight we are having mac and cheese, which is Felix's favorite meal, but the salad could ruin everything. He only eats white food. Bread, pasta, white cheddar cheese, vanilla cake. The helicopter drone buzzes angrily over all the lettuce.

And when you say your field staff will pay a visit to cut off our power, would that be you? Miranda is saying. Because maybe I wouldn't mind if you paid a visit. We could sit down face to face and discuss, human being to human being, the inequality of this situation. And you have such a lovely phone voice. I roll my eyes and Miranda shrugs. She spoons up the salad onto two of three plates sitting on the counter.

Miranda heard a theory a while back that you should put a little of everything on the side of a picky child's plate and gradually his palate will develop.

It's a theory that goes against everything my mother believes in. This trying to trick a child into doing what *you* want,

this method of bribing or starving or forcing food down un-
willing gullets.

That may have been the inspiration for her to start her parenting blog in the first place.

I see, Miranda is saying. So what's the least amount I could
possibly pay without having your field staff come to cut off the
power? Because it is getting cold out there. And I do have two
children. We're actually having trouble keeping food on the
table. Miranda is tearing off squares of paper towel for napkins
and she has the ketchup bottle and a jar of pickled beets.

Okay, yes. I can pay that, she says. By October tenth, you
said. Yes, I understand. Yes, I got your notices. You're being
very understanding. She puts down the beet jar and points her
finger down her throat and pretends to gag. I cross my eyes.

You're going to *pay* the heat bill? I ask when she finally
hangs up the phone.

You heard the conversation, Flan. They're going to cut off
the heat. The electricity. I can't let that happen. Don't worry, I
should have a check from the Arts Council by then.

And then we can get my biology book too, right?

We'll have to see how much the check is for, Flannery. You'll
have to borrow somebody else's book for little while longer.

At that moment the helicopter drone nosedives into the
sink, which is full of soapy water.

Black Hawk down! screams Felix. He rushes over and pulls
out the dripping helicopter. It's probably fried. We could have
sold it at Traders when he got bored with it. The pawnshop
might have coughed up just enough for my biology book.

I need a schoolbook, I scream. Is that too much to ask? I
wrench open the closet door and let it slam against the wall,
grab my windbreaker, shove my feet into my sneakers and
slam the front door behind me.

Magnificent Mothering with Miranda

Your child knows what his body needs. Trust your child. Listen to what he tells you. Really listen. Don't say broccoli when your child says s'mores. We muddle the child's innate understanding of his nutritional needs by foisting upon innocent taste buds dank, limp, hairy, over-boiled vegetables and unripe fruit. The particular, slimy texture of banana is revolting to some children, don't forget that. People say the potassium in a banana is good for them. If the kid doesn't like banana, to potassium I say Pshaw!

Think of the carrot in the bottom drawer of the fridge. Think of the sweating plastic bag the carrots are crowded into, brownish juice in the plastic folds and wrinkles, the breathy stink of earth when you tear the plastic. This could ruin a child's appetite for a lifetime.

Do not insult your child's intelligence. The raw carrot stick is not a fun snack. Even if you smear it with peanut butter. Who would eat that? Who thought to call a celery stick with processed cheese and raisins Ants on a Log? Your child knows that calling them Ants on a Log doesn't make them taste any better.

Here's another piece of advice: Your kid doesn't like crusts, you cut them off.

Warning: A single Brussels sprout contains within its tight, balled-up little leaves enough despair and loneliness to destroy a childhood forever.

Don't do it.

Don't give your child a Brussels sprout. Your child will grow old and wither before your very eyes.

Next week: The Evils of a "Time Out."

9

It's very cold. I'm only wearing a hoodie and a wind-breaker and it's already dark. My ears are burning and I'm walking as fast as I can until I calm down. I can see stars above the white oil tanks on the Southside Hills. The digital clock at city hall says it's 7:06, and the temperature is minus 5.

I'm mad at everyone — mad at Amber, mad at Tyrone. Mad at Miranda for buying the video helicopter instead of my freaking biology book. Even though Felix has been making some pretty good videos.

And I'm mad at the power company. I mean, heat and electricity, shouldn't that be free? Doesn't everyone have a right to shelter? That's part of shelter.

I cross the street and head down to Water, past the construction on Waldegrave. The backhoes are abandoned at this hour but glow bright yellow in the floodlight of the excavated pit.

I'm jogging past the antique shop and the flower shop and those grungy, ancient bars down there where the bikers hang out. I'm on the west end of Water, across the street from the site of the new parking garage, next to the old train station.

A car passes on the other side of the street, and — *boom* — I see the graffiti. It's on the plywood wall around the parking garage construction site. The headlights of the car run over the mural, making it flare.

The Snow Queen. Tyrone has been doing a series of angry Snow Queens all fall, but this is the most extravagant thing I've ever seen him do. It runs the length of a whole block.

This Snow Queen is mostly silver and aquamarine and her hair flies around her head in silver tendrils and she has high comic-book cheekbones and a kind of silver bodice of scales and a flowing cape. There's a team of horses and flashes of lightning and a dragon covered in silver scales just like the ones on the Snow Queen's bodice.

All of this appears out of the dark in the few seconds it takes the car headlights to pass over the plywood wall, and at the very end of the wall, shaking a can of spray paint, is Tyrone O'Rourke. I see him, and then I think I can hear the ball bearings in the can doing their mad dance as he shakes it.

Hey, I call out. I do some jumping jacks, crisscrossing my arms over my head. Hey, hey, I'm yelling.

His arm is raised with the paint can. He's spraying in the Snow Queen's left nostril.

Another car goes past, and another. His shadow stretches up high and sinks back down, the stallions rear, the whites of their eyes show, the dragon's claws sparkle. The mural is like a living thing, teeming with action and life.

Now a car slows on my side of the road and pulls to a stop beside me. Its engine is idling. Two burly men sit inside, one with a shiny film of short gray hair that glows in the streetlight. The other man has a black moustache and is so tall his head touches the roof of the car.

I freeze, mid-jumping jack.

The men are staring at me. What do they see? A sixteen-year-old freckled, buxom, near frostbitten, gangly kid doing jumping jacks in a desolate part of downtown, and she's jumping up and down to gain the attention of...? Who?

Their heads both turn in unison to look across the street and they spot the graffiti.

Tyrone is making the Snow Queen's nostril flare just like Miranda's, actually, when she's cleaning the fridge and she finds a package of liquefied asparagus. It's liquefied because who has time to clean out the fridge when you're busy carving life-sized polar bears out of ice to protest global warming?

Or like when the pipes freeze and she has to go down in the basement with a blowtorch.

In those moments, Miranda's nostrils do their thing. They go flat and wide and quiver with flibbertigibbet determination.

Speaking of mothers, Tyrone's spray-painted Snow Queen looks a lot like his own mother, in fact, except that so far the Snow Queen has only one perfectly flared nostril instead of two.

I hear Tyrone shake the paint can again. The wind has died down a little and I really can hear it from all the way across the four lanes, a traffic island and a few skinny trees. I can even hear the hiss, the spraying of silver.

The one nostril makes the Snow Queen look like she has been waiting for that other nostril all her life. A lot is on the line for her. Her eyes are nearly bulging out from her dramatic cheekbones.

Tyrone is wearing a black hoodie and black jeans and a mask — like a gas mask, so he doesn't breathe in the fumes, and goggles, so the paint doesn't get in his eyes. He looks like E.T. or a cricket.

The silver-haired man on the passenger side of the car reaches down around his feet for something and slaps a siren on the dash and it whoop-whoops and throws out an arm of red light and blue light and they screech away to pull a U-ey farther up the road.

I yell, Run, it's the cops. *Run!*

Tyrone turns and sees me and sees the cops and he bends and sweeps up his knapsack full of paint cans and takes off around the corner of the construction site.

They saw him because of me.

Because I was jumping around and waving like an idiot. It's my fault.

Behind the construction site there's the Waterford River and Symes Bridge. Tyrone's already sprinting over the bridge by the time the cops get their car pulled around the traffic island that divides the road. Now Tyrone is racing up through the forest on the Southside Hills, and I keep losing sight of him, but then I can see the tree branches swaying all their orange leaves as he climbs along the overgrown path that leads through the woods.

The cop car has skidded to a stop on the other side of the road and they've jumped out of the car and they're on foot, running up the same path behind the construction site. They're closing the distance between themselves and Tyrone pretty fast.

Then there's an engine revving up. I see the fan of a single headlight blinking as it passes through the tree trunks.

He's got his motorcycle! After a moment the cops come running back down around the building site and they get in the car and pull another U-ey, the siren going, and they're heading up to the Southside Hills.

The siren is very loud and high-pitched and it fades away. I stand there waiting, but there's nothing else to see.

The Snow Queen glares down at me from across the street. She's all haughty jaw and smolder. Sharp angles. She manages to look malevolent and smug, even though she still has the one-nostril problem.

All of Tyrone's Snow Queens are voluptuous and this is a comfort to me. If I'm not mistaken, Tyrone's queen wears a double-D.

10

A text from Amber! She wants me to walk to the Arts and Culture Centre with her after school. She has received permission to borrow from the costume bank for Gary's music video. They're only open until five and she really has to pick out a lot of stuff.

She really, really needs my help.

They're thinking ten female dancers in the video and fifteen male dancers and of course the whole band. And, most important, Gary, because he's the lead singer.

I have to meet her on the front steps of the school as soon as the buzzer goes. Melody can't make it. She has detention. Gary has basketball practice but he'll show up as soon as he can.

Oh thank God, Amber says when she sees me coming down the stairs.

We really have to hurry, she says.

I have to work hard to keep up with her all the way down the sidewalk, past Brother Rice and the Lions Club and the university residences on Allandale Road and across the lawn of the Arts and Culture Centre which is covered in orange and yellow leaves.

Amber talks the whole way, hardly stopping to breathe.

Gary says this. Gary says that.

Gary's mom brings them down a tray with two glasses of lime crush and a bowl of barbecue chips every day and they have to listen for the door to the basement opening at the top of the stairs if they're making out.

Gary's basement is renovated and he lives down there and there's a little bar and flatscreen TV and Gary's little brother is really cute and Gary's Pomeranian is just like a little mop.

Monique, Gary's Pomeranian, really loves Amber. Monique licks her ankle and her little tongue is like sandpaper.

Gary's Pomeranian tickles. Amber tells Gary, Your dog is tickling my ankle, but what can Gary do about it?

And it's hypoallergenic and doesn't shed and Gary wants them to get matching tattoos (Gary and Amber, not Gary and the Pomeranian), and Gary's band is playing an all-ages show on the weekend. Gary can't see her on Tuesdays or Thursdays or Fridays, because of the band.

And the video for their unit is going to be really wicked, Flannery. They're renting a limousine and the band is going to climb out of the limo and there are fireworks all around it, except for Gary, who stays in the limo but his window goes down and there he is with a cigar and a fedora and sunglasses and then the window goes back up. Gary thought of that part.

Amber is going to shoot it with Gary's new GoPro camera. Gary put the GoPro camera on Monique and got some really deadly shots. Gary rode his mountain bike down the Signal Hill trail and some old grandmother got mad because he was coming down the stairs and her grandkid was going up and Gary knew he wasn't going to hit the kid but they ruined his GoPro shot. And the grandmother was yelling and shaking her fist and Gary said it was really funny, this little old lady, her bifocals crooked, her gums flapping. You should see Gary on that mountain bike though, he can really go.

Gary says Amber could lose a pound or two, like, just here, on her hips? And she would look, you know, *skinnier*. It wouldn't surprise Amber if Gary's band gets really big. Gary says that there's a label that's been in touch because they saw an all-ages Gary and the band did and the guy was really nice. The guy said Gary really has something. The guy wants to see the video when it's finished, which is part of the reason they really need good costumes.

Gary wants her to get a tattoo with the name of his band on it. *The Squalls.* In a heart. With an arrow piercing it. Like, just a pound or two because Gary says she's starting to fatten up.

Gary doesn't like it when she talks to other guys because he's really sensitive and shy and it just makes him feel uncomfortable and most guys are jerks. And nobody understands Gary because he's really talented and sensitive.

Without Gary that band would just fall apart.

Gary listens to really cool music. It isn't true that Gary wouldn't let her dance with Tony Heffernan at the party, Tony was being a jerk and everybody was drinking and Gary just got a bit upset.

Gary is listening to the White Stripes right now.

Gary is thinking about growing his hair.

Gary is listening to M.I.A. right now.

Gary really likes some rap but not all rap. Gary's grandmother is deaf and sometimes she comes down the stairs when they're on the couch and they have to jump up. Gary really likes art films. He's seen all of Kubrick.

Tony Heffernan was twirling her around and he and Amber did a move from *Dirty Dancing* and she could see Gary on the couch with his arms crossed, the couch with a broken leg, and he was really pissed off but they were having so much fun dancing.

She knew Gary'd had too much to drink, so she decided to leave. He pushed himself up off the couch and stood in the doorway, blocked the door, yes, okay, that happened, he wouldn't let her walk home by herself because it was late. I mean, it's dangerous. At night. To walk by yourself, obviously. If you're a girl.

Amber wouldn't actually call it a shove. He put his hand on her shoulder. He did *not* shove her. That was just Elaine Power exaggerating. Elaine with her third-wave feminism which she will never shut up about.

Gary caught Elaine on the GoPro camera mouthing off and it's really funny. She's really shrill and Gary might put it in the music video but just, like, turn down the sound so it'll just be Elaine's big mouth going.

And Tony Heffernan was exaggerating and they shouldn't have written that on Facebook. It just made it worse. Gary called him a fag, yes, that's true, right up in his face, a faggot, and it's true that spit came out of his mouth and landed on Tony's face, and Tony *is* gay is the problem, and he's studying ballet, so it wasn't nice of Gary, that's true, he got carried away because he felt so jealous. But he apologized later to Tony, Sorry about that man — bros, right? And okay, so he's not totally perfect, he's very sensitive, and sometimes he loses his temper a little bit because, it's because he really loves her, and Gary wrote a song about Amber that's really beautiful.

Gary, Gary, Gary, Gary.

What a weird word it is. Gary. When you hear it over and over. There's only one word worse than Gary.

And that word is *we*.

Since when did Amber become *we*, I want to ask her. I used

to be half of *we*, I'd like to tell her. I hardly knew what she meant, when I first heard her say it.

We have to study for biology. *We* think what's going on in the Middle East right now is scary. We both got 89 on that quiz. We think it's dangerous for girls to drink because they're vulnerable. We think that when girls get drunk, like, what do they expect? We think sexual assault is not okay, obviously, but, like Gary says, we think you have to take care of yourself. You can't just go passing out all over the place. Like, who goes down to George Street dressed like that? Like, let's not get all victimy here. We think it's okay to protest, of course, but graffiti is destroying public property. Like, is vandalism okay all of a sudden? I mean it's fine, obviously, but somebody has to pay for that, Flannery.

Amber, what's going on with your face?

Pardon?

Your expression, you look surprised all the time these days. Wait a minute, did you pluck your eyebrows?

I had them waxed. So what?

You had them waxed? You paid for that? You know your eyebrows don't grow back, right?

I think it looks nice. Gary paid for it, if you must know.

Let me guess. Gary thought your eyebrows were too hairy?

We think you should get it done too, actually. You're getting a unibrow, Flan.

We're in the basement of the Arts and Culture Centre by this point, surrounded by tons and tons and tons of costumes. There are a gazillion giant white Sugar Plum Fairy dresses with tulle skirts and lots of sequins and feather boas and faux-mink stoles. I'm wearing a red saloon dress with a giant bustle on the back, and Amber has on a mermaid costume. She's standing in front of a giant mirror framed in lightbulbs, trying to flap her tail. I've just put on a hat that has a big pile of fruit on the brim — apples, oranges, pears and bananas. I lift the netting that hangs off the brim of the hat. Amber is staring at herself. She looks so beautiful, but somehow even more tired than usual, the circles under her eyes darker than before.

We better get this stuff back on the hangers, she says. It's already quarter to five. I'll just tell the lady what we've decided to borrow. She has to tag the stuff, and then we'll come back and get it on the day of the shoot.

I'm putting all the hats back on the top shelf while Amber lists off everything she needs to the costume lady in another office.

Neither of us mentions, on the walk home, that Gary didn't show up. Instead Amber wants to talk about losing your virginity with someone you love, when you're ready, of course. The person you're going to spend your life with. No big deal, right?

Obviously, it doesn't have to be that way, she says. I mean, you don't have to love the guy or girl or whoever. I mean, it can be casual. It can just be fun, you know. That's what Melody Martin says.

But if you happen to have found the guy you're supposed to love for your whole life, might as well be him, right?

I think I will be in love with Tyrone my whole life, I say.

Tyrone is just a passing thing, she says. I'm talking about love.

11

I was almost nine and Tyrone had just turned ten. Almost seven years ago. Before Felix was born. Before everything. Or almost everything.

Tyrone was a scrawny, already too-tall kid with big eyes and dark lashes and black curly hair, waterskiing for the first time.

He was way out on the glassy lake. The boat was rocking gently in a blast of white sparkles. Tyrone's stepdad, Marty, was in silhouette because the sun was a big maraschino cherry behind him, sinking fast.

I could see Tyrone's head floating above the water and the tips of the white skis and the line the rope made floating on the surface. The day was almost over and soon the wedding guests were going to help gather up the chairs from the lawn and the dancing would begin.

A carpet of white sparkles had unfurled on the water from the speedboat to me. I was sitting on the dock kicking my feet through the shimmer, and it looked like I could have stood up and walked out on it, all the way to the boat and Tyrone.

We'd been told weeks in advance that there would be waterskiing for the kids at the wedding. The invitation had demanded, .

in curly gold script: *Kids, bring your swimsuits!!!* Miranda said they'd gone a bit overboard with the exclamation marks, but other than that she didn't say anything about the invitation.

If she was upset that Hank was getting married so soon after they'd broken up, she wasn't going to let it show. I think she decided to go to the wedding to prove she was okay with being jilted — which she definitely wasn't. Or maybe she needed to be there to prove to herself he was really gone.

Tyrone's stepdad was a groomsman. He had promised Hank he'd be in charge of the waterskiing. There was Marty, one hand on the wheel, beer bottle in the other hand, still wearing his tuxedo with a pink carnation on the lapel.

Tyrone had been obsessed with the waterskiing from the day he got wind of it. He had never waterskied before. But he and I watched YouTube videos and read tips and talked about what it must feel like to fly across the surface of the water.

By the day of the wedding, Tyrone's excitement had a voltage of about a gazillion megawatts.

Don't get all worked up about reducing your ski angle, Tyrone was telling anybody who'd listen (even the adults, who had no intention of ditching the open bar for the lake).

Square your shoulders over your knees, he was saying. That's a big part of staying up.

As soon as Marty got the speedboat out of the boathouse, a lineup formed of all the kids at the wedding old enough to waterski. Tyrone was the first in line, but Marty kept ignoring him, taking the kid behind him, and then the kid behind that kid.

Okay, who's next? Marty kept saying. Everybody's hand shot up and they were hopping up and down, jutting their hands into the sky and screaming, Me! Me!

Tyrone had been swimming and I could see beads of water on his bare shoulder, burning with sunlight. He was shivering.

But there was a steady current of anticipation flowing out of his brown eyes. He kept his eyes on the boat and he didn't jump up and down like everybody else. He raised his hand and held it straight while Marty's eyes slid right over him.

Parents kept wandering down to the shore to thank Marty, standing at the edge of the wharf and cheering when it was their kid's turn. Marty was every kid's best friend: "Let Uncle Marty help you with that life jacket!"

But Marty made Tyrone wait until the very last. Tyrone had wanted to impress everybody, but the other kids, blue-lipped and shivering in their damp towels, had all wandered back up to the house to change. Tyrone would have an audience of one. Me.

The dancing was going to start soon. Marty looked at his watch. There was a four-piece band on the lawn and they were warming up. The sax sounded like a bawling moose. Marty was drunk, which meant he had to stare at his watch a long time before he could compute the hour. He finally said he didn't know if there was time for Tyrone.

I've been at this all afternoon, Marty said. It's time for me to get myself a real drink.

Tyrone didn't answer. They were just looking at each other. Tyrone on the dock, Marty on the seat of the boat, looking up. Marty had been Tyrone's stepfather for five years, but maybe this was the first time they were recognizing the hopelessness of the situation. Marty drained his beer, tossing the bottle into the bushes.

A short one, he said. You'll have to get it on the first try. I've had enough of this.

And finally, they were out there.

Marty let the engine idle as Tyrone got his skis into position. A cloud of blue smoke hung in the air.

Every move Marty made was deliberate and slow. He'd finished off a half-dozen in the boat.

The bottom edge of the sun was very close to the rim of the lake. The sky was flamingo-feathered. Tyrone was floating behind the boat, not saying anything at all.

Marty revved the engine and the boat flew. The rope pinged out of the water in a straight line and water drops flew out in a misty spray.

I watched Tyrone rise out of the white wake. The nose of the boat spanked down hard.

Marty increased the speed. He seemed to be going too fast on purpose.

But Tyrone was up. He was bent forward with his bum sticking out and then he was leaning way back, like he was trying with all his might to stop the runaway boat in its tracks. Then he nearly fell face first, his knees in big shackles of foam, and then he was straight up again.

They roared around the other side of the lake. They flew past the wharf where I was jumping and clapping and when Tyrone was passing me, he lifted one hand off the wooden bar and waved at me.

I could see the thrill of it and how audacious to let go with one hand, the fastest wave you ever saw, and he slammed his hand back down on the bar and his whole body crumpled, one ski lifting off the water, wonky and boneless, bent and tipping, left, right, and then he was up straight again.

He righted himself. He was still up.

Marty had seen Tyrone's little wave to me. He did a double take. That wave must have enraged him.

Marty cut the speed, letting the boat slow down so the rope went slack, and Tyrone was sinking down to his knees, almost down to his waist, and once he was good and low in the water,

Marty thrust the boat into full speed again, and it jerked Tyrone so hard his body flicked like a whip and his skis smacked down on the hard surface and bounced up over and over.

The sun was so low that its reflection was a perfect bright red circle on the water's surface and as the boat swung around, the circle was smashed into a thousand pieces that skittered away from each other and then floated back together, making the perfect circle again.

Tyrone was still up. It was as though his hands were welded to the wooden bar.

It seemed there was nothing Marty could do to ditch this ten-year-old kid.

Was this when I fell in love? Was it that little wave?

He was a head taller than everybody else in our class, just a couple of months older than some of us, and the loneliest person I had ever met. A prankster, begging for attention. His freckles. His curls. The space between his front teeth. He just believed if he worked hard enough at it, people would see what a great kid he was. He needed them to see it.

I think I was his only friend.

Marty and Tyrone had hated each other pretty much from the beginning.

I'm still trying to figure out the reason Marty hated Tyrone.

Why Tyrone hated Marty was easy. Tyrone hated Marty because Marty had told Tyrone to chew with his mouth closed.

I don't want to see what you're chewing, what are you, a little pig? That's what Marty said. He said it front of me and he said it in front of Jordan who was over for lunch too and Chad Yates-O'Neill. And Marty mimicked Tyrone, and we all giggled, because somehow Marty had managed to look just like Tyrone.

The man's face had turned into a boy's, and it was a magic trick and there were gobs of peanut butter and bread tumbling

around in Marty's mouth like clothes in a dryer, and some fell
out on his plate.

We giggled. But I regretted that giggle pretty fast because
Tyrone had clapped his hand over his own mouth and he was
blushing.

After that Tyrone kept his lips pressed together in a funny
way whenever he chewed. Almost like he was trying to watch
his own lips. Lips that were pressed very tight together in a
small hard line.

And Tyrone's mom had just sat there not saying anything.

It had been a moment when she might have taken her son's
side against a stranger who stank up their house with a cologne
so strong it made everybody's eyes water, and who insisted
on being served first at the supper table, and who took over
Tyrone's video games, saying, Hand over that controller, and
whose silence, when the garbage wasn't put out on time, felt
like a weather system.

And meanwhile, in school, none of the boys would sit with
Tyrone in the lunchroom because they said it was gross how
his food showed when he was chewing, even though he now
chewed with his lips pressed tight and very slowly, and only
a single bite before he threw his sandwich out. Or he just unwrapped the Saran off his sandwich and didn't touch it at all.

But the boys made fun of him anyway and he had to go sit
with the girls. They just barely put up with him.

He'd do annoying things. He tipped Tamara Gordon's pudding cup over her head and he had to go to the principal for
that. The office called his home for an emergency meeting.

I was called to the office as a witness because I'd been at the
table. Tamara was already there. She had washed her hair in
the nurse's room but it was still wet. So were Tyrone and the
vice principal, Ms. Kearsey, and one of the women who served

in the cafeteria, still in her hairnet and white plastic apron.

And Marty was there doing all the talking. He informed us that Tyrone was exactly the same way at home, that he, Marty, and Tyrone's mother didn't know what to do with him, but he, Marty, would make a promise to Tamara and to everyone else present that there would be no Xbox for Tyrone for the rest of the year.

In fact, he was going to be throwing the Xbox out the second-story window as soon as they got home. He wanted very much to see how Tyrone would like that.

There'd be no nothing, according to Marty. For the rest of the year. No allowance and no soccer and no art lessons. No nothing.

Marty said that Tyrone's mother was too soft. That was the problem. Tyrone got away with murder because of his mother. What he needed was a good smack.

But you can't do that anymore, Marty said. That makes too much sense.

Tamara said, I'm not even sure it was Tyrone.

But you said just a moment ago that Tyrone emptied your chocolate pudding over your head, said Ms. Kearsey.

It wasn't even him, Tamara said. Of course she knew it was. But Marty had frightened us all.

Who was it, then? the vice principal asked.

I didn't see, she said.

Somebody saw, Marty said. Somebody bloody well saw.

The cafeteria woman said she was just a volunteer.

The vice principal asked Tyrone and me to leave the office. I'll have a word with Tyrone's father alone, she said.

Step-father, Tyrone and Marty corrected her, in unison.

But for some reason Tyrone was immune to Marty's hatred that day out on the waterskis.

His body was like a lightning bolt of joy. He couldn't believe how good he was at keeping his balance.

Neither could Marty.

Miranda has her faults. She gives me peanuts and kiwis for lunch even though you're not allowed to bring them into school because some people have allergies and will blow up like balloons and clutch at their throats with both hands and writhe on the floor until their heads explode and they die, if they get even a faint whiff of a peanut or kiwi. When I explained this to Miranda she said, Oh, for God's sake, it's just a little kiwi, take it.

She didn't give me piano lessons even though Felix gets karate lessons, and she can't buy the grade-twelve biology textbook that is, as I may have mentioned, required.

But I had been shielded from a particular truth that was coming over me there on the grassy bank of the lake, watching Tyrone waterski when I was nine years old.

Adults could be evil.

Evil was something Miranda had made sure, up until then, I knew nothing about.

It was a lie by omission.

Miranda had a lot of boyfriends, but every one of them was kind to me. Every one of them offered to cut my steak, or they carried me on their shoulders. Every one of them was the kind of guy that daubed blue icing on the end of my nose if we had a birthday cake from Sobeys, which you could get cheap if it had somebody else's name on it written in icing and it hadn't been picked up or if it was three days old. We've had cakes that said Happy Birthday Declan or Raoul or Jasprit, or Keira or Fiona or Sally or Molly.

Every one of the boyfriends showed up with Miranda on Sports Day, sitting with her on the patchwork quilt with the picnic basket. They all did the egg-on-the-spoon race, on my team, and tied one leg to mine for the three-legged race and ended up on the parents' side of tug of war when it was the parents against the teachers.

Every one of them made me a part of the conversation. They asked me what I thought. They used big words, and they explained the big words. They told me about politics and explained what elections were, even though I yawned the whole way through the explanations, and sometimes actually and truly fell asleep.

Here's the word that explains my relationship with every one of Miranda's many boyfriends: cahoots.

I was in cahoots with them.

Never in cahoots against Miranda, not really. But we pretended. Yes, I'll read you another chapter, but don't tell Miranda. Yes, you can put that broccoli in the garbage, but wait until your mother turns her back. Stage whispers, with Miranda right there in the room pretending not to hear. Or if they were babysitting me: Quick, before your mother gets home, let's get these dishes cleaned up, it'll be a surprise.

But sitting on the edge of the lake as the sun was setting, with my toes kicking through the water and Tyrone skimming along behind the boat, watching Tyrone so full of happiness, and his stepdad at the helm, I realized something. Marty was evil.

On the last spin around, the boat turned hard and Marty told Tyrone to let go of the rope. He yelled it at him. His voice hoarse and angry.

Let go, he yelled.

Tyrone was coming for the wharf too fast. Maybe his stepdad really did think it would be cool for Tyrone to have a dry landing. That's what he said later. Kid was doing so well out there, Marty shouted at Tyrone's mother, he's a goddamn natural.

The truth is, my mother was in love with Hank at that wedding. Of course I didn't understand that in quite those words.

Use your words. I didn't use those words back then. I was nine.

In love.

All I knew was that Hank used to sleep over. Hank had been around the house for what seemed like an eternity, but it was actually only three years. I had experienced peanut butter and honey for the first time because of Hank. And tie-dyed T-shirts, because we did that on the back deck. And I'd acquired a taste for curry and olives (not at the same time).

He'd read me to sleep sometimes. He started coming around after *Charlotte's Web*, which was a short-lived guy named Dave, the boyfriend before Hank, but was there for *Harriet the Spy*.

And he let me cuddle into him on the couch when Miranda had to work late waitressing, and he carried me out of the taxi if they were coming home from parties and once a drop of rain fell on my forehead and woke me up and I was wrapped in my Mickey Mouse blanket and Hank was smelling like Hank and Miranda was paying the driver and they were tipsy and she caught up with us and leaned in for a kiss in the red taillights of the taxi and my head was squished between their chests.

Hank was only around for three years but it felt like everything I'd ever known, except for *Charlotte's Web* Dave, who was also nice. But Dave wasn't love.

Hank was love for Miranda.

Real honest, go-for-it, live-it, be-in-it, give-everything-to-it love.

Miranda and Hank broke up around the time the second Harry Potter came out, because he wanted to go to law school in Nova Scotia and he couldn't "do long distance," he said, and Miranda wouldn't go with him because I was in school, and four months later Hank was marrying someone else.

Someone who had no kids and who could go with him to Nova Scotia and who was also accepted to law school and who had dark hair and big eyes and wore the pearl engagement ring belonging to Hank's great-grandmother which Hank had previously given to Miranda but which Miranda had given back because they were breaking up and she'd used butter to slide it off because her fingers were swollen which should have told stupid Hank something.

The sun was almost completely down as Tyrone came plowing toward the dock on the waterskis, and it made a final dark-orange flare on the dark water.

I was feeling funny because I'd had too much sun. Not since the words "You may now kiss the bride" had anyone asked me where my hat was or if I had on sunscreen. All day it seemed the adults were not themselves. Nobody paid any attention to me. Nobody counted how many glasses of Orange Crush I had or told me to wash my face.

Hank, though, had picked me up and kissed me on the forehead. Of course I was too big for that.

I'd seen him getting ready. He was wearing a tuxedo and standing before a full-length mirror, absorbed in the carnation he was putting in his lapel. Sticking in the pin. His mouth drawn down in a frown.

I'd seen Miranda pat his chest earlier with her patent-leather clutch. She tapped him with it. She asked if he'd still change her spark plugs now and then.

He just said her name. He said it softly, but he waved her purse away from the spot where it had come to rest on the accordion pleats of his white, white shirt.

I'd come upon him fixing his carnation in front of the mirror just before the actual ceremony. Everyone else was outside sitting on the white chairs in the hard heat, lined up in rows on the brilliant green lawn, but I'd gone through the back door because we'd been sitting there so long in the sun I felt funny and I needed to go to the bathroom.

There he was in the last bedroom just before the bathroom, and he saw me in the mirror behind him, leaning on the doorframe. He turned and grabbed me up in his arms and hugged me. I almost screamed because he was hurting my sunburn so much. He kissed my forehead and I couldn't move because of the burn and also because I wanted him to hug me. One of my gumshoes fell off. He set me down on the floor and I stood for a moment just looking into his eyes. I was trying to say something with my eyes. I was trying to say, Don't you care about us? I thought you loved us. And, You're hurting my mother's feelings.

Hank pointed to my collar and said, You spilled something on your shirt. Is that ketchup?

When I looked down, he chucked me under the nose. I fell for it every time.

Very funny, I said. And then I felt tears coming and it made me mad to cry in front of Hank and I hissed at him, You look stupid in that suit. It's too small for you.

I grabbed up the gumshoe that had fallen off when he hugged me and I stormed down the hall to the bathroom, trying for some funny reason to look dignified and grown up, except I was hobbling along because I was only wearing one shoe.

Miranda was wearing a floaty chiffon number that day, loose at the waist, and she wasn't crying a bit. She also wasn't drinking. There were children everywhere and the cake was really something.

It had five tiers and the little plastic bride and groom dolls were on surfboards in white bathing suits, because Hank's new in-laws were giving them a honeymoon in Hawaii for a wedding present.

Maybe that was the icing on the cake for Miranda, because she couldn't travel with Hank when they were together because she had me and I had school and she was broke and her mother had died young and left her nothing in the way of an inheritance and her father, like my own, had never made an appearance.

I had the feeling Hank had left Miranda because he couldn't face the responsibility of me. Who wants to take on somebody else's kid? Miranda had a big student loan and a degree in fine art and not a whole lot of prospects, financially speaking.

Personally, I thought she had blown his mind for a while because she was an artist, because she was dazzling in her *numbers* night and day, because she knew someone who was growing poems in a laboratory with mold cultures and scientific equipment, because she could throw a pot on a pottery wheel and she could throw a party where everybody came and sang in the kitchen until dawn, with banjos and ukuleles and bodhrans and bells and the spoons and guitars, shouting about politics and all the kids charged the adults money to use the bathroom and we made a fortune and the adults went skinny-dipping in the Bannerman Park pool at dawn.

But something had given Hank a fright. He had been accepted at Dalhousie for law and gave up auto repair. Then he was spending time with this woman whose parents were a retired politician and a judge and who had lots of money and who had also been accepted to Dal. The woman was kind of crisp at the edges, with ironed straight hair and tailored suits and new hiking gear, and she somehow made Miranda look shabby and frayed.

Beside that woman, Miranda's glamor dimmed and maybe she just looked poor to Hank. Poor and rundown. I heard him shouting one night that it had been a nice dream, but that's all it was, *dreaming*.

I had no idea what he could mean. It frightened me and I pinched myself just to make sure I was awake. I pinched myself to make sure I existed.

Did he think that not having money made people unreal?

Maybe he was right. Maybe we were invisible.

Tyrone's face, as he was flying toward that dock after he let go of the rope, was still full of the thrill of getting up on the skis for the very first time. I think that's what pissed Marty off. But I saw the joy switch to terror just before he hit the dock. The edge of the wharf broke one of his ribs and made a total mess of his clavicle which would require a metal plate and some permanent screws and would possibly give him arthritis in his thirties, the doctors said.

I had to shout for help, but I felt like I couldn't even make a squeak. I felt my voice was coming out in a whisper. But I must have actually shouted pretty loud because I was quickly crowded out of the way.

Tyrone's mother was swaying on the outskirts of the crowd that had gathered around Tyrone, and then she just sank down into the grass, her skirt riding up so it showed the control panel of her stockings, her champagne flute still upright. She was pinching the skinny plastic stem of the glass and one of her pinkies was curled out. She hadn't spilled a drop.

She knocked the champagne back and tossed the glass into the bushes and got herself standing back up again and smoothed down her skirt and followed the crowd back up to the big house. Tyrone was in some other person's arms, and

Marty was cursing and swearing under his breath and trying to steer the boat back into the boathouse.

My arms and legs and belly were stinging. I had goosebumps, and the hair on my arms was standing up.

I had understood about evil. I had seen how it was ordinary and stupid and there was nothing magical or fairytale-like about it.

It was just a grown-up taking his problems out on a kid. Because he could. Because nobody stopped him.

It was easy to hate Tyrone. He was too huggy. He hugged everyone and Marty thought it was girly. Knock it off with the hugging. Grow up. Even at ten Tyrone could draw. He was goofy and when he laughed really hard sometimes Orange Crush would come out his nose and his whole body would shake with it. He hooted when he laughed. Whoo-hoo-hoo. He did sometimes chew with his mouth open. He had a big vocabulary and Marty didn't. He never ran out of energy. Except when he ran out of energy, which happened all at once, and then he would be hard to wake up, because he could sleep very deeply.

Everything he did was all or nothing.

Tyrone was driven hard through the water, and his skis popped off, and he was lucky he had missed hitting the dock with his face because he would have lost every tooth in his head.

Just before he hit the wharf, he screamed.

His freckles, his deep brown eyes.

After they carried him up to the house, I was alone. I leaned over the water and threw up all the barbecued hotdogs I had wolfed down and gallons of Orange Crush and a cucumber sandwich and I have never eaten hotdogs since or cucumber and I've switched to Lime Crush.

Can you picture the very particular pink-gray color of a thrown-up hotdog, floating, as it was, on the surface of the lake and bright bits of thrown-up orange processed cheese?

I was in love.

I knew I was in love with Tyrone O'Rourke.

This is how hopeless the situation was. I still believed in Santa Claus. I believed that my father would show up one day out of the blue, even though he didn't know I existed.

I believed my mother was a goddess and that she was always right and that Hank had something wrong with him for leaving us.

How could he not love Miranda and me? Hank, who had hugged me when my skin was so sore from sunburn, and how much I would miss him.

I still hid my baby teeth under my pillow for the tooth fairy, but I had begun to doubt the tooth fairy.

I knew Miranda put the money under my pillow and some-times she forgot and once I'd just held out my hand with the tooth and she reached in her pocket and took out five bucks and put it in my hand and dropped the tooth in an amber-colored pill bottle on the top shelf in the kitchen cupboard behind a broken toaster. The pill bottle had all my other baby teeth but I had forgotten to stop believing in the tooth fairy. (My mother had forgotten to stop believing she would ever get the broken toaster fixed.)

Not believing in something requires a lot of effort. It is eas-ier to believe. Once I have accepted that something is true, I have a hard time losing faith in it.

I believed in Tyrone and I will always believe in him. I mean that there is something in him, something I can't even say or put into words that makes me love him and it's so scary, loving someone.

It's a big, out-of-control, jumping-jack love that makes me crazy and lonely.

Of course it went away when he went to a different junior high. I joined the drama club and the school newspaper at Brother Rice, and I was busy with Amber, and there was the birth of Felix.

Or maybe I just put it on hold. Because when Tyrone O'Rourke comes into a room I find it hard to not believe we are meant for each other, because I know him inside out, since forever.

12

———

Mr. Payne has announced Part B of our Entrepreneurship unit. We have to approach a person, or persons, in the business sector and conduct a recorded interview about the promotion and sales of our units. We are supposed to choose a business representative who has marketing experience related to our particular projects.

Mr. Payne makes it sound like there are gazillions of business people out there just dying to share their time and sales strategies with a bunch of grade-grubbing high-school students.

And he's giving us only two weeks.

Amber and Gary have already decided they're interviewing some big film producer who happens to be in town filming a battle re-enactment for a documentary about the First World War. Even Elaine Power looked impressed when she heard that.

But who am I supposed to interview about magic potions?

On top of the interview, Mr. Payne wants us to hand in revisions to our project proposals next week and have the prototypes of our actual projects ready on November 2nd. We have this very demanding timeline for the project because, as

Mr. Payne says, he's teaching us how manufacturing works in the "real" world. He seemed to sort of love my plan for the potions, though — I mean *our* plan — except he said it was too ambitious for a start-up. Choose just one kind of potion, he said. We can diversify later if the product is a hit.

It's been two weeks since Tyrone has been in school. He doesn't answer my texts and he's probably lost his phone. He's probably couch surfing at the apartment of some university students he met and sleeping until one because he's playing video games all night and getting stoned.

His mother told Miranda that she's getting daily automated phone calls from the school. *A person in your household named TYRONE ...*

She says he shows up every day before Marty gets home from work and tosses a few pizza pockets in the oven and then he's gone again on his motorcycle, leaving her to yell out the front door about wearing a helmet.

Since Miranda won't let me take the cell phone to school (she's waiting for a call from a journalist who wants to talk about her new project — she's working in neon now), I have to wait to get home to text Tyrone.

I text him after dinner: *Payne says we need to choose only one potion. What do you think?*

I certainly don't expect to hear back from him.

But before I go to bed I go up to Miranda's study to check the phone. And there's a two-word message from SprayPig. It says, *Definitely Love.*

Boom. Boom, boom.

Okay, I know it doesn't mean that Tyrone definitely loves me. I *know* that. I know it doesn't mean he's *not* serious about that parrot-haired girl I saw him with at the mall or that they've broken up.

It does not mean that he'll show up at school to help with our *Definitely Love* potion. And it doesn't even mean he'll lift a finger to help us get a good mark on *our* project. I'm not a total fool!

So why is my heart trying to beat its way out of my chest? Why am I clutching the phone so tightly in both hands, holding it over my very-loud-pounding heart?

Well, what's a girl to think? After weeks of silence — *Definitely Love.*

I put the phone down on the desk, right where it was. But I pick it up again and read the text again. SprayPig — that's Tyrone. *Definitely Love.*

What are you doing in my office? Miranda calls up from downstairs.

Oh, nothing, I say.

You sound funny, she says.

Really? I say. There's no worry about Miranda reading the text. She doesn't know how to open them. She's never texted in her life, though I've certainly offered to teach her. But she has materialized silently in the doorway of her study.

What's up? she says. And steps into the room and lays her hand on my forehead.

You're all flushed, she says.

Just heading to bed, I say. And I trot down the stairs and get in under the blankets and layers of dirty laundry piled on my bed and stay awake for a long time, thinking in the dark.

It doesn't really mean anything, I keep telling myself.

It probably just means that I am going to feel seriously f--ked up, as Miranda would say if she were writing this, only she of course would spell out the whole word, which I refuse to do.

Miranda believes there is no such thing as bad language, only the inappropriate use of language in a given circumstance.

She believes curse words, including some very disgusting ones, have a radical power and they can make huffy, uptight people uncomfortable, which Miranda believes is generally a good thing to do.

Miranda thinks these sorts of people are, generally speaking, too prissy for their own good and a well-placed curse word can have the effect of a "laxative for the soul." Loosen up all those stoppages. She has blogged as much.

I refuse to use the F-word because I believe f--king, should I ever have a chance to engage in that physical/spiritual/emotional activity, is a beautiful thing, or has the potential to be a beautiful thing, maybe, and that it should be treated as if it's secret and sacred, and it should definitely not be spoken of in such harsh language, or so casually, or without respect for its beauty, actually, and maybe not even spoken of anywhere at all.

Because I think it should be private and maybe wordless, if you know what I mean. Something between two people. But if you do have to speak of it for some reason, I think *making love* is a really nice way to describe sex if one has to describe it.

Miranda thinks this is a very silly idea. Which I think is ironic given that when it came time for her to explain sex to *me*, she failed pretty spectacularly.

Miranda sat me down on the edge of the bathtub with a picture book about sex when I was eight. I don't know why she chose the bathroom. But there we were, sitting on the side of the tub, the clear plastic shower curtain covered with angelfish tugged back so the fish looked like they were swimming somewhere in a big hurry, all banging into each other.

Miranda's policy was, If kids ask, you answer.

With the truth.

She's blogged all about this theory too, of course.

Apparently I'd asked about the box of tampons in the cupboard under the bathroom sink. What are those things? was probably all I said.

From tampons, Miranda's thinking must have gone, It's time for the sex talk.

Miranda decided to present the whole thing with a library book. A picture book. I thought it was strange when I saw it in her hands because we'd already progressed to I Can Read chapter books.

But in the little book there was a drawing of a man and a woman. The man was on top of the woman. They were kissing. It showed their outlines, but it also showed what was inside them, as if their bodies were transparent.

It showed the man's penis fitting snugly into the woman's vagina. It showed little sacks inside the woman with lines drawn from the sacks to words like *ovaries* and *womb*, and it all looked painful, like there wasn't room inside the woman's vagina for that ugly-looking penis, and what the hell were they doing, why was the man on top of her, probably squashing the life out of her? How had these two people ever agreed to this, how had they found themselves with each other without their clothes on, and what was the bizarre exchange of words, to end up in this position with his penis sticking into her vagina?

I was *flabbergasted.* That's the word. It's a word that shows up in the old yellowed Agatha Christie novels you find at your friends' summer cabins. There are British people in those novels with big green lawns and rock walls and there are little old ladies who murder people with arsenic or by stabbing them straight through the forehead with an ice pick, and portly butlers with double chins and cooks with bright red faces and rectors, whatever they are. Those are the kinds of people who get flabbergasted.

And little eight-year-old girls sitting on the side of the tub in the midst of a school of terrified angelfish, with their mothers and a library book about sex.

I thought about Miranda going to the children's library to borrow the book. The chat she and the librarian must have had.

I would never go to that library again.

Why would anybody do that? I shrieked. Why?

I felt betrayed. I felt like there was a big secret and I was mad it had been kept from me and mad that I had been told about it.

I was deeply angry with whoever had invented this crazy thing. I knew, without being told, that the line drawing in the little pastel book with the organs and the eggs and the kissing people was a cover story for a horrendous, crazy explosion of emotion and weirdness.

Now that I knew about it, there was no *not* knowing about it. No going back.

Then it hit me.

That was the way I had come into existence. People sit down on the sides of cold bathtubs everywhere, with their mothers and with books that begin deceptively with a picture of flowers and some bees hovering, and it's *la-la-la* with the pretty drawings, and a box of tampons tucked into their bathroom cupboards near the snaking, cold, sweating pipe that curls out of the sink — the pipe that's there to get rid of toothpaste spit and germs and scum. People find themselves in that situation, because those people have mothers who have had sex.

That's how I had come into being.

Miranda had done this terrible thing.

To make me.

I stayed far away from any book that might have to do with sex until grade seven. That's when Amber and I got our hands on a fat paperback called *Love's Tender Fury* and we sussed out the steamy parts and read them over and over. Every time something was about to happen — something hotter and more anatomically complicated than a kiss — the heroine swooned.

As far as we could gather, the swoon occurred because of the extreme tenderness of the kiss.

First there was a struggle on the woman's part to avoid the kiss. She'd fling her head to the side and all her long tendrils would fly around, covering her face, her shoulders, her soft, plump, heaving breasts. She had a lot of hair. It tangled and coiled as she thrashed. But the hero held her arms firmly in his grip. He was calmness itself.

Then she'd just happen to look in his eyes, totally by accident, and she would pull an emotional one-eighty. Instantly, she'd be all for the kiss. She couldn't get enough of it.

What the hell, we thought.

She didn't want the kiss. She wanted the kiss. There was nothing in between. Then she swooned.

Swooning was generally followed by some of the fury mentioned in the title. But the swoon part, that was love, dawning in all its glory.

Now I think love must be more like a strike than a swoon. You get *struck* is the way I imagine it, is the way I feel about Tyrone. Struck with awe by every single thing about him, his army surplus knapsack, the way the cuffs of his jeans are worn down to white threads on the back, his big eyes and the curly black hair and the way he walks, long limbs all over the place and how tall he got in grade ten and his eyelashes and his freckles and once, when he first transferred to Holy Heart and saw me by the lockers, and we were talking just like when we were kids, as if no time had passed, he pushed my hair back with a finger, just tucked a loose strand of my hair behind my ear and my ear burned even though we'd known each other since car seats. Our moms went to movies with us in the middle of the afternoon and breastfed us in the back row, which is kind of weird but I'm just saying — pretty much since we were born.

Lying in bed, under all that laundry, thinking about his *Definitely Love* text, I also remembered that little wave while he was waterskiing.

But love is not just something that befalls you. It's also hard work, the work of believing in someone. This is another theory of Miranda's that she's drummed into my head. It's been pretty hard this past week to believe in Tyrone when he has been so absent — from school, from our project, seemingly from the face of the earth — and I am depending on him to help me with this project. Amber has Gary helping her and everyone else has their partner helping and I have no one, basically.

So love is work and it's always changing and it's making and noticing and needing and giving and definite. It's definite.

Definitely Love.

It's a start.

13

The school secretary is eating a tuna sandwich behind the counter in the principal's office. She's sitting in a swivel chair and she has her high heels up on the desk. The wedged heels of her shoes are clear plastic and have tiny nuts and bolts and miniature wrenches suspended in the wedge.

My mission here is complex. I have to figure out a way to get the voice recorder from the secretary while also faking sick so I can miss Healthy Living, a course I am required to take and which I loathe.

This week, for example, we are going to be put into pairs and given a bag of eggs to take care of. It's supposed to show you how much work it is to have a baby. The eggs are always loose in a paper bag, and if one gets broken you must discuss the symbolic significance of the spilled yolk in an essay lamenting the evils of teen pregnancy.

Since I am the product of a teen pregnancy I find the whole idea of the project insulting. And I don't want to get stuck dragging around a bag of eggs.

So I have to miss class, but I can't go home without getting that voice recorder. My appointment with my "marketing expert" is tomorrow night and there's a sign the size of a bill-board outside the principal's office saying that Fridays are equipment-inventory days and no materials will be given out for loan on those days.

Since it is Thursday, it's now or never.

The secretary is reading a fat novel with a hologram on the cover. There's a picture of a beautiful girl with flowing blonde hair and a white nightdress in a meadow full of flowers.

The secretary is deeply engrossed. She licks her finger and turns the pages slowly.

There's a little silver bell and a note taped onto the desk beside it.

Ring the bell, the note says.

I put out my hand and smack the little knob. It makes a vibrating *ting*.

The secretary lifts her eyes from her book very slowly. Her eyes are commanding. They're dark brown, or maybe even black.

She tilts her book against her chest and the hologram of the innocent fairy girl in the meadow changes so that the girl now has eyes with vertical black slits like a snake and her teeth have turned into fangs, dripping blood, and her white nightdress is now red — soaked with blood, I guess — and the flowers have turned into bats.

I came to borrow a voice recorder, I say.

Flannery Malone, the secretary says. Aren't you supposed to be on your way to Healthy Living?

She very slowly clomps one wedged shoe onto the floor, then the other. She stands up and puts her hands flat on the desk. Even with the heels, the secretary is shorter than me.

For my Entrepreneurship project, I stammer. We have to interview an expert in the field of sales and promotion.

What are you doing for your unit? the secretary asks.

A love potion, I say.

Of course, she says. And what makes you think you're allowed to borrow this equipment?

Mr. Payne said I could?

Is Mr. Payne in charge of technical equipment?

I don't know, I say.

He is not, says the secretary. I am in charge of technical equipment.

Well, could I borrow a voice recorder please?

I am on my lunch break, the secretary says. She carefully lifts a triangle of tuna sandwich off a nest of tinfoil sitting on the counter, her long red nails sinking into the white Wonder Bread. Then she takes a bite. Just so I understand.

A crumb of tuna drops into her cleavage. She glances down and wiggles every part of her body and flaps the bottom of her blouse and I guess she must have shaken it free because then she clomps over to the table with several digital recorders piled on top. And comes back to hand me one.

I drop the little recorder into my knapsack and the secretary pushes a button built into the desk. The buzzer rings out through the whole school.

Now go to your Healthy Living class, she says.

I touch the back of my hand to my forehead and flutter my eyes.

What are you doing? the secretary says. Get to class. Go. Shoo. She flicks her hand at me.

It's just I feel slightly...

Slightly what, she says. She takes a step backwards.

Warm, I say. It's probably nothing. The secretary pulls her sandwich toward her.

I mean, I'm sure it's not contagious, I say. Not the bird flu. Or H1N1 or Ebola or part of a pandemic or anything. Just, warm. And dizzy. I feel suddenly very…

Suddenly very what?

Funny, I say. I feel funny. It's probably nothing.

I touch my throat.

And my throat feels funny, I say.

Do you want to sit down? she says. Over there? She points to chairs on the far side of the room.

I cough, just an *ahem*. A slight *ahem*, *ahem*. Then I cough a little harder. A hack. I let loose with a *hack-hack-hack*. I let my face get red, I let my eyes bulge a little. I force my eyes to water. I double over in a coughing fit.

It's *cough*. Probably *cough*. Not *cough*. Contagious, I say.

Okay, go home, Leave. Out, the secretary says. She tosses the rest of her sandwich in the garbage.

Get, she says. Evacuate the premises.

Well, maybe I will just sit out my next class, I say. Healthy Living. I'll just, you know. Recover in the library. I'm sure I'll be fine after that.

Radio silence from Tyrone, so it looks like I am going to have to do Part B of our Entrepreneurship project on my own. Which really means, of course, that Amber has to do it with me. At least it was always that way before Gary. Besides, I'm helping her with the costumes for her project so I figure she owes me.

Amber, what are you doing tomorrow night?

Going to Gary's basketball game.

Because I have to go interview my expert…

No way, Flan. Forget it.

I don't think it'll take very long. What you could do is, when the game starts, you could be there in the stands cheering Gary on.

Oh, thanks a lot. Thanks, Flannery. Phew, I was afraid you wouldn't permit it.

You can wave or blow kisses or whatever.

I do not blow kisses, Flannery.

Once the game has started, you sneak out.

Gary will kill me.

Gary won't even know you missed the game. You'll be back before it's over, waving your pompoms or whatever.

This explains how Amber and I have ended up with an appointment to see a Wiccan fortune-teller tonight.

The Wiccan was Miranda's idea. She says that a love potion falls under the business category of "Occult Services" and we need a person well versed in the practice of harnessing magical energy.

A Wiccan, I say.

A who?

A practitioner of Wicca, Am.

Of what, Flan?

A form of witchcraft with feminist leanings, Amber.

Oh, that's a relief, she says. For a second I thought it was just an ordinary witch who submits to the patriarchy all the time.

Gods and goddesses, equal power.

Awesome.

It *was*, though. I'd done a pile of research and narrowed down the number of practicing Wiccans in town — surprisingly large! — to a choice of two.

There is an intriguing-sounding witch near the Avalon Mall, The Amazing Gloria, but in the end I decided on a woman named Ms. Rideout. Ms. Rideout, according to her law firm's website, is also a lawyer specializing in personal injury.

Which makes it sound like she'd be really good at punching you in the eye, or that she takes your injury really personally.

What Ms. Rideout actually specializes in, her website explains, is getting compensation for people who are injured in car accidents or who slip and fall or otherwise hurt themselves on ice or sidewalk cracks or poorly marked or unprotected construction sites.

The clincher in Ms. Rideout's favor, though, was that her house is just a ten-minute walk from our school.

Amber could definitely make it back before the end of the game, I figured. Especially if we took the shortcut down Water Street.

So, here I am waiting for her by the back door of the gym on the coldest October evening in history with hundreds of cigarette butts at my feet. I can hear the muffled roar of the crowd inside. The basketball thumping on the floor like the heartbeat of an ogre. An ogre with an arrhythmic heart murmur. The boys' feet hammer the floor, chasing after the ball.

Amber said I couldn't wait inside. If Gary saw me with her, he'd know something was up. Gary has decided, apparently, that he doesn't like Amber hanging out with me.

Just as I'm beginning to think she isn't coming, the door creaks open and here she is with half a hotdog hanging out of her mouth, talking, chewing and dripping mustard. She strides past me out onto Bonaventure Avenue.

Hurry up, Flannery, she says.

What took you so long?

Gary got a foul, so he had to sit on the bench and he kept looking over at me the whole time so I couldn't leave. I couldn't even text or he'd ask later who I was texting. Of course, you don't even have a phone. Anyway, he tripped this guy on the other team. I mean, obviously, it was a mistake — his foot accidently stuck out in front of the guy. But the ref is totally prejudiced against Gary because he's such a strong player and keeps getting all the baskets.

That's when I feel a snowflake on my cheek. I look up and snow is spiraling down from the heavens.

Hey, first snowfall of the year, I say. No response. I can barely keep up with her. Maybe if I said the snowflakes looked like Gary's big white-pudding face, she'd be interested. But that gives me a better idea.

Big fluffy flakes, like duckling down, I say.

Last year for an English assignment we had to think up a hundred similes and metaphors about winter. We turned it into a competition, seeing how many we could each come up with on our walks home from school. The duckling one was Amber's.

And it works — sort of. Amber doesn't say anything, but she does slow down a little and gives me a sort of smirk-smile. I take it as encouragement.

We are trudging through the fallen leaves like the voyageurs of yore, I say, except we are *sans* canoe.

Amber is a sucker for when I speak French.

It's the kind of cold that gets the hair on your arms standing up at attention, like an army raising their bayonets when the commander yells *hup*, I say.

Just as I'm saying *hup*, a transport truck roars past and I see the orange dice doing the Highland fling below the rearview mirror and the truck's back tire hits a frigid puddle and a splash flies up all over Amber's sneakers.

She sucks in a big breath and shuts her eyes as if she's been slapped.

I brace myself for her anger. What will Gary say when he notices her sneakers are soaked? He'll know she left the gym! But instead, miraculously, there's the Amber grin. Ear to freaking ear.

My sneakers are so wet I could wring out half of the Atlantic Ocean from each one, she says.

They are as wet as seedless watermelons, I say.

And my feet are cold. My feet are each a tub of ice cream so frozen it bends the spoon, Amber says. Wait, where are we going?

Shortcut, I say. Come on. But Amber stops suddenly and I bang into her.

That's the bar I told you about, she says. That's the Wild Irish Rose. I told you I didn't want to come on this stupid interview with you, Flannery. Look at it. That's the bar.

Come on, Amber, I say again. Let's get out of here.

But she stands for a moment with her hands buried in her pockets, her head tilted back looking up at the sky.

It's really coming down, she says.

The snowflakes are big and soft and tattered, like my exam notes on *A Midsummer Night's Dream*, torn up and tossed in the air on the first day of Christmas holidays, I say. She ignores me.

Or, wait, they are pot-smoking ballerinas, I try again. Ballerinas with white tulle skirts and pointy-toed little slippers with rhinestones on the toes, giggling their little heads off, drifting away from the ballet company to do their own private *Swan Lake*.

Flannery, please stop, Amber says. Just stop, okay? She's staring at the Wild Irish Rose.

At that moment a very drunk man in a leather bomber jacket saunters out of the bar. He takes a wool hat out of his pocket and puts it on his bald head and continues up the road toward Subway.

It's almost funny now, she says. It sure as hell wasn't funny then.

I know exactly what story is unreeling itself in Amber's head. She first told me about it one Christmas holiday when we were both twelve and I was sleeping over at her house.

She's thinking about another Christmas, when she was only eight. Amber was listening to the audiobook of *A Christmas Carol* on her iPod in the back seat of her mom's car. Which happened to be parked in pretty much this very spot.

She was just getting to the part about the Ghost of Christmas Future, when a swaying man, whiskered and with wet purplish lips, pitched forward from the sidewalk and slapped his hands against the car window. He'd probably dived toward the window to stop himself from falling flat on his face, but then he tried to see into the dark car, as if looking for something to steal. His skin was the color of pea soup.

So she screamed and then he screamed and he reared back into the darkness.

He must have slipped on some ice, or just from the fright of seeing her little pale face and her big blue terrified eyes surfacing from the dark interior of the car. His arms started windmilling, his feet flying up and landing him on his ass in the snow bank.

Once he was back up he stumbled over to her window again. Probably he was just trying to calm her down. But Amber was so scared she could hardly move. She realized one of the back-seat doors wasn't locked and he'd gone around to that side, trying to get in. At the very last millisecond she flung herself across the seat and pressed down the lock just as he was flicking the door handle.

Locking the car might have been the wrong thing to do, she realized, because the guy became furious. Like he hadn't just tried to see if there was anything to steal in her mom's car. He was smashed. He didn't know what he was doing. But he recognized Amber and he started yelling.

Your mother thinks she's something special. She thinks she's better than the rest of us. Let me tell you something, kid, there's nothing special about Cindy Mackey. She's as common as dirt.

That's a simile Amber is not likely to forget.

And that's when Amber's mom came out of the bar. She started swinging her purse. She walloped him on the back and again on the shoulders and on top of his head and there was eight-year-old Amber in the back of the car watching it all, convinced that her mother and this stranger were about to kill each other.

We were parked next to that concrete planter, she says now. She points at a planter containing a single skinny tree trunk no bigger than my wrist, and with just one amazing withered black leaf covered by the freshly fallen snow. A leaf hanging on like a frightened kid.

Like a kid who will, after her mother's drinking incident, have a social worker take her out of class and interview her about her mom. How much does your mom drink, you can tell me, what about your dad, are you wetting the bed, do you have nightmares, I'm here to help, are you afraid, has anyone ever hit you or hurt you, do your mom and dad fight a lot, and let me see your fingernails, and have you ever been left alone, and what do you have for breakfast, and the teacher says you are very tired in class. Do you sleep at night? What time do you go to bed?

The cops pulled Amber's mom over a block from their driveway that night. Amber had to watch her mother get out of the car and get into the cop car and she honestly thought she'd never see her mom again.

When Amber got home it turned out Sean had made his special meatloaf with oranges and brown sugar which I have had several times and I can tell you, it is disgusting, but he got the recipe from *Canadian Living* and he's so proud of it he makes it all the time and no one has ever told him how awful it is.

The look on Dad's face when we came in with the officers, Amber says now. He kept saying, There's some nice meatloaf, Amber. Go sit at the table. And he's running back and forth with that stupid apron on, spooning out my meatloaf and rushing back out to the front porch to see if the cops are going to take Mom off to jail and rushing back into the kitchen to get me the ketchup.

I toy with providing a few metaphors for that meatloaf but then think I'd better keep my mouth shut.

Have you ever seen your mother collapse, Flannery? Amber asks. When you're eight, you think she has died. I mean, she just sort of collapsed in the hallway. Just the whites of her eyes showing. And she stank of that very bar over there. She stank of letting everybody down.

Your mom's been sober for ages, I say quietly.

Six months, she says. Six months and two days tomorrow.

Maybe this fortune-telling Wiccan lawyer will predict a happy future for us, Am, I say. I take her hand and drag her away from the Wild Irish Rose.

Look, the snowflakes are getting lighter now, I tell her. Now each snowflake is like a single square of biodegradable toilet paper, crumpled in its own unique way.

Or they are like snowflakes, Amber says. They are just exactly like snowflakes that speed up and spin out of control in the backdraft of each passing car, like snowflakes in a backdraft, and not like anything else.

14

Once people see how talented Gary is, Amber is saying. I sort of wish he'd hang out with me a bit more, but he has to spend all his time practicing with the band. He's writing another song for me. It's about when we first got together. It's really romantic.

She sings a little bit. Apparently Gary is trying to rhyme *Amber* and *ember*, and the ember turns to a *flame* and he stakes his *claim*.

His claim?

Yeah, like he claims me as his true love. His heart would break, so he makes a stake.

What are you, a gold mine?

Stop being so literal, Flan. It's sounds really good with the band behind him, she says. But I do miss the way it was before, when he asked me over every other day.

She stops for a moment to consult the Google map on her phone, and when she looks up, for a second we are looking into each other's eyes.

Maybe I'll buy some of your love potion after all, she says.

She smirks ironically as soon as she says it, but I don't think she has a drop of real irony in her whole body.

The smirk is lopsided. Don't try to pull one over on me, Amber's smirk says. I know a few things. I've been around.

That's the smirk.

It's like she can't let anybody see how sincere she is, because none of Gary's friends particularly like *sincere*. They like suave and simpering gossip, they're all lipgloss and platform sneakers, and lately there have been rumors of MDMA and coke.

And then here comes hopelessly healthy Amber, all shoulders and puffy-eyed from her swimming goggles, her always-wet pale blonde hair turning green at the tips from chlorine, the lopsided smirk ready whenever her true self starts to show through.

Maybe you should get this witch or Wiccan or whatever you call her to put a spell on it, she says. On your potion. She's still smirking but her eyes are bright. Imagine if it actually worked?

It's just a joke, Am, I say. That's the whole point of our project. All about the packaging.

I know, you already told me, she says. Like canned fog.

Or pet rocks.

Or mood rings, she says.

What are you talking about? I say. Mood rings actually work. I jab her in the ribs with my elbow.

This is the Wiccan's house, she says. We are standing in front of a long gravel driveway curving up toward a giant four-story house with turrets and a widow's walk.

Amber opens the wrought-iron gate and it screeches on its hinges. Squares of yellow light from the giant windows lie flat on the white lawn.

The brick walkway leading to the front door has been

shoveled so clean it looks like someone might have taken a toothbrush to the grooves between each brick. It is sprinkled with little crystals of salt that glitter under the streetlight.

We press the bell and hear a deep rippling *bong* ring inside. The door flies open and there is Ms. Rideout.

Shhh, she whispers. I just got the baby to sleep.

We step inside and I whisper our names and we shake hands and remove our boots. I step in a puddle of icy water melting from Amber's boot and my sock gets sopping wet.

Ms. Rideout is wearing a blazing white blouse tucked into a black pencil skirt. Black jacket, high-heeled shoes. There's a gold chain on her neck with a tiny gold pentangle, a five-point star in a circle of gold, studded with diamonds. Her hair has been straightened and sprayed stiff so it moves all in one piece. Her nylons whisper as she kicks a cat toy, a little stuffed sparrow, out of our path.

Is it still convenient for you to see us, Ms. Rideout? I ask.

Very convenient, my goodness, says Ms. Rideout. I don't mind a little company, she says. Not at all. A school project. I'd love to help if I can.

We enter the wide hallway and she leads us through the living room where a fire blazes, spitting and crackling, throwing leaping shadows all over the walls. There's a near-empty glass of white wine on the coffee table that Ms. Rideout picks up as she sashays through. An oil painting of a nude woman sprawled out on a red velvet chaise longue hangs over the fireplace. I am very much afraid it is a painting of Ms. Rideout. The woman is holding a human skull in one hand and looks as though she's speaking to it. The sockets of the skull stare emptily out at the room.

This way, girls, Ms. Rideout says. We duck past the painting and walk into the dark dining room. There's the flash of two glowing green embers floating in the velvet darkness. Amber grips my arm.

There's something there, she squeaks.

Where, says Ms. Rideout.

There, says Amber, a creature. I saw it.

Ms. Rideout flicks the light. It's a black cat. A big fat cat lying on the back of an armchair.

Oh, that's Merlin, says Ms. Rideout.

What a charming kitty, says Amber.

Don't look Merlin in the eye, Ms. Rideout says, or he'll fly through the air and land on your back. If you make eye contact, he thinks it's an invitation to play. I am fostering him from Heavenly Creatures. He was on the streets for most of his young life, can you imagine? Of course, he has attachment issues.

Amber and I edge past the sideboard with our backs to the wall and our eyes on the floor.

Have a seat, girls, says Ms. Rideout. Neither of you has had an accident recently, have you? Slipped on some ice coming out of a store? Anything like that?

Amber and I both say no.

Okay, Ms. Rideout says. Just checking.

I have taken the voice recorder out of my knapsack and placed it on the table.

Can I get you girls anything? Tea? Pop?

We're good, thank you, I say. Ms. Rideout sits down at the head of the table and pours herself more wine. There's a chair in the corner upholstered in cream satin. The cat has leapt onto the chair and is plucking at the fabric with his claws. First one paw, then the other. Pulling out little loops of thread with each pluck.

Ms. Rideout picks up her glass and swivels the wine around and gulps it back and then tops up her glass.

I turn on the voice recorder.

First, we'd like to thank you so much for your time, Ms. Rideout. Our school project requires that we interview a prominent businessperson about promotion and sales.

Ms. Rideout hiccups.

What about your parents? she says.

Pardon? says Amber.

Have they had any accidents lately? Hit a moose on the highway? Food poisoning? I can even work with a sprained ankle if I have to. Any cosmetic surgery gone wrong? Stress in the workplace?

Nothing like that, Amber says.

Ssshh, Ms. Rideout whispers. She points at the ceiling. Remember the baby.

Then she pulls a little Fisher-Price speaker out of a wooden centerpiece full of warty-looking gourds and miniature pumpkins. Ms. Rideout flicks on the speaker and turns the volume on bust.

Out crackles the noise of something breathing deeply. It sounds like Darth Vader — if Darth Vader were at the back of a dark, wet cave and suffering from a sinus infection.

Is that your baby? asks Amber.

I guess so, says Ms. Rideout, seeming truly puzzled. She props the little speaker up against a dark green gourd. She puts her elbows on the table and rests her cheeks on the heels of her hands, staring at the little speaker.

Amber flicks a glance at the nearly empty wine bottle and raises one eyebrow at me.

That baby is three months old now and I've never really heard her sleep before, says Ms. Rideout. Normally she's screaming her head off. But listen to that. Isn't that beautiful? she asks.

Isn't what beautiful? says Amber.

The sound of a baby sleeping.

As soon as she says it the baby starts screaming. It is a weltering wail that seems to fill the whole room.

She's awake, says Amber. Ms. Rideout snatches up the speaker and turns it off. The room is dead quiet again.

Ms. Rideout puts the speaker back in the bowl and piles the gourds on top of it. One of them falls off the pile and she balances it very carefully on top of the others. It rocks a little and then settles into place. The speaker is buried in a pyramid of gourds. Ms. Rideout drinks all the wine in her glass in three gulps and pours again, emptying the bottle.

You have to let them cry a little bit, she says. Otherwise you spoil them. Now, you're here for a reading?

We're not actually here for a reading, I say. We're here about promotion and sales.

But Ms. Rideout is removing her jewelry. Her gold rings, her pearl earrings, the gold necklace with the little pentangle. She lays it all in a pile beside her on the dark mahogany table.

I've been able to see things since I was a kid, she says. She closes her eyes and rubs her temples.

Amber and I look at each other. I'll admit that I'm pretty tempted. If there was ever a person in need of a little occult help figuring out her future love life, especially re a certain brown-eyed boy. But I know there's less than an hour until Gary's game is over.

We were just hoping for a little professional mentoring, I say. An interview, that's all.

I feel the cat press hard against my leg, and it slithers through the rungs of the chair I'm sitting on. It nudges its forehead against my shin and I lift it gently on my foot and sort of kick it away. It meows. It slinks off and soundlessly leaps up onto the sideboard, daintily stepping through the objects on the silver tea service and leaps down the other side, disappearing into the shadows.

We're here about advertising, I say, for a love potion.

A love potion, says Ms. Rideout. That's very dangerous territory.

It's just a gag, Amber and I say in unison. Ms. Rideout sits up straight and suddenly appears very sober.

It may start out that way, she says. But the power of suggestion is a funny thing. People begin to hear about your potion and they want it to work. How lonely people are, sometimes for their whole lives. They just want someone to notice their worth.

Ms. Rideout reaches back into the gourd bowl and finds the speaker and turns it on and the baby is still screeching and she flicks it off.

Pretty much everybody believes in some kind of magic, she says. They toss a little salt over their shoulder. They don't walk under ladders. Tell them your potion contains a drop of nectar from deep inside an exotic flower or some other nonsense like that, and they start to believe it works. And because they believe, it really does work. But what if a couple gets together because of your potion and they're all wrong for each other? That's playing with fate.

I think I'd like a reading, says Amber.

But Amber, we're in a hurry, remember? I say. I don't know why, but I want to get out of here.

Amber ignores me.

I'd really like a reading, Ms. Rideout, if you don't mind, she says. Amber reaches into her knapsack and pulls out a twenty-dollar bill. Ms. Rideout finds a box of matches and lights a thick white candle, which she brings to the table.

We'll hold hands, please, says Ms. Rideout.

And here we are, the three of us, holding hands.

I have to stretch a little to take Amber's hand because she's on the other side of the table. Several minutes pass. Somewhere a clock is ticking. I try to catch Amber's eye, but her eyes are closed. Ms. Rideout's eyes are closed too. We're waiting so long I wonder if Ms. Rideout has fallen asleep. I give Amber's hand a little squeeze but she doesn't respond.

Okay, says Ms. Rideout. She lets go of our hands. She blows out the candle.

What, says Amber. You didn't see anything?

Not much, says Ms. Rideout. Keep your twenty dollars. Sometimes I see things, sometimes I don't.

But you saw something?

Good luck with your schoolwork, girls. I'd stay away from love potions. You might be in over your heads.

What did you see? Amber says.

Does your friend want to hear this? Ms. Rideout asks me.

No, I say. Amber, you have a game to get back to. I'm already putting away the voice recorder.

Tell me, says Amber. What did you see?

I saw a man, Ms. Rideout says. A young man.

It's Gary, Amber says. And there's the Amber thousand-watt smile.

He was cloaked in a shroud of darkness, Ms. Rideout says.

Amber turns white, then red. She's picking up her knapsack. The smile is gone.

That's it? says Amber. A "shroud of darkness"? What's that supposed to mean? Her tone is incredibly rude. I've never heard her speak to an adult like this.

I'm thanking Ms. Rideout for her help, but I'm thinking of the beating heart of the basketball pounding toward the door of the gym while I waited out there, locked out in the cold, because Gary doesn't want me hanging around Amber, and how distant Amber has been over the past month, how I can never get her to answer my texts, and how last week I saw Gary joking with Mercy Hanrahan, being flirty by the lockers.

He had his arm out straight, resting his hand against the lockers, and Mercy had just got her books and he was leaning over her and she was looking up at him, and she put her hand on his chest as if to push him away but not really pushing. I shot him a look of disgust, and he just looked back, daring me to do something.

I haven't told Amber. In fact, it's the first time I have kept something from Amber and it makes me feel sick whenever I think of it, but I also know I can't tell her. I'm afraid she'll call me a liar.

And there's been an older guy with tattoos on his neck hanging around the school parking lot in a beat-up Sunbird and everybody says he's a coke dealer, and I've seen Gary leaning into his car, talking to the guy. And Mercy Hanrahan is often in the guy's car with her sneakers on the dash, blowing smoke at the windshield.

I feel the hairs stand up on my arms and I have goosebumps. I stand up suddenly and my chair tips over.

It's then that a snarling ball of hiss and claws leaps from the bookshelf behind me onto the back of my neck. I reach up and fling him off. He lands on all fours and stalks away, stiff with the indignity of having to attack a lowly creature like myself. I just thank God I'd already put on my coat.

Oh dear, says Ms. Rideout. You'll have to forgive poor, dear Merlin. And girls, I'm going to have to take care of my baby now, please show yourselves out.

Amber is already in the porch, yanking hard on the laces of her boots, tying them up very tight. I am right behind her, but Ms. Rideout grabs my elbow.

Keep an eye on your friend, she says.

Outside Amber is striding through the falling snow, and I'm trotting to keep up. Her head is bent down against the wind, her fists driven deep into the pockets of her jacket.

Amber, wait, I call to her. She keeps going.

Wait! I say again.

Why should I, she yells over her shoulder. What's there to wait for?

Hey, I say, why are you so mad at me? You're the one who insisted on a reading! Amber wheels around to face me.

Because you're the one who believes her, she says.

Amber, come on! That lady was drunk. And probably sleep-deprived because of the baby. She's obviously a fake. There's no such thing as seeing into the future.

Right. But still you believe her! She knew you were on her side. That's why she said, "Does your friend want to hear this?" to you. I was right there, Flannery.

Amber, that's crazy.

Tell me, then, Flannery. Tell me you don't believe Gary's a bad person. She says it like a dare, but there's real yearning in her eyes.

I don't believe "he's shrouded in darkness" or any stupid thing like that, I say. I mean, it's a total cliché. It doesn't even make any sense.

Tell me, she says again. Tell me you don't agree with that witch. That you don't think he's bad for me.

We look into each other's eyes for a moment and that moment feels like a year, longer, as long as we've known each other, "kindred since kindergarten," and then it still feels longer than that.

Finally, I say, I don't think you should trust him, Amber. That's all. But I really don't.

For a minute I think she is going to break down in front of me, and that Gary is history. I think everything will go back to the way it was between us.

But then, the smirk.

You know, Flannery, we've been talking about how naive you can be, she says. Like, don't you think it's a bit much, doing all of the work on your stupid potion project by yourself? I mean, where's Tyrone?

We again.

She keeps going. You're so desperate to get his attention you're willing to do all his homework for him. You're willing to make a fool out of yourself and follow him all over the place. Anybody can see he's interested in other girls. You know what people are saying, right?

No, I don't, Amber. Why don't you enlighten me?

They're saying you're making a love potion because you want to use it on Tyrone. She laughs.

Anyway, she says. Good luck with that.

And she leaves me standing there in the snow.

15

———

This is the way it was when Amber and I were twelve. I'd started my period at Amber's house on a very hot, sunny summer afternoon when time had pretty much stopped.

There was a major stoppage in the universe.

There was nobody home except Amber and me and all the windows were open and there was a breeze blowing the sheers out like big beer bellies.

We had nothing to do that day. Everybody we knew was gone to the country or they were working at Tim Hortons or their cell phones had died. Amber had already been to swim practice that morning, leaving in the dark before I'd even woken up, and Sean had dropped her off at home before he went to work and she'd come back to bed.

We'd slept half the day away and woke feeling groggy and sour. The bed sheets were twisted up at the foot of the bed in knots.

I'd gone to the bathroom and there was a brown stain on my underwear.

I knew what it was, of course.

On top of that terrifying non-talk on the edge of the bath-tub with Miranda about sex and the reproductive system, we'd done the menstrual cycle in the sex-ed unit of our biology class in grade six.

The boys had been asked to leave the room and it was just girls. The boys would be doing the same lesson next week.

We felt sisterly and abandoned without the boys.

The boys were out in the sunshine having a game of basket-ball. We could hear them running and jerking to a stop, and running back the other way, yelling, but yelling in a subdued sportsmanlike way completely foreign to them. We heard when a foul was called, and the coach's whistle, and some mild expressions of concern about whether it had actually been a foul.

They knew why they were outside. They hadn't done the class yet, but they were going to do it, and maybe they were afraid.

We girls were sitting in the dark, watching an animated film of a gazillion sperms with dark crooked eyebrows and grimaces of effort and strain, snarled lips with teeth showing, all of them in a race of wiggling tails, trying to get to the egg, who was batting her long eyelashes, awaiting the lucky dude's arrival.

Is that all they could have the egg do? Sit there and wait? Why wasn't she charging around too, gnashing her teeth?

So, I knew what the stain on my underwear meant that day at Amber's.

But I also didn't know.

Because how can anybody really understand that blood? I looked in the toilet and in the cloud of pee there was a ribbon of blood sinking toward the bottom of the white toilet bowl.

I thought, What is happening to me? Even though I knew.

I wadded up some toilet paper and put it in my underwear until I got home and could ask Miranda for some pads or tampons or whatever.

Amber hadn't started her period yet. And wouldn't really start for a while, maybe because of swimming. Exercise was probably messing with her cycle, her doctor had said.

I told her about the blood, but we didn't talk about it. We didn't really talk much that summer, about anything. We were telepathic.

Amber could tell, in the same telepathic way, as soon as she opened the back door of her house, whether her mother was drunk.

It was a particular kind of low-watt tension that wafted out when the door creaked open. Sometimes it was the noise of ice tumbling down inside the fridge.

They had an ice-making fridge — very unlike Miranda's harvest gold number that was second-hand and a thousand years old, and had come from the Sally Ann and had rust all over the front, and you had to lean a chair against it to keep the door closed. The rubber seal on our fridge had hardened up and yellowed and had no suction.

I loved Amber's fridge. It was stainless-steel, ultramodern and looked like a spacecraft you could climb inside and shoot for the stars.

I loved the levers built into one of the doors where you pressed a glass and it would fill with ice, two kinds: slushy or chunky.

I loved the soft kiss of the rubber seal on Amber's fridge. It provided excellent closure.

The ice tumbled down inside a secret chamber and Amber would feel that something wasn't right.

Something to do with how quiet the rest of the house was in comparison. Silence was a good indication that Cindy, Amber's mom, was blotto.

But sometimes, depending on how drunk she was, Amber's mother would be banging away on the piano, so loud the geraniums on the windowsills would shiver. A sole white petal would drop into the dry earth in the pot below.

It wasn't the volume that gave her away. It was the precision. When Amber's mom was drunk she played without mistakes. Loud and perfect, each note crisp and glittering.

But that day, when I started my period, the house was empty. Just Amber and me.

Sitting there on the side of Amber's bed, I could feel the warm blood leaking out of me in a gush.

I'm going to bake you a cake, Amber said.

I think I'll just stay here, I said. My stomach was cramping. I felt a little nauseated. I lay back and I woke up much later to the smell of chocolate cake baking in the oven. A dense, velvety smell that had made its way into my dreams and woken me up. I went downstairs to the kitchen and there was a pile of stainless-steel bowls in the sink. I picked up the spatula and licked it clean.

Where are you? I called.

Down here, Amber said.

She was in the basement bathroom. I hated going down there. The indoor/outdoor carpet smelled moldy and there was old exercise equipment that must have cost a fortune but that nobody ever used. A pile of fur coats flung over a corduroy sofa. They looked like an animal lying in wait.

What are you doing? I said.

It's cool down here, Amber said. There was a light on in the bathroom at the back of the basement and I went to the doorway.

Amber had cut off most of her hair. All of her curls lay in the sink like a big nest. Her face looked bigger, like she'd had a growth spurt. Her eyes.

Her eyes were shiny and wet.

I'll be able to swim faster, she said.

I moved closer to her. My back was against the doorframe and I slid down so I was hunched on the floor, my knees under my chin, just looking up at her. She turned back to the mirror and fanned her hands like hummingbird wings.

I can feel the breeze, she said. It feels nice. She picked up the scissors again and then I stood up, too quickly, because I felt a little rush of dizziness and lurched forward, steadying myself on the counter. I took the scissors out of her hand.

Sometimes the pressure of competitive swimming got to her. And she was terrified her father would leave her mother, because of the drinking. And if her father did leave, she was afraid she'd be left behind. She knew the swimming was the one thing that made her father happy. So she swam as fast as she could.

16

On Saturday there's our usual family outing at the Aquarena, with the significant difference that this time, as per our new arrangement, I'll be in charge of Felix while Miranda gets in her workout.

Felix is bouncing off the insides of the truck before we pull into the parking lot, and I'm having serious doubts that any new bathing suit is going to be worth the ordeal of the next hour.

Miranda has a lifetime free pass to the gym/pool because one of her artist friends is married to one of the managers.

Sometimes the free pass includes bracelets for the water-slides, the inflated obstacle course, the five- and ten-meter diving platforms, and — though Felix hasn't worked up the nerve to try it yet — the Tarzan rope.

And sometimes Miranda's pass does not include the bracelets. The young women at the counter always check the computer for our names, which don't appear on the list, but they often say, *Oh yes, here you are*, and print the bracelets anyway.

It's pretty hard to look Felix Malone in the eye and deny him anything. His little pointy chin reaching up to rest on the edge of the counter. He widens those big blue eyes and out pours all his burning hope.

Felix cannot stand the suspense. He tries to see the screen for himself. He pouts his lower lip. He turns on an inner tap that allows the flow of a fire hose full of charm.

Incredibly, the girl at the counter seems oblivious to this pressurized charge of adorableness coming straight out of his eyes. It's me she's looking at instead. She has her septum pierced with a little silver ring, and a patch of her hair is magenta and another patch is green. She is chewing gum and a big pink bubble balloons from her pursed lips and breaks, draping itself over her chin. She peels it off and sticks it back in her mouth.

Then I know who she is. She's the girl who was riding the escalator with Tyrone.

The girl sees that I recognize her and then she turns to Felix and gives him a smile so big that, charm-wise, it gives his own smile a run for its money. She flicks her eyes over the list and says, Looks here like you get bracelets for full access to the waterslide.

Yay! says Felix. The printer near the girl's hip spits out a few bracelets and Felix is hopping up and down, demanding that I give him his, telling me he can put it on himself.

Thanks, I say. He loves the waterslide.

He's a cutie, the girl says. I'll probably see you around. I think we know some of the same people.

The pool is full. The shallow end is a riot of kids and parents, neon noodles floating on the surface, striped beach balls and kickboards everywhere.

The baby pool is full of little babies with water wings and life jackets, mothers with white dimpled thighs. And fathers. And fathers. And fathers.

There are fathers everywhere. I've never really noticed that before.

But the hour goes by pretty quickly. Felix even stays obediently in the shallow end when I ask him to so that I can get in a few laps on my own.

The only dicey part of the whole morning is trying to get him to go with me into the family change room. Miranda wants me to get him dressed so she can take a five-minute sauna after her workout. I finally get him to cave by promising that he can go into the men's change room by himself the minute he turns seven.

On the drive home Miranda says she can tell I'm preoccupied. I'm actually thinking about the parrot-haired girl, but Miranda assumes I'm worrying about Part B of my Entrepreneurship project, the interview. I've already told her there's absolutely nothing usable in my recorded interview with Ms. Rideout.

You know, Larry is an extremely gifted marketer, Miranda is saying.

Who the heck is Larry? I ask.

Sensei Larry, squeals Felix.

The karate instructor? I ask. What does karate have to do with love potions?

Karate is an ancient art that requires self-discipline, fast moves, balance and creativity, Miranda says. And those are some of the essential ingredients of the art of being in love as well.

Being in love is an art?

Absolutely, she says.

So you're saying that karate and love have a lot in common? I ask.

Yes, Flannery, Miranda says. She sighs as if everyone on the planet knows this but me.

17

So on Thursday evening I find myself in the gymnasium of my own school watching my little brother take his karate class. I'm going to interview Sensei Larry as soon as the class is over. That way I can get the voice recorder back to the scary secretary before inventory tomorrow.

I am sad to report that Felix Malone is not a very good karate student.

He does have a passionate love of holding up his two hands, straight as boards, in the classic karate defense position and standing absolutely still, looking all focused and mysterious. He also (and this fact was already known to me) really likes his outfit, those black pajamas with the wrap-around belt (also useful for hanging my old dolls by the neck over the stair-rail at home).

And he really, *really* likes the bow thing they do at the beginning of class.

The purpose of the bow is to act out, in a physical gesture, all the respect you have for your sensei and fellow students. This is something that was explained to me at great length over breakfast this morning after Felix found out I'd be sitting in on his class.

It turns out he has a great deal of respect for Sensei Larry and his fellow students. At the start of class Felix bends his forehead all the way to his knees and makes a point of staying that way for as long as he can, holding up the whole class.

Finally, Sensei Larry has to say, Enough bowing, Malone.

But Felix says he doesn't think he's had enough time to demonstrate all the respect he feels for Sensei Larry.

He has only demonstrated about two-thirds of it, he says. (Felix has recently come upon the concept of fractions and is always eager to display his knowledge and uses them wherever possible.) He tells Sensei Larry that if they could just wait for a minute or so he will have demonstrated the other third of his respect.

So the class waits a little bit more and finally Felix straightens up and is very red in the face and pleased with himself.

And of course he is very fond of jumping in the air and yelling at the top of his lungs and crashing into people when they are trying to work out their karate routines in a calm, orderly fashion.

But what he doesn't seem especially fond of is listening to Sensei Larry explain the precise moves and steps required to earn your yellow belt, the very first belt a karate expert must achieve.

Sensei Larry has a black belt and if there is a belt higher than black, he probably also has that.

At the end of the class Sensei Larry does a little demonstration and he kicks his feet up higher than his shoulders and his arms move like helicopter blades and it's a miracle he doesn't just lift right off the floor and float up to the ceiling.

Miranda has filled me in on several other noteworthy things about Sensei Larry as well.

For one, he was in a trad/rock band that used to play all

over St. John's and went on the road in the early eighties and once signed with a big record label.

And perhaps even more impressively, Larry collects medieval armor. It is his goal, Miranda has told me, to re-enact a medieval battle at Bannerman Park this year amid a herd of ice-sculpture dragons. He hadn't even known that Miranda was an ice-sculpture artist, but now they're thinking of a collaboration.

I have also learned that Sensei Larry isn't married and cares for his aging mother in his home. In fact, Miranda is full of information about Sensei Larry.

As you can imagine, it is my sincere hope that Sensei Larry will ask Miranda out on a date, or the other way around. Though mentioning this hope to Miranda would pretty much ensure it would never happen.

Instead, I must wait patiently to see how things unfold. Patience with your parent may or may not bring its own rewards, but sometimes you have to wait whether you like it or not.

After class, Felix runs wild around the gym while Miranda chats with Sensei Larry about wind power, fracking and a gender-studies course they both apparently did back in 2000, though not in the same class.

They discuss ice fishing and performance art and efficient wood stoves. The work of a film animator who actually scratched right into the emulsion of the film (back in the Middle Ages when they actually had film) and how Sensei Larry really must see these films. Miranda knows he's going to love them.

Sensei Larry chats back about his armor collection and the sort of pewter goblet that it was fashionable to drink mead out of in the 1400s and what it takes to be a good jouster.

He is clearly spending way more time with Miranda than is totally necessary, even ignoring the other parents, who are

milling around waiting to hear about the karate fundraiser for
the provincial all-ages meet in Gander, and what outlet sells
the cheapest karate suits.

Sensei Larry and Miranda both seem to be forgetting that
I'm here waiting to interview him. Felix has to drag Miranda
out of there by the hand. She walks backwards out of the gym,
still talking about her tiara and the feminist leanings of the
conceptual art project she's involved in and something about
dress codes in schools being sexist.

Finally the gym has emptied out and we hear the doors
slam and Sensei Larry settles himself in a lotus position right
in the middle of the gym floor, and I sit opposite him and turn
on the recorder.

I ask how he advertises his classes and he talks about Instagram and Twitter and the importance of social media. But he
says the strongest advertising tool is still the oldest one: word
of mouth.

If people start to hear good things, Sensei Larry says, they
want to check it out for themselves. We talk for a bit about
making a product that has integrity or that is especially creative
or fresh, something that has the potential to stir up excitement.

Then I hit him with the hard question. How are karate and
love alike?

He laughs, and it's a high-pitched, totally unexpected, un-
selfconscious laugh that makes him shake all over. He has
thrown his head back and I can see his tonsils trembling back
there, he's laughing so hard. But he finally straightens up and
gets serious. He talks about being thoughtful.

That's all I got, he said. You have to work at both of them,
and you have to be thoughtful.

Thoughtful, I say.

Yup, he says. Full of thought. About everything.

And in that moment, Sensei Larry looks like the kind of man who has taken the time to think deeply about life, about everything. He looks like he has a sense of humor, and he also looks kind. He makes "being full of thought" sound wise and necessary.

And I switch off the audio recorder. I have everything I need.

Afterward, I stay at the school to transcribe the interview so I don't have to fight with Miranda for the computer at home (she's been moaning about having a blog post overdue). The secretary is doing some extra filing and says it's okay.

When I'm finally ready to leave I can see that it's well past dark and the streetlights are on. The wind is blowing hard and I have to press my whole body against the door to get out of the school. There are swirls of gritty snow swaying low across the road like ghostly serpents.

The orange Sunbird is idling on the other side of the street. The engine revs a couple of times as soon as the door shuts behind me. I can hear the hole in the muffler. Music is thrumming from the inside. I decide to go back into the school so I can come out another exit. I don't trust the guy in that car, and there's nobody else around. The parking lot is empty.

But the door has locked behind me.

I detour around the side of the school so I can cut through the back parking lot. That way I won't have to walk past the Sunbird.

I'm halfway across the parking lot when a swarm of girls appears on the top of the hill that leads to the supermarket. There are at least six of them.

Mercy Hanrahan is in the front of the pack.

Hey, she says. You're that one Amber's friend. I've got something I'd like you to tell her. A message you can pass on.

I have to get home, I say. But Mercy and all the girls with her have stepped up close to me and they're in front of me and behind me too. The girl next to Mercy is texting something.

I try to step between them but they nudge me back.

Where are you going? Mercy says. We just want to have a chat. You don't have to be so rude. Why is everybody so stuck-up around here?

Her skin is golden from a spray-on tan and her hair is flying around in the wind. It flies over her face and she turns into the wind and it flies back over one shoulder, flickering out straight.

Her eyes are narrowed and watering from the wind. She's chewing a big wad of gum and the scent of simulated grape and the smell of cigarette smoke hang in every word she says.

That Amber is the most stuck-up of all, Mercy says. Some kind of swimmer or something. Who gives a fuck about swimming?

There's five or six more girls running down the hill now. They must have been in the supermarket too. That's who the girl beside Mercy was texting. Kids go there after school to get food from the deli. One of them has a greasy box of taters in her hand.

These new ones are girls from the east end. Their school has been closed because of asbestos, and they've just been transferred to Heart. They have greasy hair and too much blue eyeshadow and clothes from Pipers and everybody says they're skanks and skeets and Welfare.

Just like I'm Welfare.

People also say Mercy has done coke, and that her older sister Sienna dropped out of school to have a baby and social services took the baby and now she's working at the super-market behind the school, but I go to that supermarket with Miranda all the time and I've never seen anyone who looks like Mercy and anyway Miranda was only nineteen when she got pregnant with me.

Mercy lifts her chin at me as if she's decided that we can probably talk this thing out, whatever it is. She drapes an arm over my shoulder, drawing my neck in tight.

This won't take very long, she says. I got something I need your friend to know. Either we tell you, or we get your friend Amber back here behind the school. How would you like that? Here's the message. We don't like her very much.

The girls have moved in close and I'm in the center of the crowd. They're pressing in on me. I look up at the windows of the school, but they're black and empty. I think about what Miranda says about foul language.

Go fuck yourself, I say. I break out of the circle and stride toward the hill. I'm trying to look like I'm not in any kind of a hurry. Like I'm casually sauntering up the hill.

But I abandon that plan after a few steps and start running as fast as I can.

Somebody flies through the air at me and I'm knocked hard to the ground. They're all on top of me, and I can't breathe, I can't even move. They've got me by the arms and the legs and they roll me over on my back and there are hands all over my face. Several hands are prying my mouth open.

All their heads are together and I can only see little chinks of sky. They're grunting with the effort of holding me down and cursing, and the wind is making their hair fly all over the place.

Then I see Jessica Kelloway pushing through the circle of heads, holding something on a stick.

I got something here, Jessica says.

We got something for you, Mercy says.

I can see it's a used condom. Jessica Kelloway has pierced the rim of it with the tip of the stick. Most of it is wrinkled up and withered with little folds, except at the very bottom. There hangs a bulbous part, plump with a dense milky liquid.

Sperm.

Get her mouth open, Mercy orders. Someone has a hand clamped on my forehead and another hand is on my chin, forcing my mouth open and my head back. Several of them are holding my legs. There are knees on both my shoulders. There are many sets of arms around my waist. Someone's head is grinding into my side.

But still I am writhing like crazy. I am thrashing with fury.

They start chanting. Eat it, eat it, eat it, eat it. The stick is jiggling and bouncing and coming close to my face and then the condom brushes over my cheek.

I get a leg free and kick the girl at my feet as hard as I can and at the same time I bite somebody's finger. I can feel the bone under my teeth. I bite down hard and whoever owns the finger is screaming and people are really punching me now, fists hammering down.

Then a car drives into the parking lot. The girls all scrabble to their feet and take off up over the embankment.

The school secretary gets out of the car and rushes over to me. She says she was driving by and saw me going around the back and didn't think it was safe back there in the dark. Thought she'd just check.

We both get in her car and she passes me some Kleenex from the glove compartment and I wipe a cut on my forehead.

Are you going to be okay? she asks.

I don't know, I say. I'm shaking all over and she puts her

hand on my arm and rubs it vigorously up and down and then pats me.

We have procedures at the counselor's office, she says. If you want to name those girls. You can think about it, anyway.

I don't say anything.

I'll take you home, she says. Put on your seatbelt.

As we're pulling out in front of the school, I see that the Sunbird is still there. There's a guy bent over it, talking to whoever's in the driver's seat. The guy with his arm on the Sunbird's roof straightens up and looks in the direction of the lane leading to the back of the school.

Gary Bowen.

18

Tyrone makes an unexpected appearance — in math class of all places. There he is, long legs sticking out in the aisle. He's wearing socks with marijuana leaves on them and army boots spray-painted gold. But he's jotting down notes from the board.

I corner him in the hall while the lunch buzzer is droning through the speakers.

I have an appointment at a glassblower's studio, I tell him. To look at bottles for our potion. It's somewhere on Bond, and I'm not going there by myself. Even though the guy seems pretty nice in his texts, he is, after all, a complete stranger.

It's been a week since Mercy Hanrahan attacked me behind the school, and I'm still constantly looking over my shoulder. I haven't let my guard down for one second until now. I'm standing there trying to convince Tyrone he has to come with me when Mercy Hanrahan walks by with Jessica Kelloway. I don't see them until they're practically on top of me.

Mercy fakes this dart-jolt toward me, her sneakers squeaking on the floor, her eyes nearly popping out of her head. Her face so close to mine I can feel her breath on my cheeks.

She whispers, Boo!

Of course I nearly jump out of my skin and that sends her into a fit of giggles. She's jabbing Jessica Kelloway in the ribs with her elbow and the two of them are laughing hard, crossing their legs so they don't pee in their pants and staggering forward like the laughing might make them keel over.

Hey, Malone, Mercy says. Did you give your friend our message? Tell her she's next.

What was that all about? asks Tyrone. I haven't told anyone about the attack, not even Miranda. I feel ashamed for being stupid enough to cross the dark parking lot in the first place and I feel ashamed about feeling ashamed. Of course it wasn't my fault. But I can't help it. I feel so stupid. And the condom was so disgusting. I can't bring myself to speak about it.

What did that mean, "She's next"? asks Tyrone. What have I been missing around here?

Look, I say. I did the whole interview thing on my own and signed your name to it. Twenty percent of your grade. And I did the initial proposal on my own. And the rewrite. All I'm asking is you come with me to check out this glassblower's perfume bottles. It's the perfect packaging for the love potion. It'll just take an hour. The thing is, I'm depending on you, Tyrone. I mean it. We're already behind with this. Jordan and Brittany already have their prototype in. They're making wallets out of duct tape. They're really cool. And David and Chad are recycling old tires to make sandals. Lori McCurdy and Allie Jones are selling herb gardens. The things are already sprouting.

Tyrone ducks his head a little and scratches the back of his neck. It feels so good to be near him. Those blazing brown eyes. When he looks at me — giving me his full attention like this — I feel like one of Miranda's neon sculptures, brilliant green light zipping all through me. I'm lit up.

Can we do it tomorrow? he asks.

No, we can't do it tomorrow, I say. Everybody is supposed to have a sample of their packaging for tomorrow.

I absolutely can't go today, Tyrone says.

You sound ambivalent, I say. I reach up and pull the little thread on his Santa Claus pin and the nose lights up and there's a little tinny voice inside there that says, Ho, ho, ho.

And suddenly I find that I am flirting with Tyrone O'Rourke. Out and out full-blown hair-tossing flirtation. What's to lose, right? My days are probably numbered, when you consider Mercy Hanrahan. Desperation has made me brave.

Aw, come on, Tyrone, I say in a kind of baby-talk. Maybe we could get a cappuccino after? I feel exhilarated and unrecognizable to myself. And I can see Tyrone is taken off guard. He straightens the shoulder strap of my knapsack, though it doesn't need straightening. His finger smooths down a wrinkle in the fabric, kind of lingering there.

I am so sure I can't go today, he sighs. I've never been more sure about anything in my life.

But you have to admit there's a chance, right? There's always a chance? I mean, the guy is an artist. It could be fun.

I show him the glassblower's texts. I found him in the crafts section of *Newfoundland Buy and Sell*. He says he has a hundred handblown perfume bottles for sale, each one a unique work of art. I texted him as soon as I saw the ad. And the guy says he'll let them go for cheap because it sounds like an interesting project. Also, he's closing up shop. Moving to Italy.

Newfoundlanders don't understand glass, he texted. *They aren't ready for it. In fact nobody in North America gets glass. What I do is art.*

I could tell he must be in his fifties because he kept texting big long paragraphs.

Just then Amber walks down the corridor. She doesn't even look at me. She's talking to Melody Martin.

So you'll come? I say it loud enough for Amber to hear. And I get up the picture of the bottles on my phone.

See, aren't they pretty?

They do look sort of perfect for a love potion, Tyrone says. He takes the phone from me and flicks through the pictures.

Don't make me go there alone, I say.

This time I'm not flirting. I'm dead serious.

He's also selling swan ashtrays, Tyrone says.

I only want the perfume bottles.

They *are* cool.

So meet me by the front doors and we'll walk there after school?

I guess so, Tyrone says. Yeah, I'll see you there, Flan. And thanks, you know, for doing the interview and stuff and signing my name.

I feel intensely relieved. The truth is, I've been kind of afraid to walk home from school even while it's still light out. But with Tyrone I'll be safe.

And then I'm beaming. I can feel all the muscles in my face involuntarily align themselves into a beam. I'm humming to myself through Madame Lapointe's class on *A Midsummer Night's Dream*. I get to read Titania.

I'm still full of relief as I jam my books in my locker and hurry down the stairs and wait in the front porch of the school while all the students pour out of there.

I watch as the basketball team comes out of the boys' change room and heads into the gym for practice.

I'm not smiling quite so much at 3:45 when Amber and Melody get out of Amber's father's car with armloads of the costumes Amber and I picked out at the Arts and Culture Centre three weeks ago.

Flannery, still waiting for Tyrone? she asks.

Amber, I say. Can I talk to you a minute?

I don't know, Flannery, she says. I'm kind of busy.

I have something to tell you, I say.

My arms are full, Flannery. Gary is upstairs waiting to get to work on our project.

I'm worried about you, I say. I want to tell her about Mercy.

Oh, I know, she says. You're worried about me. You want to protect me from my boyfriend. Thanks a lot, but it all seems to be working out fine. I don't think we need your help. Maybe you should worry about yourself, Flannery.

Sean, Amber's dad, sees me at the door and waves and toot-toots the horn before driving off. Amber breezes past. The school is emptying out now, and I really have to get going. I guess I'll be going to the glassblower's alone.

Just then Kyle Keating comes up to me and thrusts a brown paper bag into my hands.

Here, he says. I've been carrying this thing around for a week. Now it's your turn. You and I are partners in Healthy Living. Mr. Follett put us together while you were supposedly sick, as I'm sure you know, since I've been texting you all week.

You know something, Flannery? he says. I didn't ask to be partners with you. But I was glad when Mr. Follett put us together because I thought you were cool. I didn't think you were the kind of person who would let somebody else do all the work on a project.

I didn't get your texts, I say. (That's a lie, of course. I did get them, but I didn't pay attention to them.)

Sure you didn't, Kyle says.

I'm sorry, Kyle, I say. God, I'm really sorry.

I take my hand away from the bottom of the bag of eggs and there's slimy egg white webbing my fingers together.

Oh great, he says. Let me tell you something. They didn't break on my watch. You've had them for all of five seconds and now look. You can write the essay on unwanted teenage pregnancy all by yourself.

It suddenly occurs to me that Kyle Keating likes me. Like, *like* likes me. I mean, that's why he's so mad about the broken egg. I mean, he's *not* mad about the egg at all. He's mad that I have been ignoring him. I haven't been thoughtful. In fact, I've been thought*less*. I suddenly remember him asking me to walk to the Oxfam office after the Bursting Boils concert. I'm totally flabbergasted! I mean, I'm flattered and confused. I don't really know how I feel about Kyle. But I feel terrible about not being thoughtful.

I've been having a bad week, I say. I hope you can forgive me. I really am sorry. I had this really terrible thing happen.

And suddenly I'm telling him all about Mercy Hanrahan. I can't stop myself. I tell him about kicking and biting and even the condom. I cry a little bit. And I laugh too. And when I'm done I see that he has walked me home. I still have the bag of eggs in my hand.

And I'm sorry about our metaphorical baby, I say.

I hold up the bag. The bottom is completely soaked through now, and it tears apart and all the eggs fall out on the sidewalk.

Some of them break and some roll away.

19

―――――

$\mathcal{I}'d$ come home from a sleepover at Amber's one day when I was nine. This was after Hank had married the soon-to-be-lawyer lady and the happy couple had both headed into the sunset on their surfboards. I got the key out of the mailbox and opened our front door and all of a sudden I noticed the house was very quiet.

Our house was never quiet.

Miranda likes to have music blasting and it was the height of her tango phase, when she was taking tango lessons and sometimes I would come home and there would be six couples — mostly women though there was one gay male couple — charging across the living room with their arms out straight and grim looks on their faces, cheek to cheek, turning on their high heels just before they smashed into each other or the opposite wall.

Or she'd have her feminist consciousness-raising group over and they'd be yelling about social justice, equal pay for equal work and sexual freedom. At the very least, she'd have several pots boiling away on the stove, the lids rattling, the fire alarm set off by whatever she was burning in the oven.

But on this day, I'd come home and it was very, very quiet.

I called out to Miranda.

The window was open in the living room and a square of bright sunlight lay over the hardwood floor and a billowing curtain had knocked over a plant.

The pot had cracked and the roots of the banana plant were poking out through the black soil and the roots were white and hairy.

Something about the great mass of those twisting hairy roots and how very translucent they looked gave me goosebumps.

I went up the stairs and every room was empty and all the curtains were open.

I was afraid to look in Miranda's study so I stood on the landing. I could hear a jackhammer several streets away. I could feel the vibration of it in my teeth.

And then I peeked into the study. Miranda was sitting at her desk, but her head was hanging down and a thin strand of drool had dropped from the corner of her mouth to her chin.

I had never in my whole life seen Miranda asleep in the afternoon. I had never seen her drool.

I knew at once that Miranda had been enchanted. Something powerful had cast a spell and drawn her away. She had been possessed. Or taken over by an alien life form.

What was left at the desk was the husk of my mother. She had become a host or a shell.

She looked like my mother, sure, but — like the Big Bad Wolf after he'd eaten Little Red Riding Hood's grandmother and put on her clothes — there was something unfamiliar in her expression, in the flush of her cheek.

I tried to say her name and nothing came out, and then I tried it again and said it very loudly and her head jerked up with a snort and she said, Oh!

She saw me standing there in the doorway and she smiled at me. Even the smile was weird. It looked as if I had already grown up and left her and she was smiling at the kid I used to be.

The heat must have knocked me out, she said.

I knew if she spoke again everything would change forever but there was no way to stop what was coming.

Flannery, she said. The alien put out my mother's hand and wiggled my mother's fingers, beckoning me to come toward her. I stepped forward against my will.

This wasn't Miranda and the knowledge made me miss Miranda so much I couldn't stop my feet. They moved, one heavy clodhopper at a time, across the room. Miranda had put up a fight, that's why her cheeks were blushing and radiant. But she had finally succumbed.

Come here, girl-child, Miranda said. Which is the name the real Miranda sometimes called me. Girl-child, Flana-Banana, Buckwheat, Bucktooth, Lover Lumps and Malone-Face. But there was still the telltale glimmer of drool on her chin, which she wiped at with the back of her hand.

She drew me close to her, rested her head against my chest.

I didn't care if she was an alien then. She was all I had.

She yawned and rubbed her eye with her knuckle.

Miranda said, I'm going to have a baby. You're going to have a little baby brother. It's not just going to be the two of us anymore, Flannery. We have a beautiful new baby on the way.

I felt the sting of tears. They were rolling down my cheeks and my neck.

She was my mother. Mine. Not somebody else's. I didn't want to share. Why should I? Why did we need somebody else? Wasn't I enough?

I thought of her footprints in the flour spilled on the kitchen floor when she was making pizza dough the week before Hank's wedding and the flour print of her hands on her hips.

I thought about us both sitting on the side of the bathtub with the book about sex. I thought of all those sperms with their angry faces in the animated film the teachers had shown us.

And the egg, preening in front of the mirror, putting on mascara, batting her eyes. I thought about my dad, Mr. X, sailing the high seas in his boat of plastic bottles and tin cans and chip bags.

Miranda was pregnant with Felix, but she hadn't told anybody — least of all Hank. She'd been hiding it in loose clothes. Even at nine years old, I think I might have understood that she would only have wanted Hank to be with us if he was in love with us. It doesn't feel good to be somebody's obligation.

One other thing I suddenly understood. Something had come between us now. Between Miranda and me.

There was something definitive in the way she said it wasn't going to be just us.

And the third thing that dawned on me that day was that there should be a magical phone you can call when things are bad, and someone on the other end who can fix just about anything.

There should be a special red phone with a flickering red button that you can use only once in a lifetime, when all is lost.

Not when all is almost lost.

Not when a few things are lost.

This would be a phone that you'd use on that very singular occasion when *all* is lost.

Say you are on the highway in your beat-up old Toyota truck with your very pregnant mom on the way home from a picnic in Northern Bay Sands and a rain has started. A rain so dense and hard that no matter how fast the windshield wipers flick back and forth, ridges of water pile up on top of each other and you can't see. The trees are the same gray as the sky.

It is getting dark and Miranda says she has to pull over because we might hydroplane and on the radio they are saying there are accidents and to stay off the highways and so Miranda pulls over because she can't go any farther and she's having pretty intense contractions.

You are nine years old, almost ten, but you know what contractions are because ever since you can remember you've had to know things most kids don't.

You've had to know that the heat bill might not get paid and that some people are slightly uncomfortable with children who don't know who their father is, don't even know his last name for God's sake.

You've had to know not everybody can afford the school trip to Quebec at the end of junior high, and that sometimes perfectly respectable people have to get welfare and go to food banks and that there are welfare police who sit outside your house in their cars and spy on your mother to see if she has a boyfriend sleeping over on a regular basis, so they can take away her welfare check.

You've had to know and pretend you don't notice that there's a guy in greasy glasses and a black-leather bomber jacket who is an undercover welfare cop and who sits outside your house in his car every day with his daily slice of takeout pizza and a can of pop, watching your front door hoping to see a boyfriend of your mother's come out.

Because welfare moms are not allowed to have boyfriends because that might mean they are being *supported* (an idea that causes Miranda to snort like a horse).

And you've always had to know that it costs the government more to have him sitting there, with strings of melted mozzarella cheese sagging between his glossy lips and his pizza slice and the car gradually filling up with his pop cans and after-pizza cigarette smoke, than the amount of welfare your mother receives, and all the while she's trying to make art which the world needs in order to make life worth living.

You have had to know that someday you might find yourself trying to wave down a transport truck in the middle of a rainstorm at the edge of the highway because your brand-new baby brother is coming.

The hard wind and gritty mist of a passing transport truck will nearly knock you down and you will watch the taillights zoom away while your mother is having contractions.

A red phone should appear on the hood of your new/old Toyota, with a red blinking button that puts you in touch with somebody higher up.

You would pick up this magic phone and somebody would say, This is big stuff, kid. Life and death. This is a job for adults. Step aside.

Okay, forget the phone. The clouds should part and a ray of light, the hand of God. Somebody should take over.

There was a phone, of course. Miranda had an ordinary (though second-hand) cell phone in her purse and she dialed 911 and she told them where we were and that the baby was coming and that it was a month premature and that she only had her daughter with her, her nine-year-old daughter.

She was looking at me while she said all this, except when she squeezed her eyes shut. She was in the middle of speaking and she shut her eyes and she didn't look like Miranda at all. She didn't look like my mother.

Our next-door neighbor had had a home birth a little while before this, which I thought was gross, and they'd invited all the neighbors to stop by for a visit during the labor like a big party, and they kept the placenta in the freezer because in some cultures everybody fries up the placenta later on and eats some of it as part of a ritual to welcome the new baby.

I was so scared Miranda would make me go over and watch the birth I forgot to ask some important questions that might have come in handy there on the side of the road in the rainstorm.

Miranda hung up the cell phone.

They're coming, she said. Then she said it over and over. They're coming, they're coming, they're coming.

Which is what I mean about the special phone, because anybody could see that they weren't coming.

They would never come, whoever they were, but I was there. I was there already, and that's the part that was profoundly unfair. I was going to have to deal with it.

Miranda grabbed my hand and she squeezed it hard and she said, Flannery, this baby is going to be born very soon.

And I thought, All is lost.

Perhaps it would be helpful to list some of the many things that were lost.

We had been hiking in the woods in our rubber boots and mine had wild horses on them and there was a waterfall with mist coming up all around it and the squelch of the mud and lots of pitcher plants and the long grass was golden and there were rust bushes with glittering frost and a few trees that were so orange they looked like a fire.

Miranda was huge and she had a big felt hat with a striped feather and an overstretched unraveling sweater that used to belong to Hank and a red poncho and our picnic basket had olives and peanut butter and honey sandwiches and chocolate chip cookies. It was supposed to be *our* trip, a mother-daughter thing. A day in the woods together before the baby came. We'd even had a little bonfire.

I had seen Miranda's belly wobble. I had felt Felix move under my hand. I'd been at the baby shower.

All the diapers and powders and blankets and sleepers.

But did I believe there was going to be a baby?

I did not.

Not until that transport truck whipped past me on the highway in the rain and I heard Miranda's door open and she was pacing back and forth behind me and moaning and panting and yelling and leaning against the side of the Toyota and at one point she got down on her hands and knees which was the scariest part, but she got back up and she sat down on the truck seat with the door open and her head hanging down.

The rain was lashing the divided highway. It looked like steel ropes swinging down from the heavens when cars driving past on the other side of the highway lit it up in their headlights. The headlights lit up the tops of the trees and the big empty sky and, for a brief moment, the wrenching pain on my mother's wet face, and then she was plunged back into darkness and there was a floating spot hanging before my eyes, and there was nothing but forest and my jacket was soaked to my skin and I was shivering.

Miranda stood up again and was resting her back against the tailgate of the truck and she threw back her head and screamed into the sky as loud as she could, *The baby is coming.*

And then I believed, without a shred of doubt. The baby was coming.

Also, there was going to be no red phone. What was lost was the life we had before, Miranda and me. What was lost was just the two of us.

I had loved just the two of us.

But later, on Saturday mornings, when Felix and I would wake up early and get two big bowls of vanilla ice cream with bananas and chocolate sauce and maraschino cherries and watch cartoons, I had to admit. All had not been lost.

All had almost been lost. Sure. And maybe something had been lost. Miranda screamed her head off and then we heard the siren. We heard the siren before we saw the flickering red lights.

An ambulance was coming out of the dark.

20

After Kyle Keating and I watch the last unbroken egg trundle as fast as it can toward the curb, totter with indecision at the edge and finally topple into the gutter, its yellow yolk slithering free of its broken shell, there is an awkward moment.

We're just sort of standing there, facing each other but looking down at the sidewalk.

So, yeah, says Kyle.

Yeah, I say. I know.

Kyle's hands are dug down deep in the pockets of his jeans. I can see his knuckles pressing against the tight denim. He's rocking back and forth on the balls of his feet. I'm still holding the torn and empty paper bag.

Even though I've talked my head off the whole way home about Mercy Hanrahan and the love potion and the glassblower I've got an appointment with about bottles for the potion, and Amber and Gary, I suddenly can't think of a single thing to say.

Neither can Kyle.

But then he gets a text and says he has to head off to work. He's a lifeguard. I tell him I'll talk to Mr. Follett about maybe getting a new set of eggs and starting the project over (any-thing to avoid writing the essay about teen pregnancy).

Thanks for walking me home, Kyle, I say.

You're welcome, Flannery, he says. And then Kyle is jogging up Long's Hill, and I burst into the house slinging my knapsack off my shoulder onto the pile of boots, yelling for Miranda.

I've got to go to this glassblower's studio. So can we drive?

There isn't much gas.

We don't have to go very far.

Can't someone else take you?

Miranda, you'll enjoy this.

It sounds like shopping.

It's not shopping, and I need the truck so I can bring back the bottles. Plus, do you want me to fail Entrepreneurship?

How are you paying for this?

The guy said I can pay after the fair, out of my profits.

Awfully optimistic, this guy.

Believes in the love potion, it seems.

He said that?

He implied it.

When Miranda and I finally pull up in the truck there's a squat cinderblock building with a blinking red sign in the window that says *Glass Studio*. The door has a wrought-iron ring for knocking.

We knock, but there's no answer, so I pull the door open.

The heat hits us in the face. We can hear the furnace breath-ing fire like Tyrone's dragon.

Inside, a man is lifting something from the huge furnace with what looks like a giant pair of tweezers. He's wearing denim overalls and a plaid shirt with the sleeves rolled up and a trucker's cap that says *Kingsbridge Auto*. He has wireless octagonal glasses that sink into his apple-red cheeks, and he appears to have no teeth but lots of fine white nose hair. He's got to be at least eighty-five.

Look! says Miranda.

The man is holding up a tiny, delicate glass bottle. It's shaped like a bottle but it appears to be liquid fire. It is pulsing like it is a heart, and the heart is flushing with blood that is not blood but white boiling light with a yellow halo.

The man dips the little vessel into a vat and there's a hiss and a cloud of smoke and he lifts the glass heart out of the vat and it's a perfect bottle for a love potion.

He sees us watching and comes to meet us with one hand out for shaking and the other still holding his treasure in the tweezers.

I broke one of the hundred packing them up and had to make a new one, the man says. I'm Fred MacLachlan, pleased to meet you. Now, which one of you is the mother?

Oh, stop, says Miranda.

Two ravishing beauties, he says. What a pleasure.

I introduce myself and Miranda and within seconds they're deep in conversation — about the new parking garage on Water Street, and the graffiti, and how the construction is blocking traffic. And Fred tells Miranda about his upcoming move to Europe.

You should come along, he says.

Oh, I have my kids, she says.

Well, I guess they'll grow up sometime, he says. This comment annoys me, naturally.

We don't want to hold you up, I say to him. After all, you have to get ready for your trip. You're leaving soon, right? Leaving the province? Going to some place where they understand glass?

Huh? he says. He's having a hard time taking his eyes off Miranda.

Oh yes, he says. But wait. Let me see what I have for this beautiful lady. A memento.

He's gone to the back of the warehouse and we hear something that sounds like a shelf of glass tipping over and smashing.

He's laying it on a little thick, isn't he? I whisper.

Oh, I don't know, says Miranda.

He comes back holding a little glass figurine out before him. He puts it in Miranda's open palm.

It's a polar bear, Miranda says. Oh, my! Flannery, look! She is clearly moved by his gesture.

A little glass polar bear, Flannery! Like my ice sculptures.

Global warming, the guy says. I read about your project in *Canadian Art.*

You read that? Miranda says.

Of course I did. Two-page spread, how could I miss it. Very nice picture of you, too, on the beach with the bonfire.

You're too kind, Miranda says. So. But. You're leaving, though?

We actually have to get going too, Miranda, I say. Got to pick up my brother, I tell the guy. That's Miranda's other child? She has two, actually. And he's very young. He's not going to be grown up any time soon. I look at the guy to make sure this is sinking in.

Well, what a pleasure, Miranda says.

Me too, the guy says. It's an honor. An artist of your caliber. It really is an honor. You're doing such good work. Keep it up. And good luck with your love potion, Florence.

Flannery, I say.

Indeed, he says. Good luck.

21

There's a Halloween party at Brittany Bishop's tonight but I don't want to go. I don't want to run into Tyrone after he's stood me up *again*. He probably thinks he's too cool to go to a party at Brittany Bishop's anyway. Everybody says her parents are going to be home.

Amber has the big swim meet to decide if she gets to go to the Nationals this weekend, so she won't be going to the party. Besides, she's hardly talking to me.

But everyone else has been planning their costumes for weeks. Brittany Bishop's parents always rent a chocolate fountain for her parties. And halfway through the night a pizza guy delivers a gazillion pizzas.

Elaine Power is going as a monarch butterfly, of course. Andrew Sullivan is going as a soap bubble. His costume is apparently made of chicken wire and twenty-seven boxes' worth of Saran Wrap. Ella Sloan is going as a block of Swiss cheese.

Even Felix has a party. A little girl in his karate class is having everybody over. Felix is a devil. His face is covered in red makeup and he has a plastic pitchfork and a red satin costume with a tail, and horns on the top of his head. He also has a glue-on goatee of black synthetic fur and fake nails, long and curling.

I'll be staying home all alone, dressed as myself. Leggings, Morrissey T-shirt. Same old, same old.

But right now I have to finish the prototype of our unit because it has to be submitted to Mr. Payne on Monday or Tyrone and I lose fifteen percent. I'm in my bedroom with all my notes and one hundred beautiful glass bottles.

Tyrone hasn't done one single thing for this project. I hate him.

Love, definitely *not*.

Then there's a knock on my bedroom door.

What are you putting in this potion? says Miranda. She sits down in the middle of all the clothes on my bedroom floor and the stuff I've gathered for the project. I've been online and I'm determined to make the potions totally eco-friendly.

I already know that people will reuse the perfume bottles because they're so beautiful. But I want the potions to be non-toxic too. Artificial food-coloring is actually pretty nasty. It can cause disease.

You need to boil some fruits and vegetables, Miranda says when I tell her all this. Beets for red, carrots for orange, spinach for green and blueberries for blue, she says, because I've also told her my idea for four different kinds of love.

I happen to have some blueberries left over from last summer in the freezer.

Soon we're down in the kitchen chopping carrots and beets, boiling spinach, squashing blueberries and straining everything through four separate pieces of an old cheesecloth blouse of Miranda's. She says it had a hole under the arm. When we're done, we pour the four different kinds of colored water into four different bottles. We seal them with the frosted stoppers that came with each bottle. The potions have some sediment floating around in there, but that just makes them look more authentic.

They don't taste very good, I say, when Miranda holds out a teaspoon of green potion for me to try.

But a customer only needs one sip for it to work, Miranda says.

Tyrone is supposed to be here, I tell Miranda. I slump down into a kitchen chair. It's already late and I still have to label the prototypes. Miranda can see I'm upset, even though I'm trying really hard to sound unfazed and blasé and generally like I couldn't care less about Tyrone.

I believe people are the best people they can be, Flannery. I believe everybody is trying to be good. But it's harder for some people. Tyrone has had a hard time. They're going through some heavy stuff over there.

So are we, I say. I don't even have a biology book. And we're going to have to go to the food bank again. Do you know what that feels like? I mean, they're asking everybody in school to donate to the food drive. And I can't donate anything. I'm the one they're donating to, for gosh sakes. It's humiliating.

Miranda closes her eyes for a second. When she opens them, she says quietly, Flan, oh boy. Okay. Look...

But then she doesn't say anything for a minute. I wait quietly, looking into her eyes, until she takes a big breath and starts again.

Tyrone's stepdad, Marty? she says. Is physically abusive, Flannery. He's hit Tyrone's mom. He's blackened her eyes. Once he broke one of her ribs. Marty is a terrible drunk. I'm trying to talk to her, get her out of there. But it's not easy. There are shelters, but she's not ready to leave yet. She's afraid he'll come after them.

She lets out another big breath. This is confidential, okay, Flannery? But you have to understand. Things aren't very easy for Tyrone. He's not even at home half the time. Maybe his grades aren't the most important thing in his life right now.

It's not *grades* I'm worried about, Miranda, I say. I really care about him. My voice goes all funny.

Oh — oh, I know that, baby. I *know*.

But it hurts. Like, why doesn't he care about me? What's wrong with me? Why not love me?

I love you, kid.

I know.

I love my babies a lot. She hugs me and it feels good. Well, it feels better.

I'm about to start my period, I say. Maybe that's why I'm so emotional. I mean, that's part of it. And then I shed a few tears.

Me too, Miranda says. We're synced. But we have lots of reasons to feel emotional. Life isn't fair. There's nothing wrong with emotion, Flan. That's how we know we're alive. It's good.

It doesn't feel very good, I say.

Now, what's the plan for the love potion labels? Miranda asks, straightening herself up.

Labels? I say. It's just colored water, Miranda. It's only a gag.

Sure it is, she says.

Okay, I say. I go and get my notes and show her what I have written down so far, what I am calling the *Four Elixirs of Love*.

1) Blue: fast-acting befuddling crush-inducer, effects last two to four hours.

2) Red: eternal love, effects include marriage and anniversaries up to ten years.

3) Orange: good for securing a prom date.

4) Green: for provoking an unending stream of compliments from the one you love.

Miranda jumps up and I hear her rummaging around in
her studio and then she comes back with these huge sheets of
thick, bumpy, beige-ish paper.

Look, Flannery! Left over from my paper-making phase,
she beams.

I don't say this, but the paper sort of looks like the paper
towels in our washrooms at school.

But then Miranda gets the idea to attach some kind of written spell to the neck of each bottle.

Just a phrase or two, she says. For promotional purposes.
Like a label, but more mysterious.

I had already thought maybe a gold cord with little gold tassels for the price tag, I tell her. They have them at Fabricville.

Gold tassels are all wrong, she says. You need twine.

She jumps up again and bangs around in the laundry room
cupboard this time and while she's doing that I cut out a tag for
the blue potion and I write:

This love potion has a short and bittersweet bite,
One little sip and it's love at first sight.

It's complete foolishness but it sounds good. And that's
what marketing is all about, right?

Miranda comes back with a ball of twine. It's brown and
bristly with rough little hairy bits sticking off.

But the gold tassels, I say.

We want to conjure up medieval times. Those gold tassels
would scream kitsch, she says.

I think they'd be classy.

Picture, Miranda says, a castle on a craggy moor, nothing
for miles but jagged rock and tufts of dead grass shrouded in

fog. Ancient fog. Fog that has been creeping across the earth for centuries. Bleak, sopping, sorry-looking fog.

Fog with cat feet, I say.

Panther feet, she says. Fog that steals and swallows and sucks and —

Yeah, I got it. Fog. What's that got to do with tassels or twine?

Medieval, Flan. More medieval, more magical. Picture fairies flitting in the shadows or riding the backs of butterflies, she says. Leprechauns dancing jigs; fireflies glowing in the dusk. Never mind tassels. Twine is more "of the common folk."

Okay, I say. The twine.

Picture in the distance, a castle, all towers and . . . what do you call them?

Moats?

Not moats.

Ramparts?

Yes, ramparts. And drawbridges.

Yeah, okay, the twine.

And in the shadow of the tower window, which is just basically a hole in the wall because they didn't have glass windows, a young lass, forlorn. Is she going to be impressed by gold tassels?

I'm guessing no?

Think of what she's going through, Miranda says.

Is she in love?

Yes, but thoroughly unrequited love. Picture the face on her.

She's annoyed.

She's forlorn, Flannery. There's a difference.

Forlorn.

Like, heartbroken because she's in love with a guy who doesn't return her affection.

Is he maybe in her Entrepreneurship class?

Oh, he's in a different class from her altogether.

She's got it bad.

And not only that, it's medieval times, she has to eat her food with her hands because they don't have utensils yet. Half the time she has chicken grease smeared all over her chin.

Which has got to be a drawback if you're trying to get a guy's attention.

They can't text, or Instagram, there's no Tumblr or Google glasses or email thank God and I won't even go into the plumbing situation. Also the castle could use a space heater. Place is like a fridge. Talk about visits from the field worker. Costs a fortune to heat that place. So, you can see, these tassels you mentioned are all wrong. And she's sixteen, so she's already suffering a midlife crisis, they died so early back then.

Wouldn't the silky gold tassels cheer everybody up a bit?

Sending the wrong message, Flan.

The twine is sending a message?

Absolutely. It's authentic.

Gotcha. The twine is better than the tassels. And we don't have to go to the mall. The twine is right here.

Exactly, says Miranda, looking at her watch. It's nearly midnight. The spirits are roaming. I'd say it's the perfect time for our spell.

I've already written the first one, Miranda. See —

No, Flannery, we need to *say* the thing. An incantation. So the potion works, you know?

She's smiling slyly, daring me.

All right, whatever, I say.

After all, it's just a gag, right?

So let's have the eternal love one, she says. I set out the bottle of red potion and she clears her throat with a little *ahem*.

We call upon all the goddesses of love in the universe and beyond...

She looks at me expectantly. I roll my eyes.

One sip of this potion, Miranda continues, *and you'll grow eternally fond ... of the first person you see. Better than fond. After one little sip, you'll play your part.*

And I chime in with the ending: *The first person you see will steal your heart.*

What about the green potion? I say. My pen is ready, hovering over the bumpy paper.

One sip of this green potion, says Miranda, *and your true love will turn into a poet. You'll be ravished with compliments before you know it.* I write it down on the bumpy paper and attach the little note to the neck of the bottle. I try to make my writing look all medieval-like, pointy and jagged.

And the orange potion? she says.

Easy-peasy, I say.

One sip of this and any Dick, Mary, or Tom
Will instantly ask you to go to the prom.

22

Elaine Power holds the door for me on Monday when I'm taking the love potion prototypes back to my locker after Entrepreneurship class.

And then she stops me. She looks at each of the bottles.

Let me try the red one, she says.

But that's eternal love, I say. Why not go for blue? With the blue potion you get a crush, it's milder, the effects wear off after a few hours.

Elaine looks up at me and I see that, for just one millisecond, she's actually buying it.

I mean, go ahead if you want, I say. But whomsoever you happen to gaze upon after a sip of the red potion — that's it, you'll long for them forever. The. Rest. Of. Your. Life. It's kind of a big decision.

Elaine seems kind of awed. But then the old Elaine — scientific-genius Elaine — floods back, eclipsing soft-vulnerable-believing-romantic Elaine in a nanosecond.

Great sales patter, Malone, she says. Gimme the red one.

Okay, I say. You asked for it. She takes a moment to read the label.

"Steal your heart." Yes, bloody likely, she says.

I take the frosted glass stopper out of the bottle and hand it to her. She swirls the bottle and sniffs it.

How did the prototype app for saving butterflies go? I ask, embarrassed, because it's a project of such obvious eco-political merit, especially compared to mine, a mere sight gag.

One butterfly at a time, Flan, one butterfly at a time, she says with a sigh. She tells me that she and Mark Galway are doing a live demonstration in Mr. Payne's office this very afternoon.

Then she takes a glug of the potion. Wipes her mouth with the back of her hand, smearing her black lipstick. Her eyes are squeezed shut for a moment, no doubt formulating a chemical analysis/critique of the potion.

Hmm, she says. Just what I thought. Colored water. Beets? Nice gimmick, Malone. Low overhead. I think these will sell big. You're going to have a tidy profit —

At that very instant, Mark Galway comes through the door and bangs into her. I mean, he has his head down and the brim of that stupid fedora must be blocking his view and he just *collides* with her and her eyes fly open.

And there they are, eye to eye.

Elaine Power is wearing wishbone earrings. I mean, like actual dried chicken bones, and they are dancing with indignation under her earlobes. She is clearly ready to lacerate Mark with a single, elegant, precise and vicious comment about what a graceless douche he is.

I feel a horror/fascination. What will remain of Mark Galway once Elaine Power is finished with him? A fedora floating in an oozing puddle of gristle on the floor? A puddle that used to be Mark Galway?

But all she says is, Oh, hi, Mark.

And Elaine Power sounds dreamy and doubtful about all she has hitherto understood of the universe and everything in it.

Mark and I exchange a glance. He's cowering. We both figure she's holding back so she can deliver the full force of her attack aided by the element of surprise. A tactical move for which Mark is not going to fall.

I'm so sorry about that, Mark says.

It was an accident, I say.

Well, *duh*, says Elaine. Obviously. But, hey, nice to bump into you.

Then she giggles, well, like a schoolgirl.

After that, I keep seeing Elaine Power and Mark Galway, sworn enemies of yore, together, and every time Elaine is giggling her fool head off. Yes, apparently Elaine Power has a giggle mode. Who knew?

More astonishing, it's always something Mark is saying that's making her laugh, causing her glee. Once she even hip-checks him right there in the hallway, just as if they were actually friends, or more than friends, even. I have to admit, it's giving me shivers to think of her lifting that love potion bottle to her black lips.

Of course, the transformation can't have had anything to do with the potion.

But Elaine starts telling the story of taking a sip of the prototype seconds before Mark came through the door and banged into her. And when she gets to that part of the story she stretches up onto her tiptoes and kisses him on the cheek.

And I've been head over heels ever since, Elaine says. I can't get enough of him.

Yup, that's true, says Mark. He actually seems pretty chuffed. She *is* the smartest person in the entire history of the school, after all. He's stopped coming to school in the Hummer. Now he's on a skateboard. Talking nonstop about butterflies.

The story about Elaine and the potion spreads around the school pretty fast. Next Brittany Bishop is coming up to me in the corridor.

I'll try the blue potion, she says.

But that's just a crush, I say. Don't you want eternal love?

Not on your life, she says. Give me a hit of that crush potion. The blue, green and orange prototypes are still in my locker, so I take the blue one out and hand it to her. And as soon as she takes a sip, Melody Martin shows up.

Melody, Brittany says. You've got to try this. She hands the bottle to Melody who takes a sip and a little drip of blue potion runs down Melody's chin, and Brittany touches it with her finger and catches the drip.

Want to pip off and walk Signal Hill with me? Brittany says.

God, that's exactly what I want, says Melody. How did you know? They walk off down the corridor holding hands.

Just before math class Kyle Keating is coming out of drama, where they've been rehearsing *Romeo and Juliet*, and he runs into me near the lockers. Sort of ridiculously/gorgeously, he's wearing tights and a jacket with big puffy velvet sleeves and a slouchy velvet cap with a feather which looks sort of cool with his dreadlocks. But definitely not a look everybody can get away with. Turns out he's playing Romeo.

He announces loudly that he wants to try the green potion right there in the corridor. Everybody is rushing off to class but a little crowd gathers around us.

I don't know, I say. We've got to get to math. But I take

the potion out of my locker and hand it over.

Kyle takes out the little frosted-tipped stopper.

So what's this one supposed to do? He reads out the tag. Compliments? I'm supposed to start just coming up with compliments on the spot? Come *on*. You don't expect people to believe that?

Well, it's kind of a gag, I mumble. Like canned fog. He takes a sip.

Just like I thought, he says. Tastes like spinach. It's spinach water, everybody. Just spinach and water is my guess. Is that right, Flannery?

I can feel my shoulders slump a little.

Yup, I say. He swirls it around. And takes another mouthful.

I'm getting nutty undertones, he says. It's fruity, am I right? Hints of cherry? Maybe some oak in there? Definitely an oak base. And it follows through with a hint of anise. Light but full-bodied? (When he says *full-bodied* he actually lets his eyes slide all the way down my body and back to my face, and wiggles his eyebrows.)

Actually it tastes pretty good, Kyle says. This is probably the best spinach juice I've ever had.

Nobody asks if he's ever had spinach juice before. Who drinks spinach juice? But he's looking straight into my eyes and takes another sip.

You have green eyes, he says. I never noticed that before. Really green. Not many people have green eyes. Not like yours. Like, a stormy sea-green. Like the green in the Northern Lights. Your eyes are beautiful, Flannery. I guess you get that all the time.

I can feel a blush flooding into my cheeks. I mean, I know he's joking around but he doesn't look away and he sounds dead serious.

And your freckles are like cinnamon. (Now he's really hamming it up.) Shall I compare you to an October's day in Newfoundland? he says.

You have the most beautiful freckles I've ever seen, Flannery Malone. Like autumn leaves scattering in the wind.

I punch him gently on the arm.

Aw, shucks, I say.

Everybody is laughing.

A door swings open down the hall and Mr. Green sticks his head out of the classroom.

Mr. Keating, he says. You have exactly three minutes to change out of that costume and get to class or you're in big trouble. Ms. Malone, get in here and stop causing congestion in the corridors. You others, move along. The buzzer has sounded.

Kyle hands me the bottle and stopper and exits stage left, male bathrooms.

The next day orders for the green potion are through the roof.

Three more people want to try the blue and red potions so they can fall immediately in love with the first person they see.

And then I get wise. No more free sips. I start taking back orders. Everybody wants a bottle. After just a few days of taking orders, the red potion, eternal love, sells out.

Then there's an announcement over the PA that the student council is looking for volunteers from grade twelve for the grad committee. After school there's a big run on the orange potion, the one that gets you a prom date. Prepaid. It *definitely* looks like I'll be able to pay back Fred the glassblower and maybe even get a new order of bottles before he takes off for Europe.

It's word of mouth, just like Sensei Larry said. And like Ms. Rideout said, everybody believes in at least a little bit of magic. And at the same time, everybody knows it's a joke. But a charming joke.

Talk about the love potions spreads like crazy. And because people start to believe, even a little tiny bit, the potions actually start to work. They work instantly.

23

Amber Mackey! snaps Madame Lapointe. She has been wandering up and down the rows between the desks, the shrapnel cracks of her high heels on the tiles ricocheting off the walls.

Up and down, up and down.

Madame Lapointe is eight months pregnant but she's still in stilettos. While it may seem crazy that we have a woman from Paris, France, teaching us English, we're also learning about the hairpin turns one can make in very high heels. Madame Lapointe is the most beautifully dressed woman I've ever seen. Her wardrobe is wasted on most of these lumber-jacket-wearing louts in grade twelve.

The classroom is dark with the curtains drawn, lights off. How can they expect Amber to stay awake when the lights are off?

We are watching a film clip of the three witches from *Macbeth*. One of the witches wears a black skullcap that ties under the chin, with holes cut out for the ears. Very fetching.

I can see Elaine Power eying it, like it's just the thing to go with her construction boots and her black skirt with dried chicken bones dangling off the hem.

The wide blue eye of the projector sends out a fan of light that grazes the top of Amber's blonde hair. She's snoring softly.

I have stopped talking to Amber. I haven't spoken to her for two weeks. Even when she sits in the desk in front of me — not a single word. Not even to congratulate her on qualifying for the Nationals at the swim meet in Toronto last weekend. Or to say how great it is that everyone in her dad's office had doubled their money on those stupid bets. Nah-ah.

At first it was just to teach her a lesson. You wait, I thought. Wait until you see how dull and full of despair life is without me, your best friend since sippy cups.

Since milk moustaches.

Since we were infants in the hospital born five hours apart and our mothers took pictures of us with big satin bows on the sides of our little bald heads, which was a thing to do with babies back then.

Why did Amber need to learn this difficult lesson, you ask?

For one thing, she stopped texting me. Completely. She just stopped. Another stoppage. The friendship needed a plunger. We were gucked up.

Okay, there were a few scraggly little texts, like, *Busy, sorry.*

Or, *Can't, Flan.*

Or, *Not tonight.*

Then she just didn't answer me at all! And then I ran into her dad at the supermarket and he asked me if I wanted to come over for supper.

Did Amber invite me? I asked.

No, Sean said, but she's been having so many sleepovers at your house that I assume she's eaten you guys out of house and home.

It took me one long baffled second, that's all. I must have had a funny look on my face because Sean said, Like, last weekend she slept at your house. And the weekend before that. And the one before that.

Then I recovered.

Oh, that's okay, Sean, I said. Don't worry about it. My mom doesn't mind. She loves having people around.

Really, Flannery, thank you for being there for her. Cindy and I know she's going through a tough time right now, but she won't open up to us. She's been swimming her whole life. I know she thinks we're angry with her for missing a few practices. A lot of practices, actually. But we just want her to be happy. What do you think of this guy Gary?

Gary? I said. Gary is ... Amber really likes Gary.

Yeah, okay. That's what I thought. Thanks, Flannery. Say hi to your mom.

Then I had to head for the produce section just to get away from him because I could feel tears starting. There I was in the supermarket, my eyes watering the organic bok choy.

I tried to think about what it was I felt.

First of all, shock. Amber skipping practice? Now she has to prepare for the Nationals. That's what she's been working toward. I know that she partly competes to please Sean, but she also loves it. She's part fish. She's happiest in the water. It's like she can breathe under there. It's who she is. Ever since I can remember. It's her thing.

And then, "sleepovers"!? I felt used. I hated lying to Sean about her sleeping over. And I felt hurt.

Simile: My chest felt like someone had lit a birthday sparkler right under my breastbone and it was firing off a gazillion splinters of cold burning pain. That was my heart.

The truth is, I felt lost without Amber. Who was I going to tell stuff to? The weird stuff that happens every single day. The stuff I used to save up to tell Amber when we were walking home from school.

And now when we see each other in class or in the halls, Amber pretends I don't exist. Like *I'm* the one who's done something wrong. She's like the little boy in the Snow Queen fairy tale. A splinter of ice in her heart has made her cold inside and out.

So I did the only sensible thing I could. I decided not to speak to Amber ever again in my whole entire life.

Or at least for a couple of weeks.

That'll show her, I reasoned. Bring her to her senses.

The morning after this decision I was brushing my teeth really hard and I was foaming at the mouth and I just stopped and said out loud to the bathroom mirror, This is for your own good, Amber Mackey.

Felix banged on the door and yelled, Who are you talking to in there?

I thought the cold shoulder would have her on her knees after a week, begging for forgiveness.

But that was two weeks ago and I don't think she's even noticed. She's always with Gary, or Gary and his band, or — much more often, actually — the girlfriends of Gary's band.

I broke my vow of silence three days into it and sent her a text saying, *What's wrong? Have I done something?*

It was like she didn't even get the text.

But, I thought, she'll still need me for the music video. When it came down to it, I knew Gary would do nothing to help except sing his songs with the fake tremolo he likes to throw in on the high notes. The tremolo, the thing he does with his hips. Gary has a way onstage. He sort of rocks his hips. I find it particularly unappealing. The newly acquired black-rimmed hipster glasses? Please. Also, to tell the truth, I think his voice sounds a little nasal. You know that kind of singing high up in the nose?

So I figured, I'll rise above and help Amber with the big shoot and prove myself indispensable to her and the costumes and the bazillion dancers and even to Gary if that's what she wants and then this whole Ice Queen thing will finally melt away. I knew that Melody Martin had dumped her band-boyfriend for Brittany Bishop, so *she* probably wouldn't be helping with the video anymore. Amber would need me more than ever.

But then, on Monday, I saw on Facebook that Jordan Murphy had put up pictures from a shoot that had happened on Tuesday night. It was *the* shoot.

And no one, including Amber, had thought to tell me about it.

From the pictures it looked like everybody in our school was there. There was even a picture of Elaine Power with a clipboard, pointing at something on stage with her pencil.

There was a photo of Amber looking through the viewfinder of a camera, and then another of her giving instructions to the videographer. And in another photo she was laughing and looking like she was having a lot of fun. There was no hint on her face that someone important was missing. She hadn't given me a single thought.

Then, a few days ago I went to the bathroom in the middle of math class and I heard the door creak open and I caught sight of Amber's shoes. I came out and she was leaning with her back against the sink, facing my stall. Her arms were crossed. She looked exhausted and pale.

I went to the sink next to her and turned on the taps. I pressed on the soap dispenser three times and washed my hands under the running water.

She was sort of jiggling one leg as if trying to hold back whatever she had to say.

I pulled three pieces of paper towel and dried my hands very slowly and balled up the paper and tossed it in the garbage. If she wanted to apologize she didn't have much more time. There was nothing else I could do.

I had already opened the door when she finally spoke.

I want a bottle of the red love potion, she blurted. I think it would make a nice present for Gary. I'll pay you.

So there wasn't going to be an apology or an explanation about why she'd left me out of the video shoot, or why she was letting Gary ruin a friendship that had once been the most important thing in both our lives besides our families.

They sold out, I said.

That's not true, she hissed. I know you must have some. You're just jealous of my relationship. That's why you don't want to give me any.

Nope, I say. Sorry. Sold out. You can't get it, not for love nor money.

And I let the bathroom door slam behind me.

Macbeth's witches are trundling across a long beach. This is a very old movie. It takes them quite a while to get to where they're going. A seagull circles, squawks. There's a whining noise that sounds like somebody getting their fingernails pulled out, but it's only the creaking wheels on the little wooden cart that the witches are dragging behind them.

The sun gleams on the wet sand. One of the witches stops and draws a circle on the ground with her walking stick, and then all three witches get down on their hands and knees to dig the hole.

The youngest witch gets a package out of the cart, something wrapped in filthy rags.

Whatever the youngest witch has, it isn't any of the ingredients mentioned in the Double-double speech.

What *is* that thing the young witch is cradling near her breast like a baby? It's too big for an "eye of newt" or the "toe of frog" or a "lizard's leg." Could it be some "wool of bat"? Do bats even have wool? I thought they were more rubbery. The youngest witch unfolds the rags to reveal...

It's a man's hand! Severed somewhere around the elbow, and the witches drop it in the hole they've dug in the sand. A man's hand is not even on the list of ingredients for the evil potion! Unless they're trying to pass it off as the finger of the babe "ditch-deliver'd by a drab."

I mean, it's bad enough to give birth in a ditch, which Miranda almost did with poor Felix, but if the "babe" has an arm that size, I'd hate to think about how big the rest of it was.

Must be very disturbing for Madame Lapointe, who could pop her own baby out any second.

The witches lay a dagger in the palm of the dead hand and they bury it. Then they pour some very dark liquid over it, maybe the baboon's blood.

And they're all business, these witches, spitting over their shoulders, first over the left and then the right.

They stand up and look at the sky. All in a day's work. They are apparently checking the weather because they have places to go, people to see. Other severed limbs to bury. Lots of toil and trouble to cause. They make Ms. Rideout look like a slacker.

Madame Lapointe is standing in front of the classroom slapping a ruler against her thigh. She's noticed Amber is asleep.

Amber Mackey? asks Madame Lapointe. I hear a chuffling, groggy snore.

I am *not* going to wake her like I normally do. Amber doesn't want us to be friends anymore.

Forget it, Amber. My days of saving you in class are over. If you want to forget about that summer Miranda took us to Northern Bay Sands and we stayed in the ocean until our lips were blue and our teeth chattered and afterward we had a bonfire and jumped up and down on the bed until we broke the bed frame, and we had to sleep with the bed on a tilt and we kept rolling onto the floor, that's fine with me.

Or if you want to forget about going to circus camp together when we were seven and spotting for each other when we were learning somersaults on the trampoline, go ahead, forget all about it.

Or when we got those glasses that are actually clear plastic drinking straws and you put one end in your lime crush and suck and the crush goes up the straw and circles one eye, and goes across the bridge of your nose and then it circles your other eye and behind your ear and into your mouth and we sat there watching each other's glasses until we were laughing so hard lime crush came out our noses. Go ahead, forget it.

Or when Miranda's former boyfriend Hank made us stilts and we climbed the fence to get up on them and then learned to walk through the boulders at the edge of the ocean in Broad Cove looking like elegant flamingos, okay, go ahead, yup, forget all about that too.

I'm not here to be walked all over anymore, Amber Mackey. You're on your own. You can spend the rest of your life in detention for all I care. You're not the friend I thought you were.

And the truth is, you stopped talking to me before I stopped talking to you. I haven't been able to sleep since you stopped talking to me and it isn't fair to just walk away from a friendship like that without an explanation.

I can't even draw a full breath because my chest hurts so much and it's because I've lost the best friend I ever had. You're mean, Amber Mackey, capable of anything. How can you just forget me? You're like that witch with the skullcap, except it's my heart you buried in the sand.

Fine. Okay. I get it. We're not friends. We're like strangers. I would probably help a stranger. I tried to tell you about Mercy Hanrahan, but you wouldn't listen. In fact, I'm worn out trying to help you. I give up. I am not helping you out of this one.

I am not waking you up just because Madame Lapointe is about to lose her poo, and probably fail you for falling asleep in her class. She is French, after all, and very passionate, and she doesn't take kindly to that sort of thing. She's flunked people for less.

I get it already. Gary is more important.

Fine. Let Gary wait outside the school in the snow and dark for you to finish detention. Let Gary be attacked by a bunch of girls who want him to eat a used condom. Let Gary hear all the stories about your mother being a drunk. Let's see how Gary manages when it comes to being a real friend. Because we're not friends anymore, right? I'm never saving you again, Amber Mackey.

And then I jab the pink eraser of my pencil between Amber's shoulder blades and her head bobs back up and she has a full body shiver.

Isosceles triangle, says Amber.

It's *English* class, I whisper.

Atticus Finch, Amber says.

I haven't asked the question yet, says Madame Lapointe.

Macbeth, I whisper.

What did the witches put in the cauldron? asks Madame Lapointe.

Cinnamon hearts? asks Amber.

The buzzer rings.

Miss Mackey, Madame Lapointe says. See me after school. You have detention. She gathers her purse and storms away, the roses on her dress rippling with the breeze.

Somebody turns off the projector and the cooling fan at the back of the machine sounds really loud in the dark. Somebody else turns on the classroom lights. That's when I see it. Amber's hair has fallen over one of her shoulders in the front and I see a mark on her neck that was hidden by her long hair. Some kind of lettering.

I can't help myself. I do it without even thinking. I reach out and pull down the neck of her sweater so I can see what it is.

It's a big tattoo. A big red heart with an arrow through it and the name *Gary* in yellow on a bluish rippling banner.

Amber jumps up and tears the neck of her sweater out of my hand.

Let go of me, she spits.

Amber, what have you done? I say.

And then it's out of my mouth before I can stop myself.

It looks more like a brand than a tattoo to me, like he owns you.

Amber's face goes very pale. At first I think she's going to faint, but it's a white-hot rage. Her eyes narrow but she's biting her lower lip as if in an effort to hold back what she's about to say. But it bursts out of her anyway.

I am sick to death of you, Flannery, she says. I'm sick of you trying to make me feel guilty all the time. Looking at me with those big stupid puppy-dog eyes. I'm busy, okay? Do you get that? I have a life. I have a boyfriend. It's not my fault nobody's in love with you.

And stop salivating over my biology book. I'm sick of that too. It's not my fault that your mother doesn't have any money and my parents do. You can just stop rubbing that in my face. My parents work. That's why they have money. Why doesn't Miranda get a job like everybody else? You're not my problem, Flannery.

Trying to pretend there's something superior and *chic* about vintage clothes from the Sally Ann. They aren't "vintage"; they're just *used*. And they smell. Just leave me alone. Just stop, okay? I don't have time. You're Welfare. Stop hounding me. Do you think I don't notice that look on your face in the corridor every single time I walk past? I'm not going to be stuck with you anymore. I have moved on. I have new friends. People change. Get over it. I didn't want to say this. A normal person could take a hint. But here goes. Just. Leave. Me. The. Fuck. Alone. Do you think you get it now? Are you satisfied? Are you happy?

Her eyes are wet with tears, making them even bluer than they normally are. She is trembling all over. I have never seen her so angry. My blood is thumping in my ears. My face feels like it's on fire.

Everything between us is ruined. She has ruined it. She has ruined it.

The few stragglers who were left in the classroom gathering their books are now in a big hurry to get out. It's clear I'm about to cry too and nobody wants to see it.

Amber is shoving stuff into her book bag. Papers, pens. A clear green plastic ruler snaps in half against the edge of the desk and she hisses under her breath, Now look what she made me do.

I am pretending to be getting my stuff together too. I keep flipping through my exercise books like one might be missing.

Like it's absolutely imperative that I find that particular exercise book right now. Then I close the binder. My tears fall on my blue binder cover. *Plop, plop, plop.*

Finally I've packed all my stuff together. Of course I have biology next. Mrs. Krishna tells me if I don't have the book by the next biology class, I'll get a week's detention.

I decide to cut class. I head down two flights of stairs and out the front door and down Bonaventure, half expecting some teacher to call out after me to come back this minute.

I can just hear the automated phone call now. A child in your household named FLANNERY was absent from fifth period and she walked home all by herself, snuffling and bawling, and it was a very long, lonely, miserable walk.

24

At first I tell myself, it cannot be.

What is that? I ask Felix.

What is what? He looks up at me with his big blue evil/innocent eyes, a spoonful of Cheerios halted just below his pouty lips. Cheerios are his bedtime snack. He's wearing flannel pajamas with a hamburger print. Hundreds of little hamburgers with sesame seed buns and lettuce. And each hamburger has eyes with little hearts exploding from the pupils. They are his favorite pajamas.

Never mind the pajamas. There's a smudge of chocolate just under his lip, and I can feel my stomach flip over.

On your chin, I say.

A beard? he asks, touching his chin.

No, I say. Not a beard. A smudge. A chocolate smudge.

Felix lowers his eyes, trying to see his own chin.

And then he looks back up at me. He is unblinking, doleful, angelic. His curls are bouncing with halo light.

I know that look.

I tear out of the kitchen and take the stairs two at a time. I throw open my bedroom door.

At first it looks as though everything is in its place — exactly how I left it.

There's a layer of clothes tumbling off the bed and more clothes spilling from the bookshelf. Clothes churn in the open drawers of the dresser and a balled-up lacy skirt froths over the sides, all of it pooling on the floor.

I dive through the crumpled chip bags and books and belly under the bed and grab my jewelry box of treasures.

Even from under the bed I can hear Felix downstairs by the front door, zipping into his ski jacket. The whisper-whisper of the nylon.

I lift the lid on my pink and black velvet jewelry box with the pop-up ballerina balancing herself on her tiny wire spring. She turns in a jerky pirouette. Music tinkles out and the ballerina glances over her shoulder at the little square of mirror glued to the pink satin backing.

My own giant hazel-green eye is in the mirror. I wiggle my fingers through my beads and rings and the peacock feather earrings Amber gave me for my tenth birthday.

I pick up the jewelry box and shake it, and all the contents tumble onto the bureau.

Where is it? I scream.

I hear Felix fling open the front door, and it slams behind him.

I run out of my room screaming, Come back here, come back right now. I'm going to kill you, Felix Malone.

Miranda comes out of the living room.

What is going on here? she says.

I crumple on the staircase and I am sobbing a big wide opened-mouth sob that has no sound. I can't even get any breath in my body. I rest my head against the banister.

Flannery, for goodness' sake, Miranda says. What's happened?

He stole my heart, I sob. My mother comes up the stairs and puts her arms around me. He stole my chocolate heart that my dad gave you.

Flannery, my mother says.

It was the only thing I had of my father, I say. It was all I had.

Okay, listen. I know it's been hard on you, Flannery, without a dad. But I'm doing my best here, Miranda says. I have no regrets. I was eighteen when I met him.

Tell me the story again, I say. Tell me.

Okay. Okay I'll tell you, Miranda says. But she doesn't say anything, she's just sort of gently rocking me. So I have to start her off.

My father had big brown eyes and long black lashes like a girl, I say, to make sure she starts at the beginning. My tears are running right down my cheeks and hanging off my chin before they fall on the ribbing of Miranda's pale blue cotton sweater and add to a growing wet spot.

Or else they were green, Miranda says.

Were they green or brown, Miranda?

Hazel, sort of greenish-brown, Miranda says. Like yours. I don't know, it was dark.

My father had hazel eyes and beautiful thick curly black eyelashes like a girl, I say.

That's definitely where you got those eyelashes, Miranda says. We are practically eyelash-less on my side of the family.

He was tall and handsome.

I came to his shoulders, Miranda says.

And my father had a mysterious smile.

Well, he had very even, white teeth.

An even, white, mysterious smile.

I wouldn't say mysterious. I'd say he had braces as a kid.

You first saw him climbing the mast of the eco-ship tied up in the harbor.

They were all worried, she says.

About the hole in the ozone layer, I say.

They were sailing a magnificent ship made of garbage across the sea.

Like something out of a fairy tale, I say. The mysterious visitor from away, rising out of the North Atlantic.

Well, we met on the dock of the harbor, yes. And I told him there was a party happening at a place out in Topsail Beach that night, and I gave him the address. I told him he should bring his friends.

And you were dancing with your girlfriends when he walked in, right? And there was shag carpeting and stucco on the ceiling. The Bee Gees were playing, right?

Yes, because it was a retro-disco party, Miranda says.

You were listening to the Bee Gees singing, *Ah, ah, ah, ah, Staying alive, staying alive.* The one with the life-saving rhythm, I say. (When I did my CPR course for my babysitting certificate, they told us the rhythm of that song is exactly the one you use for thumps to the chest of someone needing pulmonary resuscitation. I sing it when I'm scared.)

And we were both wearing identical mullets, Miranda says. Blue metallic tinfoil, with thick blue bangs cut very straight.

And the identical mullets were a sign that you were meant to be together, I say.

Well, actually several people at the party were wearing those wigs. They had a big load of them at the Zellers, Miranda says.

And before you even spoke, he held up his hands in front of him to show there was nothing in them and then he reached into the tinsel tendrils of your blue mullet and gave your ear a little tweak.

We were speaking, Miranda says, kind of shouting over the music. Where was he from and all that.

And then he opened his hand, and right there before your very eyes was the chocolate heart wrapped in red foil.

Big spender, Miranda says.

And later that night you decided to go for a swim together on the beach, and you ran over the beach rocks holding hands in the moonlight.

Well, actually there wasn't any moon, it was kind of foggy.

And plunged into the icy water and foam and your hearts were pounding and in the house across the highway where the party was happening the music was pounding too, *Staying alive, staying alive*, and there amidst the creamy surf you kissed in the moonlight and your blue tinsel mullets floated away together like two lovelorn jellyfish on the waves.

We lost the mullets when we got smacked by a wave.

Never to be seen again.

Well, we didn't really look for them.

And the very next morning my father returned to his eco-ship made of plastic barrels and Coke bottles and old bric-a-brac garbage to continue along with his fellow sailors to make a statement about how we are destroying the planet. (And the press came out to see them off and there was fanfare and camera flashes and the one picture that has survived in the Newfoundland archives shows just my father's shoulder. He happened to have his back to the camera, but it's a beautiful shoulder, all strong and round in an ordinary black T-shirt which doesn't tell me much, except my shoulder looks sort of like his, more or less. Maybe? He's out of focus so it's hard to tell.)

Then they tugged out through The Narrows into the bright red dawn, I say.

I think it was actually still foggy that morning, says Miranda.

And he left the beautiful maiden he'd fallen in love with behind in order to take his message about saving the planet to the whole wide world.

Well, yes, says Miranda. But what he didn't know, poor idiot, was that he'd left a little something behind.

And she grabs my chin in her thumb and finger and gives it a little waggle.

And I'm so glad he did, she says.

That heart was all I had, I say.

And then the doorbell rings. Miranda unwinds herself from my arms and stands to let Felix back in. It's minus ten out there and his cheeks are blazing red and his nose is running.

I'm sorry, Flan, he says. I never meant to eat your heart.

We'll get Flannery another chocolate, Miranda says.

I am suddenly furious.

"Another chocolate?" Can't Miranda understand that this is *hard* on Felix and me? Going without the things other people take for granted, like paying the heat bill on time or at all? Worrying about the groceries, schoolbooks, fathers? I've had it! I want her to tell Felix who his father is. I want Felix to know. I want Hank to know.

Miranda thinks it's her decision. It is not her decision.

Forget the chocolate heart, I say. Get me a biology book. And I stamp up the stairs and slam my bedroom door.

After a few minutes I hear Felix knocking.

Flannery, I'm sorry.

He waits.

Flannery, I said I'm sorry.

Go away, I say. I don't ever want to talk to you again.

I am deep asleep when I hear Miranda yelling through the house, calling for Felix. Then she bursts into my room. She is yelling at me.

He's gone, she says. Get up.

Who's gone? I say, but I am already out of bed pulling my jeans on over my nightie. One leg of my jeans is twisted at the knee and I have them half hauled up already and can't get my foot through the twisted leg. And I have to hop around with the jeans leg flapping like the broken wing of a Bowring Park duck.

Finally I get my leg through and I'm pulling on a sweater and my toque and one boot and the other boot is downstairs near the front door. The wind is making the window rattle and the snow is pinging against the glass. There are frost feathers all over it and the night beyond is as black as black can be.

Felix is gone, Miranda says. She's slamming the drawers in the bathroom, looking for the keys to the truck.

He's not in his bed, he's not asleep under the dining-room table, his ski jacket is gone, and his boots. His mitts are gone off the heater in the front porch. There are footprints in the snow.

It's because I didn't forgive him.

It hurts my forehead, like an ice-cream headache.

We go out into the stormy night. Miranda hasn't even done up her coat. His footprints are mixed up with the track of something smoother. It's like he was dragging something heavy — a suitcase or a toboggan. But the prints disappear altogether at the end of the street.

I scrape the windshield of the truck and go to scrape the back but Miranda yells for me to get in. We go to Felix's friend Lila's house and Miranda rings the bell, but all the lights are off. Eventually they come on — a bedroom light upstairs, the lights over the front door. Miranda is talking to Lila's mom.

She steps inside and is in there for a while. She has left the truck running and I notice the gas is close to empty.

Then she comes out.

I've called the police, she says. And she drives down to Water Street. She is gripping the wheel and leaning forward.

It's a Saturday night and there are lots of people out. She pulls onto George Street, where couples are walking in the middle of the road. Some kind of hockey game must have got out from Mile One.

Move, Miranda hisses to them under her breath. Get out of the way.

Something is blocking traffic at the other end of George Street. There is a giant crowd. Maybe a hundred people.

Is it an accident?

Then we both know what it is at the same instant, we jump out of the truck and run at the same time. Miranda leaves her door open. There's a cop car behind us with the lights spinning around, and another one coming up the other side of George Street.

We push our way through the crowd. I hear bells. It sounds like bells. It sounds like "Hot Cross Buns" and some kind of crazy made-up jazz and *"Au clair de la lune"* all at once, and I break through the crowd, and there is Felix Malone, right in the center of a circle the crowd has made, blocked from the wind, playing the glockenspiel. In front of him is the velvet-lined glockenspiel box and it's filled with loonies and toonies, like a pirate's treasure chest brimming with gold and silver coins, some of them spilling over onto the snow. Farther down the circle I see Miranda break through the crowd, and she spots Felix too.

Felix does a little crescendo with the hammers and that's when he sees us and there are police officers on both sides of him now, trying to clear the crowd away even while they're all still applauding like mad.

Flannery, he says. Look! I have enough money for your biology book. It's your Christmas present!

25

I'm walking Felix home from school with my new biology book in my knapsack and we're talking about how Sensei Larry can karate chop a block of wood in two, and how one day Felix will be able to do the same. A motorcycle turns the corner onto Livingstone Street and, in a flash of chrome and snowflakes, there's Tyrone O'Rourke. He flips up his tinted visor with a gloved hand. Tyrone O'Rourke's brown eyes.

Hey, Flannery, Tyrone says. He tilts his chin in the direction of the back of his bike.

He's wearing his black leather jacket and a black helmet, and the chrome on the engine is gleaming in the winter sun.

I take Felix over to the front door and tell him to go inside and play.

I'm telling on you, Felix says. He stamps his boot on the step. We both know Miranda would never allow me on that bike. Especially in winter. Even Felix knows it isn't safe.

But I'm tired of safe. I want some fun.

Don't be such a baby, Felix, I say. We're only going for a little ride around the block. I'm already swinging my leg over the back. Tyrone hands me a helmet and I put it on.

I'm tired of listening to Miranda. I'm tired of taking care of my little brother.

All I care about in this moment is Tyrone. And besides, I've been worried sick about him. Miranda told me yesterday that his mother hadn't heard from him for days. And that the last time he was home, he said he wasn't coming back again until Marty was gone.

Tyrone makes the engine rev with a shift of his wrists, and the vibrations shoot through my legs and chest and I don't know where to put my hands.

He drives to the end of Livingstone and roars up Long's Hill. I grab two handfuls of his leather jacket and hold on tight. I lean against Tyrone's back and it would not be a lie to say that I find myself brushing my lips against his leather jacket.

The sky is darkening, the deepest blue, the blue before black. The blue of blueberry jam, the blue of a frozen pond where the ice is thin.

The ice on the trees shoots out a gazillion sparks. The bike sways beneath me and I'm happier than I have ever been in my whole life. To hell with Amber Mackey. To hell with everything.

Tyrone drives past the mall and we are out on Thorburn Road and nearly in St. Philips when he comes to an over-grown laneway. It's a dirt path with frozen puddles. A strip of dead yellow grass running down the middle, thistles pushing through the snow, ATV tire tracks hardened with ice, everything silver with frost.

The motorcycle flies over the ruts and the back tire skids sideways and straightens out. A few tree branches scrape against my arm. After a while Tyrone has to slow down and sometimes he has to put his foot down so we don't tip over and he rocks the motorcycle gently out of the deepest potholes.

A few times I have to get off and walk, and I watch him

working the motorcycle through the path, a cloud of smoke from the exhaust pipe.

Finally he comes to a stop at the edge of a clearing. He gets off the bike and removes his helmet, shakes out his hair. My legs feel watery, but Tyrone has set off down a path, whacking bushes out of his way with a stick that had been leaning against a tree trunk. I take off my helmet and hurry to catch up with him.

Where are we going? I say.

You'll see, Tyrone says.

A few crows fly through the trees and call out and the air smells of fresh snow and fir trees.

Then we come to another path that goes down a steep bank to a river. Tyrone takes my hand to pull me onto the narrow ledge he's standing on. There's a waterfall frozen solid. Three tiers of black stone and frozen white foam.

I'm sure I'm blushing because he's still holding my hand, but he isn't looking at me. He's pointing straight ahead.

Then I catch my breath. On the smooth rock face near the waterfall is one of Tyrone's paintings.

A girl with black hair, washing a red dress in the river. The girl's knee is painted on a protruding boulder, one that is itself shaped like a knee, and her shoulder sticks out on a nub of rock jutting from the face of the cliff. She's glancing up, as though we have surprised her. But she looks happy.

I recognize her. It's Tyrone's mother when she was a young girl. Tyrone must have used one of the high-school photographs of her that I remember seeing on top of their TV when we used to hang out as kids. But she's also the same girl in the Snow Queen graffiti. Except here she isn't silver and muscled and powerful. I guess Tyrone O'Rourke wants his mom to be like a superhero.

I did it last summer, he says. I haven't shown it to anyone else.

Tyrone sits down on a fallen log and pats it for me to sit down beside him. In that moment I forget all about the potion and the unanswered messages and even the girl with the parrot-colored hair who may or may not be his girlfriend.

It's the way he offers me the seat. He does it like the kid-Tyrone, the one I went to Queen's Road convenience with when we were both six. We'd pooled our money, a great fortune in pennies that weighed our pockets down so we had to keep hauling up our jeans, and we bought five dollars' worth of rainbow gummy worms, waiting with anticipation as the man behind the counter slid each penny under his index finger from one pile to the other, moving his lips as he counted.

We ran back to my house and up the stairs to my room and under the covers to spend an afternoon dividing the worms into piles according to length and color like two biologists going through specimens.

That boy-Tyrone has all but disappeared.

The person sitting next to me on the log is a man. He's changed. Not just physical changes, though believe me, I am quite aware of those.

He's self-possessed. That's the word.

He owns himself.

Tyrone takes out a baggie of weed from a pocket inside his jacket and he's rolling a joint on his knee. He flicks a lighter.

The marijuana smells sharp and green and smoky in the cold air. It smells like camping and Christmas. His eyes squint up against the smoke, and he's holding his breath in.

As he exhales, he says, What do you think?

I look back at the painting but don't say anything.

Do you want some? Tyrone asks. He holds out the joint. But I don't want any and I just say so and it isn't a big deal.

I haven't shown this painting to anybody, Tyrone says. But I wanted you to see it.

I'm starting to shiver. The tips of my ears are burning with the cold. I take out a little flashlight I have on a keychain and let it play over the painting. It has become dark without us noticing. The faint yellow spot from my flashlight falls on the young woman's cheek. The painting has a thin skin of ice over it, like varnish on an antique oil painting, gleaming and crackled.

Tyrone tosses the end of the joint into the river and stands to leave. He puts his gloves back on and slaps them together to get the snow off them. I stumble forward a little and he catches my shoulder.

Then he kisses me.

Tyrone O'Rourke kisses me. It's full of tenderness. A thoughtful, tender kiss. I have never really known before now what the word tender means.

When I get home Miranda is slamming pots and pans around the kitchen. She tears off her shoe and throws it at me. She misses by a mile but it leaves a mark on the wall.

She's never thrown anything at me before.

How dare you get on that motorcycle, she screams. How dare you?

I have never seen her so angry.

You could have been killed. The roads are full of ice. It's dark out. I had no idea where you were. And he was driving that thing stoned, wasn't he? I can smell it on you! You are grounded, young lady. You are grounded for the rest of your fucking days.

I thought you didn't believe in grounding, I shout right back at her. I thought it wasn't *creative* fucking parenting?

Don't you use that language with me, young lady, she says.

I thought it was okay to swear as long as you were *creative*.

You are pushing your luck, she yells.

You can't ground me anyway, I say. I'm sixteen. I can do whatever I like. I could leave if I wanted to, and who would take care of Felix while you're off making art that doesn't sell?

Okay, you're *not* grounded, screams Miranda. You are just a disappointment.

I am stunned. These words, from Miranda, are such a low blow. Does she mean it? If she had smacked me in the face it would have hurt less.

You're the disappointment, I say. I'm not shouting now. Everything I say is deliberate.

You are the worst mother on the planet. Did you ever hear of a condom? It takes money to raise children. It was selfish to have us. *Surprises not accidents*, my ass. You shouldn't have had us.

I can promise you one thing, Flannery, she says. If you get on that motorcycle again, you will not be welcome under this roof.

I can promise *you* one thing, *Mom*, I say.

And I lower my voice to say this. If you don't tell Felix who his father is, I'm going to do it. You're just not parent enough to raise us alone.

And I go up to my room and slam my door.

I am shaking. What just happened? Then I lock the door just in case.

In the morning I get up early and leave for school before Miranda is even awake.

26

———

Things remain cold between Miranda and me for the whole week. I do more housework than usual. She puts extra time into cooking. Makes desserts. We are very polite to each other. The sort of polite you might use with a foreign dignitary, if one moved into your house.

On Saturday we head out in the truck for our family swim at the Aquarena. I am hoping the girl with the parrot hair isn't working. What if she is Tyrone's girlfriend and she finds out we were kissing?

But the girl isn't at the desk. There's a man behind the counter and he prints out the special bracelets for the waterslide without even glancing at us.

I follow Felix into the family change room, and there's the girl with a bottle of window cleaner and a wad of paper towel. There are children changing out of wet bathing suits, children lined up in the shower stalls, mothers and fathers changing toddlers on the counters, toilets flushing, hair dryers going.

Hey, the girl says.

Hey, I say.

So are you going to that party next weekend? she asks. She spritzes the wall of mirrors over the sinks and starts wiping them clean. The wet paper towel squeaks against the glass.

What party? I say.

That music video wrap party, she says. My heart lurches like an elevator with a snapped cable. It's hanging by a thread, clanging against my chest. I knew there was going to be a party, but the last time I went to check its Facebook event page, it was gone.

Now it hits me. I've been blocked. Gary probably blocked me.

Come on, Flannery, Felix says. He is trying to tear the knapsack off my shoulders. I need my swimsuit, hurry up.

Don't you know that girl Amber? the girl asks. She's squirting a spot of glass that has something stuck on it. She rubs it really hard and then scratches the spot with her fingernail. Then she rubs it again with the paper towel until it's clean. Felix yanks the knapsack open and tears out his swimsuit and a towel. He disappears into a changing cubicle and wrenches the curtain closed.

Hey, do you know Amber too? Felix calls from behind the curtain. Amber is my sister's best friend. The girl glances up at me in the mirror.

The wrap party is supposed to be pretty big, she says. Everybody is going.

Can I go? Felix yells.

I don't think so, the girl tells him. I think it's going to be pretty wild, she says to me. She squirts the faucets on one of the sinks and starts polishing those.

Your friend Amber has some strange taste in boyfriends, she says. She pauses to wipe her magenta bangs out of her eyes with the back of her wrist. Then she leans a hip against the sink with her arms crossed and really gives me a good looking over.

Her eyes are the blue of colored contact lenses. Swimming-pool blue. Eerie and unnatural blue.

I decide I like her. Maybe she and Tyrone are just friends.

Tell me about it, I say.

He's got *her* wrapped, don't you think? Talk about controlling. I heard he knocked her phone out of her hand one night at a party and it smashed. All because she was texting someone.

I hadn't heard that, I say. She sort of stopped talking to me.

I'm not surprised. She's not allowed to talk to anybody, the girl says. I used to see her all the time here at the pool, practicing. She was pretty fast too. Everybody was saying Olympics, definitely. But she's hardly been around lately. I've heard that boyfriend is jealous of some coach who's practically old enough to be her father. And that guy, what's his name? Gary? I've seen him hitting on other girls. He's a total sleaze.

Felix bursts out of the change room in his shorts and goggles.

Come on, Flannery, hurry up! he says.

I have to hit the pool, I say. I've got my bathing suit on under my clothes and take everything else off and jam my clothes and the knapsack into the locker. The girl turns back to cleaning the next sink. I press the locker closed and drop a coin in the slot and remove the key and pin it on my strap. Felix has already gone through the showers and he's heading out onto the pool deck. I catch the girl's eye in the mirror.

I really like your hair, I say.

Thanks, she says. I'm Evelyn.

Flannery, I say. And she turns back around and we shake hands.

I hope to see you at the party, Flannery, she says. I'm going with Tyrone O'Rourke. You guys know each other, right?

Yeah, I say. When we were kids. Our moms knew each other.

And the last elevator cable snaps and my heart drops about a thousand floors.

But I have to hurry to catch up with Felix. Out at the pool there's that song by Blondie coming from a tinny-sounding boom box and a very muscled coach is pacing the deck, calling instructions to a Swimmercise class consisting of three elderly women with flotation belts on their waists, one of whom wears a swimming cap with plastic flowers, her eyeglasses jutting from the tip of her nose.

The Swimmercise coach plays the same eighties hits every Saturday morning. After "Heart of Glass" it will be "Love Is a Battlefield," "Bette Davis Eyes" and "Paradise by the Dashboard Light."

I feel cold on the side of the deck and I have to tell Felix not to run. He wants to run.

Stop running, I say. You're not allowed to run on the deck. You want to get us thrown out of here? Can't you just behave for once?

I'm wondering why Tyrone would kiss me if he has a girlfriend. Was it just because he was stoned? Though Evelyn could still be just a friend, not a girlfriend. Friends go to parties together. But he hasn't texted since that kiss. And Miranda was right. I could have been killed on the motorcycle. Tyrone ran a few red lights on the way home.

I said stop running!

Sorry, Flannery, Felix says.

Why am I always stuck with you? Tell me that, I say. You never listen.

I can see I've hurt his feelings but I don't care.

I'm listening, he says. See, I'm walking.

Look, go play in the baby pool, I say. That's where you belong.

For some reason the song "Heart of Glass" seems to be playing on an endless loop and it's making me feel like my own heart is going to shatter.

Everybody is going to that stupid party. What did Evelyn mean that Amber is not allowed to talk to anyone? I can't believe my chest is hurting so much. My heart is actually hurting. Is that really a thing?

I decide I want to jump off the ten-meter diving board. I can see Felix looking at me from the baby pool while I wait in line for the ladder.

When I get up there I gaze around for a minute and I can see Miranda. The treadmills are on the mezzanine level facing a giant window that looks out over the pool. We are both way above the world, on opposite sides of the pool. The air up here is dry and smells of cedar and the big ceiling lights are pink-tinged.

It's an Olympic-sized pool and there's a whole fiercely flickering artificial blue stretch, with squiggly black lines on the bottom, between my mother and me.

Miranda's wearing a blue Lycra body suit and a red headband and she has a silver weight in each fist. Her chin is tilted up and the weights are close to her chest and she is strutting, jerking one shoulder forward then the other — a very, very fast walk. I know she will keep increasing the speed as the hour goes on until she is running hard.

This is Miranda. Determined to get somewhere, throwing herself into it with all her might, even when there's no hope of getting anywhere at all.

I wish she'd give up on her great work of conceptual art and go back to university for a teaching degree. I'm tired of worrying about money and stealing Internet from somebody who calls himself bubbaspleasurepalace.

I jump and Felix is waiting for me on the side of the pool and he wants to try the Tarzan rope. It's a thick green rope knotted in a couple of places so you can grip it without your hands sliding down.

There's a big lineup but we wait our turn and Felix watches the girl ahead of him climb up on the platform for the Tarzan rope and lower her goggles over her eyes. She turns and gives her dad, who has been waiting with her, a little wave. She grips the rope, leaps off the platform and flies through the air, legs kicking hard.

The rope almost seems to stand still before it begins to swing back and the girl drops into the water with a big splash.

Felix steps up onto the platform. He glances back at me and I can see he's scared.

The girl is swimming out of the way of the rope and she gets to the side of the pool and turns to watch Felix through her green-tinted goggles. A lineup of seven kids has formed behind him.

The lifeguard hands Felix the rope, and everybody is waiting.

Hey, Flannery, the lifeguard says.

It's Kyle Keating.

Oh, hey, Kyle.

I've been reading your mom's parenting blog, he blurts.

What? I say.

Yeah, it's cool, he says. Your mom seems great. Then he says to Felix, No Brussels sprouts for you, right, kid? Felix doesn't seem to hear him. He's staring, transfixed, at the spot on the surface of the pool where he will probably land when he lets go of the rope. He looks like he's about to walk the plank into shark-infested waters.

Listen, Flan, are you going to Amber's party? Kyle asks.

He's wearing a bathing suit and a tank top that says *Staff* on the back in white letters. He seems to have absolutely no problem standing around in public under very bright fluorescent lights nearly naked.

I can feel myself blush. I cross my arms over my chest.

If that kid's not going to go, he should get off the platform, a parent behind me says.

Okay, Flannery, here I go, says Felix. But he just grips the rope tighter and doesn't move.

I see that Kyle Keating has no reason to be ashamed of standing around in public with hardly any clothes on. I try to keep my eyes on his face so it won't look like I've been staring at his body. But his eyes are just as hard to look at. They're *honest* is the word. And he looks *honestly* very happy to be talking to me.

Because I was thinking, Kyle Keating says.

Here I go, yells Felix. He moves his hands on the rope, holding even tighter, but his feet are still stuck to the platform.

Is this kid going to jump or what? says the parent behind us. Now there are about twenty kids waiting in line. I realize I have never seen Felix frightened before. He needs me to say something.

Go, you big baby, I say.

I am going! he shouts.

Well, go then! I say.

Flannery, he says. He says my name in a gentle way, the way he used to say it when he was a really little kid and he'd wake up from a nightmare and beg me to get in with him and he'd fall back into a deep sleep as soon as I did and his little hand would feel around on top of the blankets for me and he'd end up slapping his little palm down all over my face.

He looks back regretfully at the lineup behind him.

Just go, I say. I stamp my foot.

Here I go, then, he says. I almost don't hear him. And then he yells at the very top of his lungs, *Hiiiyaaaaa!*

He runs a few steps and goes flying through the air. He swings far out over the water.

Because I was just wondering if you'd like to go to the party with me, Kyle Keating says. We could go together.

Felix has reached that stretchy moment when the rope seems to go completely still, just before it heads back toward the platform.

Unless you are already going with someone else, Kyle says.

How long does it take, you might well ask, for Kyle Keating and me to realize that the Tarzan rope has swung back and that Felix isn't hanging onto it anymore? Nor has he swum to the side of the pool.

The answer: Actually, it takes quite a long time.

The answer: Too long.

The answer: Not very long at all. Maybe fifteen seconds. Maybe a half a minute.

There is a lot of noise in the pool. Lots of splashing and kicking and the boom box is now playing "Love Is a Battle-field" and the old ladies are swaying their arms over their heads in the Swimmercise class and people are shooting out of the waterslide like human cannonballs.

Okay, maybe it is even a full minute. Maybe longer. Like an eternity? I have been fiddling with my locker key and the pin comes undone and it falls off my bathing-suit strap and drops to the deck of the pool, and Kyle and I both bend for it at the same time and our foreheads bump.

And for some reason Felix doesn't call out for help. He is out there kicking as hard as he can but he keeps going under and swallowing half the pool. He becomes panicked. The little girl with the green goggles is trying to get my attention, yelling at me, Hey, hey, girl!

Kyle Keating and I understand what is going on in the very same moment.

It is the same moment in which a lifeguard whistle tears through the whole building and everybody in the pool turns toward the Tarzan rope. Two lifeguards dive in and the boom box is keening *heartache to heartache* but it shuts off with a clunk and a hush falls.

Simultaneously, I understand why Miranda is always going so fast on the treadmill. She is full of fear. She's afraid of us not having money, she's afraid of the pipes bursting when they cut off the heat, and she's afraid of what will happen if her welfare check doesn't arrive in the next few days because we are low on food again.

She's running as fast as she can, even if she's just running on the spot, because that's all she can do, and she isn't about to sit around and do nothing.

And what happens is all that running bursts her out of the normal space-time continuum and before I know it she is at the poolside, just as I notice that Felix is in trouble out there.

Of course Miranda doesn't really break through the space-time continuum. What really happens is that she sees from her perch on the treadmill that her baby boy is going to try the Tarzan rope and she knows he isn't a strong enough swimmer to get to the side of the pool and she has been banging on the big glass window with her hand while I've been talking to Kyle Keating. When I don't glance up she runs down the stairs, vaults over the concrete deck and jumps into the pool at the exact same moment that Felix starts to sink for real.

So in that moment, yeah — I understand the extent of Miranda's fear, though she tries with all her might to keep it hidden. Miranda is afraid of whether or not there will be enough nutrition in our diets, and she's afraid she's going to accidentally kill Spiky and/or Smooth and that I'll never speak to her again, and she's afraid that her art isn't any damn good at all, because she really believes in that stuff, and it means a lot to her, and she's sacrificing a lot to keep making art, but she's thinking maybe she doesn't have the right to sacrifice so much when she is a mother with two kids to feed.

She's afraid that Felix and I will be made to feel ashamed because we don't have much money and it will affect the way we think about ourselves and the way others think about us. She's afraid people will be prejudiced against us, and she's afraid for our hearts, that we'll end up hurt. She's afraid I'll get killed in a freak motorcycle accident. And she's afraid she'll be alone and nobody will fall in love with her because she has two kids to take care of and can't take off to Hawaii on a whim, and the truth is I am very much afraid for her too.

She leaps into the pool in her blue Lycra suit and running shoes with the neon orange stripes and somehow swims down to grab the arm of her thrashing son.

Her baby.

Lifeguards take over and get Felix onto the pool deck. He is spewing pool water and crying and very weak.

I think of those hours when I used to play with him, making up stories, acting them out as we went along. *Troll, bring me some wood for the fire. Yes, Master! Not that wood, you stupid troll, the golden boughs! Yes, Master, right away, Master. And, Troll? Yes, Master? Tonight we will visit the lair of the silver dragon and steal the magic fang. Oh goody, Master!*

It's funny how you can know a person your whole life and

forget certain key important points about who they really are. For instance, in that moment, when I witness Miranda's fiercely blue Lycra-swathed body flying through the air like a flame from a blowtorch, I completely forget something about her that I have always known.

Miranda can't swim.

It takes everyone a minute to realize that Miranda is also drowning and then the lifeguards, including Kyle, leap in. Kyle gets to Miranda first and, in flailing around, she punches him in the face, giving him a black eye — totally by accident, she later insists.

And right about now you may be wondering what I've been doing throughout all this.

I don't move. It's as though I'm not there.

Afterwards, when we get home, Miranda promises Felix she will never, ever, ever leave him alone in the pool with me again and that yes, he can go to the men's change room next week, and that yes, she will read to him before bed tonight. She will read to him all night long if he wants, until dawn breaks and she will love him forever.

And she says that if I had been paying attention as she expected me to, none of this would have happened, and she would probably love me forever too. But taking into account my recent behavior, she's considering a little vacation from the hard work of loving me, she says. She says she will have to think about a punishment.

Your brother might have died, she says. She smacks the metal spoon against the casserole dish and touches the corner of her eye with her wrist, trying to make sure her tears don't smudge her mascara. And when she puts my plate of macaroni in front of me, the dish clatters on the table. It all seems to me to be punishment enough.

I creep into bed with Felix in the middle of the night so I can hold him. I'm holding him very tightly, because I realize how close I just came to losing him.

I'm still awake when Felix's door creaks open and Miranda comes in and gets in bed behind me, three of us in Felix's single bed with the dip in the middle of the mattress and a spring poking through.

The lit-up red S on the Scotiabank building downtown shines through the window and the trees thrash in the wind and I can hear the ice on their branches clinking.

Miranda whispers that if they do cut off the heat we might do some winter camping and she would get a very good parenting blog out of it.

I don't want to winter-camp. Miranda puts her arm around both of us. I am very squished.

Flannery, there's something I have to tell you, she says.

You have to tell me something *now*? I ask. I don't like it when Miranda *has* to tell me things. There goes my heart again, like a school of tiny fish scattering every which way in the deep dark fathoms of the North Atlantic when a shark zips past.

Do they have sharks this far north? Anyway, my heart is beating.

Miranda presses her forehead against the back of my head and pauses. Then she sits up on the edge of the bed with her back to me, her fists pressed into the mattress.

She speaks in a long single breath.

Hank and his wife have split up and he's back in town for the Christmas holidays and he's asked me out, she says.

You saw him?

Ran into him by accident.

Did you tell him? I ask.

Tell him what?

You *know* what, Miranda. Did you tell him about Felix? Did you tell Hank he has a son?

I will, she says.

And as I am drifting off to sleep another faraway but some might say pertinent thought occurs to me.

Kyle Keating asked me out on a date.

And I didn't even have to use a potion.

27

———

They'd been drinking martinis, which Miranda had never tried before.

They said you had to toss them back, Miranda says.

She speaks from her bed with her eyes squeezed shut and the back of her hand pressed to her forehead.

Orange juice, she whispers.

Orange juice? I whisper back.

Shhhhh, she says. I mix her some orange crystals. It's all we have.

Get this thing off me, she says. I take off the tiara and lay it on the red velvet pillow on her bureau where she keeps it.

I go to open the curtain and she yells, Not the light! She asks me to get her the little hand mirror on the dresser. She lifts it to her eyes, very close. First one eye, then the other. She touches the non-existent wrinkles in the corners of her eyes.

I'm old, she sobs. She slams the mirror face down on the bed.

What are you talking about, Miranda? I say.

This guy, Hank's new friend, the guy who's a plastic surgeon . . . he said I need work, she moans. She picks up the mirror again and pulls her skin near her temples very tight so she can hardly open her eyes. The hand mirror falls against her nose. She's faking a smile, but she's puffed her lips out for the bee-sting look.

Do I look younger now? she asks.

At four this morning I heard several sharp bangs on the front door. Naturally, I thought we'd been invaded by aliens and they'd probably take Felix away, and I was just wondering if there was anything I should pack for him. Would he use his toothbrush in another galaxy? It was hard enough to get him to use it in this one.

It was either aliens or Miranda had forgotten her key.

I pulled on my housecoat and went running down the stairs. The hallway was awash in red and blue light and there were a few whoops of a police siren.

This gave me a bit of a fright.

There was a police officer at the door and then I thought Miranda was dead and I would have to raise Felix by myself. She had died without cleaning the bathroom as she had promised or paying this month's rent.

But she was not dead.

She was on her knees in the snow bank, and an officer had her by the elbow, trying to get her up the front steps.

Your father home? the officer asked. I did not bother to explain about my father and/or lack thereof to the police officer. He tried to look behind me.

We found your mother on the corner of Prescott and Duckworth Street directing traffic with a salad fork, the police officer says.

I was not directing traffic, Miranda yells. I was conducting the Aeolian harp.

(Miranda believes that there are rocks on Signal Hill that make a natural harp. When the wind blows through a crack in the rocks, and when it's coming from the northeast, you can hear a gentle moaning that sounds like a woman's voice. Miranda claims when you hear it good things will happen. It's an omen, but a happy one. It means fortune, true love and creativity.)

I guessed that maybe helping me write the incantations for the love-potion labels had given her a taste for the occult.

Miranda grabbed the doorframe with both hands, shaking the cop off her elbow.

She eyed the staircase like it was a writhing serpent she was going to have to tame. Then she flung herself forward and landed face down on the stairs. She began to climb the steps on her hands and knees. Her tiara fell off and rolled on its side down a few steps and she caught it with her foot and jammed it back on her head.

That's her thinking cap, I said to the cop.

So, no dad? the cop asked. Just you?

And me, Felix said. He had just shown up at the top of the stairs in his Batman pajamas, his hair mussed to one side. He was clinging to the newel post.

And my little brother, I confirm.

Is he armed and dangerous? the cop asked. I glanced back at Felix.

That's just a Super Soaker. I don't think it's loaded.

One thing that's not loaded, the cop said. Better get her to drink some water. She talked about you in the car. Kept saying something about a magic potion? Said she's really proud of you?

After the cop left I got Miranda a glass of water but she was already snoring. Felix was asleep again, his arms and legs wrapped around his water gun which I gently pried from his grip.

As I was falling asleep I heard the engine of a motorcycle ripping up Long's Hill. Tyrone? That would mean that the Snow Queen finally had her other nostril.

Who knew what would happen, now that she could breathe properly.

I let the morning light in despite Miranda's protests. She is going to have to wake up. She has a blog post to write about when to tell your kids there is no Santa. Because, unfortunately, there is no Santa. And there won't be any presents for Felix if she doesn't find a way to "monetize" that website of hers soon.

I sit down on the edge of Miranda's bed and pry the hand mirror out of her grip.

So, how was the date? I ask. I mean, before the martinis kicked in. How was ol' Hank now that he's divorced the surfing lawyer? Did he recognize the error of his ways? Was he down on bended knee begging forgiveness?

Hank, my mother spat. Oh, Flan, they were awful. Hank was awful. His friends were awful. All they talked about was money. I mean *all* they talked about was money. It was all they talked about. There was that plastic surgeon, two doctors, a dentist, two lawyers, and the wives. Some of whom were CEOs of this or that.

So, you mean conceptual art didn't come up?

They talked about real estate. They talked about flipping houses like they were pancakes. Flipping houses and mega-barbecues and lawnmowers you sit on. What has happened to Hank? Oh, and get this. They don't call him Hank. They call him *Henry*. Before we went into the restaurant he actually warned me, "By the way, I'm Henry now." I still didn't even know who they were talking about for the first half of the evening. Apparently he's going to be making a fortune, had offers from three firms in town. He wanted me to know how successful he'd become.

But after the restaurant? Did you and Hank talk?

Did we talk? *Henry* and I did not talk, Flannery. I found a back door to the restaurant and wandered out into an alley. I had to escape. I was so drunk I could barely see. I mean, it seemed like there were three roads instead of one. Every person who passed me in the street was staggering all over the sidewalk, and they had three heads. It was alarming. Thank God I heard the Aeolian harp. It sang me home.

Actually, a police officer brought you home, Miranda, I say.

Really? says Miranda. She sits up on one elbow, and gives her long curly hair a toss.

Was he cute?

A few days later I'm in the school library after classes and I happen upon a computer screen that someone's left open and I do a double take. I see it's Miranda's blog. I want to throw my coat over the monitor until I can get the page shut down.

Someone is reading Miranda's blog? I look over my shoulder and then I slide into the chair and start reading. I haven't really been paying much attention to Miranda's blog lately.

When I'm done I'm flushed with rage.

Magnificent Mothering with Miranda

A sixteen-year-old girl with a broken heart is reckless. Those of you who have daughters in love, listen up! How vulnerable our young women are, with their too-long limbs, their new curvy bodies, and their too-big hearts.

Don't let those tulip-tender faces and those beautiful hazel-green eyes so full of trust fool you into thinking they are gentle girls. Our daughters feel desire as big as the universe and they are willing to do what it takes to get what they want.

They are changelings now, and they are growing away from us and they have to do that. They must.

They have to rebel and they have to love and they will probably get on the backs of motorcycles and smoke pot and drink too much and generally put themselves in danger, just as we did when we were sixteen, just as some of us are still doing, and we have to be vigilant and we have to watch out and we have to know what's going on and we have to hold our daughters close. But we also have to let them make mistakes. We have to let them put their hearts of glass out there on the sidewalk. Little glass hearts just waiting to be smashed. We have to trust that they will be okay. They are out there making magic, every single day, and they will find love.

28

I fling the front door open and I am about to yell my head off at Miranda.

Hazel-green eyes? Motorcycle rides? Making magic?

That is so obviously me, and it's up there for everybody to see. It's up there in cyberspace forever. I plan to go straight to the basement to get the ice pick and slam it right through the computer. I'll show her *tulip-tender*! What does that even mean?

But then I smell chocolate. Miranda is in the kitchen stirring something on the stove. I can tell, even from the front porch, that Miranda is in a very happy mood. She's got the Canadian opera singer Measha Brueggergosman playing on the iPod and she's lip-syncing, half-dancing while she stirs, jabbing the mixing spoon in the air to punctuate the beat, then leading the invisible orchestra, splattering melted chocolate all over the windowpanes.

I drop my schoolbag on top of the shoes and that's when I see the gold spray-painted army boots.

Tyrone O'Rourke is in the kitchen. What is Tyrone O'Rourke doing in my kitchen?

Guess who's here? trills Miranda. She thinks I will be happy.

I am not happy. I am stunned that he would dare to show up here.

Okay, let me back up a bit.

Yesterday I ran into Tyrone O'Rourke with Dave McGrath and Sebastian Rowe and Jordan Murphy in the mall. They were giggling and their eyes were very bloodshot and they were loping through the aisle of mirrors at Sears, gently banging into each other and finding this extremely funny.

All I could think about was Tyrone kissing me. I felt my face getting red. Seeing him coming up the aisle I could feel that kiss again, almost as if it was really happening right there amid the small appliances and ironing boards and the mirror aisle of Sears in the Avalon Mall.

Hey, said Tyrone, and he patted my back. How are you, Flannery?

I was terrified he was going to mention the kissing. Or not mention it. Or do it again. Did the kissing mean anything? Had he just kissed me out of pity, or curiosity, or mockery? Or did he understand now that our fates were intertwined for life?

All of this passed through my brain in a matter of milliseconds. Okay, we bumped into each other by accident. But there he was. And there I was! And we had kissed. By a waterfall. And he had shown me a very personal piece of art. A piece of art he had not revealed to anyone else in the whole world.

I was holding a bottle of floor cleaner. It was neon lemon, the kind with the picture of the bald guy who has an earring. It suddenly seemed like the floor cleaner was the strangest object in the world and unbearably heavy. How had it got into my hand?

I remembered what it was like when Felix was three, and I used to piggyback him. When he finally got down off my back, I would feel as though I was going to float to the ceiling. Standing in the aisle with Tyrone and his friends, I felt hot and floaty.

I thought about Tyrone's lips and how he'd tasted like the dope he had been smoking and there had been the smell of fresh falling snow. The tip of his tongue touching mine.

I was suddenly overcome with the idea that if I spoke I would tell Tyrone O'Rourke that I was in love with him.

I wanted to say absolutely anything at all that wasn't *I love you Tyrone O'Rourke*. I wanted to say, Can I do your math homework for you? Can I wash your floor with this yellow stuff? Can I help you graffiti all of downtown? Can I shine the chrome on your motorcycle? Can I kiss you again, right here, right now, in front of your goofy ultra-stoned friends?

I opened my mouth but nothing came out.

Tyrone patted me on the back again, several hard little slaps.

Okay, kid, he said. See you in the food court in a little while. We got to check out some music.

Food court, I said. Okay. Food court. Gotcha.

I ordered a plate of fries in the food court and got two little fluted cups of ketchup and sat down with my bag of yellow stuff and that's when I saw Amber and Gary Bowen and the other guys from Gary's band and their girlfriends. They were several tables over. They were laughing and talking and Amber was blowing the paper sheath from her drinking straw up into the air. Gary was trying to steal her fries and she was pretending to keep them away from him.

I know she saw me sitting by myself.

Tyrone came up behind me and slammed his lanky body into the swivel chair next to mine. He let it sway back and forth. Dave and Sebastian dropped into the two other chairs. They go to Gonzaga and I only know them a bit.

I didn't look over to see if Amber was watching, but I could feel her eyes.

Ha! You're not the only one with a boyfriend, Amber Mackey.

This is the life of a girlfriend, I thought. You're at the mall and the boys fill up the seats all around you and you're like one of the guys, except you're something better. You're a girl with all the guys around you.

I was sure everyone in the food court could see how popular I was. Even dipping my French fry in the ketchup was done just so: dip, dip, dip. Every gesture I made, every giggle and sigh, was utterly false. I was acting so that Amber could see how I was totally cool simply enjoying my French fries with the boys.

But suddenly the three boys looked like they had suffered an electric shock. They sat bolt upright and then they jumped up all at once and took off in three different directions, running. I mean, one minute they were there at the table loafing around, joking, laughing, and the next minute they had flown out of their chairs.

They were knocking into people, making them drop their bags. Sebastian actually stumbled over a woman in a wheelchair. Their abandoned swivel chairs swinging left and right with mad whines and squeaks.

Tyrone was galloping down the escalator, weaving through the people who were just standing still on the steps. When he got near the bottom he actually leapt over the rail.

That's when the security guard showed up at the table. He had a moustache and he was as pale as an uncooked cod fillet. His arms were crossed over his chest.

He asked me to come with him. He put his hand on my arm and hoisted me right out of my chair.

Hey!

With his other hand he pressed a button on a radio speaker attached to his shirt and it crackled with replies and two other security guards came running over to my table.

So, three security officers. Big men in blue shirts and black pants with a blue stripe down the legs.

Then it occurred to me. Something must have happened to Miranda. A panic set up in my forehead that felt like a knitting needle through my right eye. It was Miranda or it was Felix. Something terrible must have happened. A car accident, a heart attack.

What's happening? I asked. I wanted to cooperate, I was gathering my things, ready to follow as fast as I could.

You are being arrested for shoplifting, the guard said. And he reached inside the hood of my jacket and took out a package of earphones.

What I felt, before the shame kicked in, was the most acute sense of bewilderment.

Here's what bewilderment feels like. You have gone to the very edge of what is possible, but the edge hasn't stopped you. You keep on going. There's the word "wild" right in the middle of bewilderment, and that's where you're headed. And then you're surprised to find you've gone too far.

I remembered Tyrone patting my back.

That was the end of bewilderment.

Enter shame, stage left. Wow, shame is a hard one. Shame tingles all over and *poof* you go up in flames. The fastest-burning flames there are. Shame incinerates.

They walked me through the food court, a security guard holding each of my elbows, the third one walking behind like I was going to try and make a run for it. The food court is a noisy place but it had gone completely silent. Everybody, maybe a hundred people, looked up from their burgers and didn't say a word.

Except Gary Bowen, who said, quite loudly, See, I told you she was a welfare loser.

Amber didn't even look in my direction. She was the only one in the whole food court not looking at me. She was trying to poke her straw through the cover on her oversized cup of root beer. She had the straw in her fist, and she was stabbing the lid over and over until the straw sank in deep.

The manager's office was somewhere in the basement. I'd never been to that part of the mall. I hadn't even known it existed. We went down two sets of stairs and then a long corridor with fluorescent light and lots of doors, and actually it was scary, going down there with three men I didn't know. It seemed illegal. If I was really a shoplifter of in-ear sound-isolating wireless headphones that went for $115.99, did that mean I was stripped of all human rights and freedoms, or whatever? I was trembling all over.

It was crazy how afraid I felt. After all, it was just the mall. It was just some stupid security guards. The hallway down there was cinderblock, painted glossy white, and there were exposed water pipes, and some wrappers from takeout were spilling out of the flap of a garbage bucket. I couldn't hear the noises of the mall. It felt like we were deep underground.

Finally we came to an office and there was a man behind a desk and I was brought in and told to sit down in a chair. The man was reading a piece of paper that he held up before him. His mouth was hanging open just a little as he read. Very carefully, he placed the piece of paper in a pile to his right. His hair was a springy red afro. He had a gold signet ring on his left hand and one ear was pierced.

He looked up and spoke to one of the security guards, Did you bring those moose steaks?

Yeah, the guard said. They're out in the truck. I'll bring them in on the break.

Thanks, man, the guy behind the desk said. The wife has a crowd coming.

Any time. I got a freezer full of it.

Who's this? the guy behind the desk said.

Monitor Seven, answered the security guard, and then he and the other guards left.

The man behind the desk turned to the computer next to him and typed and then there was a paused video on the screen. He turned the screen so I could see it.

We'll have to wait for the police, he said to me. They're the ones who press the charges. Could take a while. We might as well watch some TV.

He made a phone call. He seemed to be personal friends with the chief of police. Called him Johnny.

Yeah, shoplifter. Girl. I don't know, sixteen? When can you get somebody over here? We can wait. You're welcome.

The man put the tips of his fingers together like they were a church steeple in front of his chest. He made his chair rock and it squeaked. He was obviously comfortable with just sitting there making me scared and *un*comfortable.

Now we wait, he said. Then he pressed the Play button on the computer.

There I was, in black and white, with my bottle of floor cleaner in my hand. There was a spot of glare on the bottle, like a star. The camera was above, so you couldn't see me blushing. It was a strange view. It felt like I was the guardian angel of myself who had forgotten to take care of me.

And then, the handsome Tyrone and his crew. And you

could see, in spite of the angle, how happy I was to see him. The mirror aisle. Round mirrors, mirrors with big gold frames, long skinny mirrors. I was surrounded by mirrors and there was my face all over the place and what a grin. Oh, this girl had it bad.

You could plainly see Tyrone putting the earphones into my hood. You could see everybody, or bits of everybody, from all angles, because of the mirrors — and you could see us all, very clearly, from above.

And you could also see I had no idea that Tyrone had put the earphones in my hood.

The boys all turned to walk away, and when they had their backs to me, I did this stupid little wave. Wiggling my fingers. I wave goodbye even though they can't see me.

This girl, standing in the aisle of Sears with a bottle of floor cleaner, was the biggest idiot I had ever seen. No wonder nobody was in love with her.

The man stopped the video and rewound it. We watched it again. Tyrone patting my back as though assuring me all was well.

And then the manager picked up a snow globe on his desk and shook it.

This thing plays music, he said. He twisted a little key at the bottom of the snow globe and set it down on the desk. It took me a minute to recognize the Christmas carol "Jingle Bell Rock" because it was slowed down and sounded like a funeral dirge.

The two Christmas elves in the center of the snow globe had linked arms and were surely supposed to be dancing a jig. But they turned around very, very slowly in the whirling snow.

It looked like they couldn't let each other go. They could have been me and Miranda. Both of us unlucky in love, stuck to each other forever.

Care to tell me the names of your friends, young lady?

I said, It seems I don't have any friends. And I knew that that was the truth.

Those guys, he said. He moved his chair toward the computer and tapped a key and the video played again. He stopped it on my grin. He shook his head.

You're free to go, he said. I hope you have a Merry Christmas.

I've got homework, I tell Miranda.

Don't you want to have a cup of tea with Tyrone? Miranda says.

No thanks, I say.

I'm here to work on the Entrepreneurship project, Tyrone calls out from the kitchen. Isn't that due around now?

It's *done*, Tyrone, I say. I am bending down to untie my boots. I am trying not to cry and I take off up the stairs and close my bedroom door and get in bed and pull up all the covers. It's so cold I can see my breath. I can hear the oven door screech.

After a while there's a knock.

I'm coming in, says Tyrone. I leap out of the bed and jump into the chair at my desk and the door opens and I already have a pen in my hand, as if I've been writing away.

I've got homework here, Tyrone, I say.

I'm sorry, he says. About the earphones. I just couldn't risk getting caught myself, Flannery, because of my graffiti art. They'd have me then, on all those charges. I knew you wouldn't be charged. I'm really sorry.

I get up out of the chair and walk over to where he's standing in the doorway so I'm standing very close to him. I've got one hand on the doorframe and the other on my hip. I'm not raising my voice. I'm saying it as plainly as I can. I don't even know what I'm saying. I'm just talking. I'm trying to explain.

Headphones, Tyrone? Headphones? Are you kidding me?

Honestly, I didn't think they'd catch you, he says.

You and me, we know each other, Tyrone, I say. We have known each other since forever. And I actually thought this was love. And when you kissed me at the waterfall, I know this is silly, but I thought it meant something. I thought, Later, Tyrone and I will make love. We will be lovers.

Jesus, says Tyrone, and he rubs his forehead as if he can't believe what he's hearing.

Flannery, he says.

And I thought, Later we'll be lovers and later we'll eat French fries in the food court. And later we'll get an apartment. And later we'll watch movies with a bowl of popcorn. And later we'll backpack across India. And later we'll have kids. And later we'll make enough money to take care of our mothers. And nothing else matters because this is friendship, this is love, this is so big and you kissed me in front of that painting of your mother, Tyrone. That beautiful painting that you hadn't shown anybody else. I thought that was significant. I thought *I* was significant. And I've loved you since we were kids. Since we were babies.

I feel like I'm on fire here, truly inspired. For the first time in perhaps a very long time — maybe ever — every single word coming out of my mouth is exactly right. I'm giving it to him, basically.

I don't believe that some people should have more than others in this world, Tyrone. More things, more *material possessions.* That's what Miranda has tried to teach me, if she has tried to teach me anything. But the truth is, I have never stolen anything in my life.

I keep going.

Everybody has a right to food and shelter and education, and a few other things that I can't remember right now. Oh, yeah, friendship, love, respect, the chance to express themselves, be creative. But mostly love.

And I know you've had a hard time with Marty. I know how cruel he is. I've seen it. I know social services has been checking up, and they're worried about you in school. The teachers are worried. I know you've been sleeping on people's couches.

And I know I've had it easier than you. Okay? Miranda has provided love and respect for me and Felix, without dint.

Do you know the word *dint*, Tyrone?

It's a word that means a blow or mark or a hollow. You're supposed to love people without dint. That's what love means, basically. You love no matter what.

Sitting there in that security office, Tyrone, watching the image on the security monitor of you putting those earphones in my hood? I felt a dint. A big old dint right in my chest. You and I, we don't love each other. We aren't even friends.

We watched that videotape, the manager and me, in his cold office and then he paused it with your hand resting on my back. That was a pretty bad moment, Tyrone, and — no matter how bad things are for you, no matter how scared you are for your mother. Or yourself. You shouldn't have done that, okay? You really hurt me.

Now, I'd like you to leave. I don't care if I never see you again.

I close my bedroom door in his face. After I hear the front door close behind him I think about having a little chat with Miranda about a certain blog post. Maybe bring up a few issues — like that privacy might just be a human right. That she must never refer to personal-to-me identifying physical characteristics again, like the color of my eyes, for example. And she must never, ever use the phrase "tulip-tender" again. That is just bad writing!

29

Chad kicks down the footstool of the old recliner and the back snaps up and catapults him out of the chair. He strides across the room like a man full of purpose and grabs the super-sized bag of chips sitting on the dining-room table. He wrenches it open with both fists. A volcano of chips erupts into a stainless-steel bowl. He crumples the bag into a ball and tosses it into a Nerf net above the dining-room door.

There's a tub of dill pickle dip with a fierce orange sticker on top that says *Special* and another sticker that says *Reduced* and another that says *Maintain a Safe Distance of Five Metres* and another that shows a skull and crossbones, the internationally recognized sign for poison.

I have come to Amber's music video wrap party too early. I'm supposed to meet Kyle Keating here and he hasn't arrived yet. This is supposed to be our first date, but I think he's stood me up.

Here is the awful truth. I was the first to arrive at the party. I am the one and only guest.

It turns out Jordan and Devon are living here, since Chad's parents left to preach Christianity in China. They left Chad to fend for himself with a freezer full of frozen three-cheese, gluten-free pizzas.

Devon was kicked out of his parents' house because he refused to go to school. He has been smoking so much weed he's never not stoned and he's permanently fried, like forever, and he's failed everything and now he lives on Chad's sofa. In fact, they are waiting for someone to arrive with weed, because they're out.

There are crushed pop cans all over the living room and crumpled chip bags and dishes with dried ketchup swirls piled on every surface. There's a large pot with the orange remains of Kraft Dinner hardened to the sides, and four spoons. There's a pile of laundry on one side of the couch.

But there are also three very big flat-screen TVs stationed around the room. There's a bedsheet tacked to the wall so they can project the music video on four different screens at once.

This is to be the unveiling of Gary Bowen's great work of art, the project that will be screened at the Young Entrepreneurs' Exhibition and that Mr. Payne — who has had a sneak preview — says might just be the highlight. I've heard it's already available on iTunes.

But tonight is to be the big unveiling for the rest of us.

Once and for all, we will understand Gary Bowen's genius.

Here's what I think it was like before I arrived at the party. Chad and Jordan and Devon were being normal guys. They were talking normal guy talk and maybe farting. Or talking about farting or talking about breasts, but calling them tits, or they were talking about drinking or ollies they have skated, or who has a great half-pipe in their basement, funny things that happened when they were smoking weed, and famous skaters. And they were also in the middle of a chicken nugget fight. There are nuggets all over the floor.

But now they're all uncomfortable because I've showed up for a party, and the party isn't much of a party.

Nice streamer, I blurt. Someone must have thrown a streamer from one corner of the room and through the chandelier, at which point it plummeted to the floor and rolled over to the opposite corner.

The boys understand that I have opened up the streamer situation as a small-talk opportunity. They struggle to say something about the streamer.

Devon abruptly leaves the room and heads down to the basement. He can't take it anymore.

There are loud noises coming from down in the basement. Things are crashing, bouncing, tumbling.

I have known Chad and Jordan and Devon since I was at Happy Kids. We all sat on the story carpet and sang "Itsy Bitsy Spider" together, doing the little finger dance. Chad got in trouble for kicking over my Lego castle and had to have a time-out. I think that time-out may never have ended. I don't think he's had any time-in ever since.

At Happy Kids we learned about our inside voices and when we were scared or sad or lonely we sometimes used our inside voices even when we were outside. Sometimes we used our outside voices when we were inside if we were angry or when we hit each other or when things were so funny our sides hurt from laughing.

We all slept on the yoga mats for naptime and sang "Baby Beluga" and "Skinnamarink" together.

What I'm saying is, I've known these guys my whole life, day in, day out, since the beginning of existence.

But right now these guys are total strangers.

People have been texting about this party for weeks. It was on everybody's Facebook. Where the hell is Amber? Isn't this her big moment? The great reveal of the fantastic Gary's music video?

You went with pink, I say. Chad and Jordan stop what they're doing and look up at the streamer.

Girls are coming, says Chad. He sounds defensive and forlorn. As though he knows nothing about the kinds of things girls require for happiness, but has felt an obligation to learn. He has come up with this. A pink streamer.

Nice, I say. Devon comes stamping up from the basement with a giant disco ball resting in the crook of his neck, one arm curved under it. Devon looks like Atlas carrying his own private planet on his shoulder.

Jordan grabs a ladder from behind the dining-room door and Devon climbs up to the chandelier and attaches the disco ball and fiddles with some wires.

Hit the lights, Devon commands. And I do.

For a minute we are in complete darkness. Then the disco ball starts turning. We are covered in bright ovals of light. A circle moves over Chad's eyes and cheeks, over Devon's brown skin, over my face and body and hair, slipping off onto the walls behind us. We are covered in spots that swirl all over.

The swirling circles of light make us instantly happy.

Music! I shout.

Music, Jordan says, slapping his forehead with the flat of his hand. I knew I forgot something!

He puts on Bob Marley.

Wait until you see the fog machine, Devon says. He switches on some colored footlights — red, green, orange, blue — and a box in the corner of the room belches a thick fog that crawls along the floor, changing color as it winds in front of the footlights. Soon it's up to our knees.

The doorbell rings and maybe twenty-five people come in all at once. Some of them are from Heart, but some are from Gonzaga and Booth, and some of them I don't even know.

They take off their boots in the porch and they rush into the living room and change the music — Snoop Dogg — and they have beer. One of them has a forty-ouncer of vodka and they are passing it around, putting it on their heads. I'm pressed into the corner talking to Brittany Bishop about glitter nail polish — apparently she has a whole collection — and another thirty or forty people burst into the room.

Suddenly there seem to be more than a hundred people jammed into the dining room alone. The kitchen, the living room — every room seems to have people in it. The staircase.

The smell of pot mixes with the chemical smell of the dry ice from the fog machine. There's a strobe light and a black light in the living room and everything is juddering and teeth and white clothes are lit like they've been washed in radioactive milk.

The doorbell is ringing continuously now, and people are still coming into the house. In the dining room they are pressed shoulder to shoulder, dancing on the spot, just jumping up and down to the beat, pogoing, crashing into each other. The music is very loud and now it's techno and somebody shouts that there's a fire in the kitchen.

We hear there was a dish towel on fire and then people are coming out of the kitchen covered in fire-extinguisher foam.

Somebody else has a can of crazy string and people have squiggles of neon string in their hair and all over their clothes.

Even though it's minus ten outside, it's sweltering in the house and the windows are open and people are spilling out onto the deck on the second floor, dancing out there under the stars.

Then I see the guy who owns the Sunbird, and Mercy Hanrahan is with him.

She doesn't notice me. She's busy taking twenty-dollar bills from people and handing out little packages of coke and pills. The guy is just standing there with his big arms crossed over his chest, casting his glance around the room while she collects the money, and then they leave together.

Brittany Bishop says you can do coke in the upstairs bathroom. There's lots of it. People are lined up.

Forget trying to get in there to pee, Brittany shouts.

Chad has been shaking a beer with his thumb over the mouth of the bottle and he lets it spray out all over Jordan who is necking with a girl and they don't even notice.

Then a bunch of people tip over the crystal cabinet with all of Chad's mother's crystal wine glasses and fancy china and it smashes and the cabinet is lying face down and people are dancing on the back of it.

I see the shock on Chad's face. He's very drunk and he's holding a bottle of Captain Morgan by his side and he's weaving and he's turned into a kid again, looking sort of scared.

I can remember him in the Halloween parade at Bishop Feild dressed as the Lone Ranger, all in white with white vinyl chaps and a cowboy hat that kept falling over his eyes. Chad always got ten out of ten on his spelling and was obsessed with snowy owls. Even his backpack had a snowy owl on it.

He lifts the bottle of rum to his mouth and guzzles it.

The whole house seems to be throbbing, and then there is Amber standing on the living-room table. She kicks the bowl of chips off the table and it flies out into the crowd like a mini flying saucer with a serious malfunction. She has a microphone and she is outrageously drunk.

Amber has been transformed. She must have put on black eyeliner and she must have been crying because there are black patches under her eyes. She's wearing very red lipstick and a leopard-skin fun-fur skirt and high boots that go all the way up, almost to the top of her legs. The boots have very high heels.

She's weaving like crazy up there. She could definitely break her ankle. The fog is crawling up the table legs and slithering toward her feet. I can't help but think of her at the Bursting Boils concert — what? Two months ago? When she was still a serious swimmer. When she was still my friend.

Brittany Bishop shouts in my ear, Amber's on something pretty bad.

Everybody, I give you the extremely talented Gary Bowen, Amber slurs into the mike. The microphone is too loud and people cover their ears because it hurts. There's feedback and static and a slicing noise that could puncture every eardrum in the room.

Oops, says Amber. Then Amber throws her arm out toward the bedsheet behind her. Everybody turns toward the bedsheet. For a brief moment, everybody is quiet. Someone has turned off the other music.

And then the screen comes alive with Gary Bowen's music video. Though it kills me to admit this, the video is fantastic. The music is propulsive and nostalgic and sweet and sexy. There are horns and somebody playing a saw and even a glockenspiel.

There's a field at night with fireworks and a white limo bumping through the ruts on a dirt road, and then a shot of a hill. Just an empty hill with yellow grass rippling in the wind and then maybe twenty people on stilts cresting the hill.

The stilts must have been Amber's idea, from when Hank taught us how to walk on them.

Over there, Brittany says, tugging my shirtsleeve and pointing. She makes me tear my eyes away from the video. It's the guys from Gary Bowen's basketball team. They've all worn their jerseys to the party. They aren't looking at the video. They're all looking at their phones at the same time. They're all standing still, their faces lit by the blue light of their phones, and their heads are bent as if in prayer.

Brittany pushes herself off the wall and heads over in their direction. She jabs her way through the crowd. Everyone has started dancing and Amber is still up on the table, dancing by herself and wobbling dangerously close to the edge while the video plays and she's sort of singing along. Her shadow is blocking the video and it's playing all over her face and arms and white lace blouse.

I see Gary, then, and he is trying to get to Amber because he's furious. The video is running through a second time and nobody seems to be watching it anymore. Somebody switches the music then, right in the middle of the projection, and everybody starts dancing to Kanye West. Gary is screaming his lungs out at Amber to get down.

Get off the table, you fat cow, he shouts.

But Amber is still singing Gary's song into the microphone with her eyes shut. She's off-key and screechy.

Tyrone and the girl from the Aquarena, Evelyn, come into the room then. Tyrone is trying to make his way toward me. Evelyn follows. They are holding hands. Tyrone is dragging her through the crowd. Brittany is talking to one of the guys on the basketball team. No, she's screaming at him.

I see Brittany grab the guy's phone and she's heading back over to me. Brittany gets to me before Tyrone and shows me the picture on the phone.

It's Amber, completely naked. Brittany scrolls up to show the texts.

Pretty hot, right? Now you guys send pictures of your bitches!

Gary has sent Amber's picture to the whole basketball team.

And that's when I notice Gary shouldering his way toward the projector, grabbing people by their shirt collars and wrenching them out of his path. He's at the computer and the desktop screen is projected onto the bedsheet for an instant, and then there is the naked picture of Amber, the picture on the phone in Brittany's hand larger than life all over the wall behind her for the whole party to see.

All the guys in the room start a whooping noise. They scream for Amber to take it all off, take it all off. She stumbles a little, confused, and her hands are fluttering near her head.

Let's see those tits, bitch, somebody yells.

Amber reels and she's about to fall off the table, but she catches her balance and turns around to see what everyone is pointing at on the screen. The image reaches all the way up the wall and part of her forehead is projected on the ceiling. She turns back to look through the crowd, to look for Gary, and she sees him at the projector.

I said get *off* the table, you fat cow, Gary shouts.

I trusted you, she says into the mike. But her voice sounds small.

Tyrone has finally made it through the crowd. He's grabbing me, saying, Come on, we have to get out of here. The cops are coming. They'll arrest me if they find me here. Somebody gave them my name about the graffiti. Flannery, come on.

You go, I say.

Come on, he says. I'm afraid you'll get trampled.

I can't leave Amber, I shout. For a second Tyrone stands absolutely still, looking up at Amber and the projection. He looks back at the doorway. And then he starts fighting his way through the crowd toward Amber.

I'll get her, he shouts over his shoulder.

Amber turns back to look at herself, then starts backing away from the projection. She has covered her mouth with one hand.

And that's when we hear the deck.

It's a high-pitched wrenching. The wood cracking and nails screaming as they're torn from the house and the screams of all the people on the deck. The deck is coming away from the house and for a brief moment it seems to sway on its struts like the whole deck is on walking stilts and it's going to walk all those stoned, drunken, dancing people across the city and over the Southside Hills and far away into the sky and the stars.

Then it crashes through the maple trees tossing forty-three teenagers out of it as it falls.

Cops, someone yells. Cops! We can hear the sirens on the street.

Everyone in the house is rushing toward the back door. People are climbing out all the ground-floor windows.

Amber whirls around to face us again and there is no Amber. Whatever drugs she has taken, or whatever Gary might have slipped in her drink, she isn't Amber anymore. She is searching the crowd for Gary and she sees him.

Fat fucking cow, he's shouting over and over.

Amber suddenly tears her shirt open. Buttons go flying. And she wriggles out of it and whips it around in circles over her head and tosses it.

I'm screaming at her, No, Amber. Get down. Amber, I'm here. I'm here.

Then she rips down one bra strap and then the other and pulls the bra down to her waist so it hangs there. She's just standing there half-naked, not moving, with the picture of her naked on the wall behind her, and she falls face forward onto the floor.

Get her, Brittany says. She'll be trampled. But I am already pushing through the crowd. And that's when I see Kyle Keating. He's moving against the crowd trying to get to Amber too.

Somehow Kyle and Tyrone get to her first. Brittany sweeps the cans and booze bottles off the dining-room table and the boys lay her down on it.

She's out cold. Tyrone takes off his jean jacket and covers her with it.

She's in shock, Kyle says. Get her into the recovery position. We need an ambulance. He's already punching 911 into his phone.

Brittany turns away and has disappeared into the crowd. Then I see the naked picture of Amber come down and I glance at the projector, and Brittany has the computer and she's shoving it into her army surplus bag.

Amber's eyes are rolled back in her head and I can only see white slits. She is clammy.

Wake her up, I keep saying. Wake her up, wake her up. And for a minute her eyes do flutter open and she looks at me. She is looking into my eyes and I have her hand and I'm squeezing her hand.

Flannery, she says. Did you like the video? Isn't it great?

But her eyes roll back in her head again.

Then the ambulance attendants arrive and Kyle tells them her breathing is slow and he tells them her pulse and one of them writes down everything Kyle tells them on a clipboard. Then they load her onto the stretcher.

Kids who have been injured on the deck are also being loaded onto stretchers. I am shaking and crying and Kyle is holding my hand.

Chad has passed out in the corner of the living room. Kyle runs upstairs and comes back with a pillow and a bunch of blankets and we put Chad in the recovery position and go to find our coats. I can't figure out where Tyrone and Evelyn have gone.

There is still a huge pile of boots in the porch. People must have taken off in their stocking feet. My boots are gone, but I borrow another pair that fit. And we step out onto the sidewalk.

It's only two in the morning. There are broken bottles all over the sidewalk. The glass glitters under the streetlight. The snow is falling in tatters. Kyle throws an arm around me, and he walks me home in the snow.

30

_____

It takes me until the next day to find out that Tyrone stayed around to help the people who were hurt when the deck collapsed. And because of that, he got arrested. Someone had posted his picture on Facebook and identified him as the SprayPig and one of the cops who stormed the party recognized him. There were pictures on Instagram of him being cuffed and put in the back of a police cruiser. He was taken straight to the youth corrections facility in Whitbourne.

Tyrone's actual trial won't be scheduled for months. But his lawyer has decided to contest the conditions of his release on bail. They're saying he'll have to live with his mother and Marty. Of course Tyrone refuses.

And so, three days after his arrest, there is a bail hearing.

Everybody piles into the courtroom for the hearing. Miranda is with Tyrone's mother. Pretty much everybody in grade twelve at Holy Heart is here. Even some of the teachers.

The crown prosecutor shows slides of what he calls Tyrone's "vandalism" over the past two years. There are slides of the Snow Queen mural, of course, and even one of the portrait of Tyrone's mother at the waterfall, washing the red dress in the river.

When that image comes up, people in the courthouse fidget in their seats. That painting, even more than the others, shows what an exceptional artist Tyrone is, and everybody can see it's a portrait of his mother. Even the judge comments on Tyrone's draftsmanship. Of course it makes me think about the kiss.

I feel sorry for him up there on the stand, talking about making art. He speaks about Marty too, and how it feels to watch someone punch your mother in the face.

But none of that is an excuse for treating people badly, he says. He looks straight at me when he says it.

I'm very sorry for those people I hurt, he says. I know my behavior has been selfish and wrong. And I'm sorry for it.

I know that I'm not in love with Tyrone anymore. But I'm ready to forgive him. And it feels good when I nod at him from my place in the audience, or whatever you call it when you're watching a person up on the stand in court.

Tyrone's lawyer talks about the history of graffiti art and compares Tyrone to Banksy — whom everybody in the courtroom quickly Googles on their phones. Except Miranda, of course, who already knows all about Banksy and doesn't know how to Google anything on her phone.

The biggest argument in favor of different bail conditions, according to Tyrone's lawyer, is his contentious relationship with his stepfather.

The integrity of Tyrone O'Rourke's living situation has deteriorated over the last several years, his lawyer says. His artwork is a creative response to this crisis, and though it is certainly vandalism and wrong-headed, Mr. O'Rourke is also a talented young man without a previous criminal record.

Tyrone looks at me again when his lawyer says this, possibly thinking of the headphones.

You're welcome — almost, I think.

Nobody is allowed to report on Tyrone's bail hearing or iden-tify him by name because he is still a minor. But that hasn't stopped the media frenzy over the SprayPig's arrest. The story is in the newspaper every day for a week, and it's the topic of three call-in radio shows and two separate segments on *Here and Now*, each showing images of his work. The newspapers have featured full-page photographs of Tyrone's paintings, and he's even had some offers — people wanting to buy his sketches. There's talk he's been contacted by a gallery in Toronto.

The judge decided that Tyrone can live in a government-run short-term housing program for youth at risk, just long enough to get himself sorted out. And just days after his court appearance, his mother has Marty charged with several counts of physical assault. So Marty has moved out too and Miranda says Tyrone's mom is starting to put her life back together — the plan being that Tyrone will eventually move back in with her.

But even though Tyrone's no longer being held in custody, he doesn't show up at the Glacier for the Young Entrepreneurs' Exhibition. I didn't expect him to. He no longer wants credit for the work he didn't do. Miranda says he's going to do grade twelve over again, but this time at an alternative school, the Murphy Centre.

The Glacier has hordes of customers and onlookers pass-ing through the fair. Everybody's parents show up, of course, and lots of teachers from all the different high schools in the city and rumor has it even the minister of finance is milling around somewhere. The duct tape wallets are a big hit. The bicycle tire sandals not so much. People say they pinch the toes. Somebody from Prince of Wales Collegiate had bird-houses that looked like the bars on George Street, and they flew off the shelves.

I'm fast selling out of the new batch of love potion. After the first one hundred bottles sold, I got to work on a fifty-bottle special edition for the fair — *Super Strength Eternal Love.* I know I could have sold even more but Fred the glassblower finally packed up his glass studio and set sail for Europe. These bottles are the last ones.

Just as I'm getting near to the end of my stock, Sensei Larry shows up at my stall and buys one, deciding to try it right there on the spot. He takes a mouthful and tips his head back and gargles, just for a joke. Then he downs the whole bottle and smacks his lips, just as Miranda's coming around the corner with Felix. My brother immediately goes into a very deep karate bow to show his respect for Sensei Larry, and he stays bent down like that for a good minute and a half.

Organic, right? Sensei Larry asks me.

Yup, I say. It's just a gag. But the bottles are pretty.

So, says Sensei Larry to Miranda, There's this thing happening, a medieval banquet at the Sheraton. People are coming from all over Canada, and I don't know if this is your thing, but there are costumes. I'll be going in chainmail. Anyway, you already have the tiara. So I was just wondering if you'd like to come with me. You know, there'll be mead, and a meal of venison and quail.

Well, I'd love to, Larry, Miranda says. Thanks for asking.

Sensei Larry puts the empty potion bottle back on the table and I start to pack up.

Right about then, Ms. Rideout, the Wiccan lawyer, shows up at my table. She has the cutest little baby in a Snugli strapped to her chest.

I'd like to make a purchase, she says. She buys a bottle of *Super Strength Eternal Love* and cracks it open right there and takes a sip.

Just then her baby wakes up and starts screaming. But Ms. Rideout just gazes down lovingly into her baby's eyes.

Well, hello there, cutie, she says. Mommy loves you, yes she does, yes she does.

Mr. Payne comes by to add up my sales so he can calculate my mark.

You've done well, Malone, he says. Especially considering you were working on your own. You're an independent young woman with a good head on your shoulders. I'm giving you an extra five marks for going solo. I just need to sample your product again for quality control before determining your final grade, he says.

Then he notices Ms. Rideout and her baby.

And who have we here? Mr. Payne asks. He tickles the baby under the chin and the baby is so surprised she stops crying.

Then he takes a bottle of potion up from the table and as he's chatting distractedly with Ms. Rideout he raises the bottle almost to his lips, but I grab it out of his hand.

I wouldn't do that if I were you, I say.

Thankfully he doesn't really notice because he is being paged over the loudspeaker. It's time for him to announce the winner of the Young Entrepreneurs' Award for Excellence.

And of course it goes to Elaine Power and Mark Galway, who receive $1,000 to continue their work in environmental activism and communications innovation. Mr. Payne explains, over the loudspeaker, that "although Power and Galway didn't actually manufacture a unit that could actually, ahem, *sell*, which was, after all, the most important requirement of the entrepreneurial units, they were brave and defiant and innovative and working to save our planet."

Also (though he doesn't say this), Mark Galway's grandfather sponsors the award.

I realize that after I wire Fred the money for the potion bottles, I'll still have quite a tidy little sum. I'd love to buy Miranda something spectacular with the earnings. Maybe a beautiful medieval ballgown. It could be her medieval number.

Two weeks later, when Sensei Larry shows up for Miranda's date, the visor on his helmet has frozen shut because it's so cold, and he clinks and clanks with every step. But I can see all the neighbors in their windows watching Miranda head off down the road in the fluffiest evening gown Value Village had to offer, with a knight in shining armor.

Epilogue

Chad and Jordan and Devon did the best they could to clean up Chad's house after the party. They got Chad's uncle to replace the back door, but the deck wasn't repaired until Chad's parents were back from China. Several people broke bones in the accident, but nobody was killed, and the ambulance attendants said that was a miracle.

The naked picture of Amber was all over the Internet and she didn't come back to school in the new year. I heard she was asked to leave the swim team, but that might not be true. It is true that she gave up swimming. Maybe she just decided, when it came right down to it, she didn't want to be a swimmer anymore.

After Christmas she was sent to finish the year at a private school in Toronto.

I went to visit her house once before she left and her dad asked me to wait in the porch (they call it the vestibule) and I stood there a long time while he talked to Amber somewhere upstairs.

He came back down and said she didn't want to see anyone. I could tell Sean was angry with me. Maybe he was angry with everyone. I know now that he and Cindy were in the middle of separating. They'd seen the picture on the Internet, of course, and I think it was too much for them. Since then Cindy has bought a new house on the other side of town.

The winter wore on after all of that, and I pretty much kept my head down.

Now everyone is getting ready for prom and I've been on a committee with Elaine Power and Mark Galway (still crazy about each other) to promote a Green Grad. We raised funds for those who can't afford prom tickets (myself!) and started a prom dress recycling program. In all, forty-two dresses were donated, in all shapes and sizes, most of them worn only once.

Elaine wanted a vegan menu too, but the meat eaters revolted. Nevertheless, I can't help but think that if my father, the stranger who sailed into town on a yacht made of garbage, somehow heard of my existence and, furthermore, somehow heard that I helped pull off Green Grad and found forty-two economically disadvantaged young women beautiful prom dresses for absolutely free, and also provided free tickets to the prom for anyone who needed them, then maybe my father, whoever he is, would be proud of me.

On the day of my last exam, Kyle Keating asks me to the butterfly exhibit at Bowring Park. Elaine Power was telling him about it in the corridor and I was walking by and he asked if I would go with him to check it out.

It hardly qualifies as a date. I just happened to be there when they were talking about it and I said I would go. I had been kind of keeping to myself all term, concentrating on my studies, figuring out about university in the fall.

But I agreed because it was sunny after twelve days of rain and I thought it would be fun to hop on a metro bus and find our way out to Bowring Park. Also, when I walked out the front doors of Holy Heart onto Bonaventure that day, I would be finished with high school forever.

I left my biology textbook at the office, for some kid starting grade twelve next year who might not have enough money to buy one. I decided not to even try to sell it.

Also, I've had a text from Amber. The first one since she left for Toronto six months ago.

She's coming home, and she really wants to get together for a coffee. That was all she said and I texted back, *Sure*, and I added an *xo*. Then she texted, *I am so sorry*.

I know Amber and I will never be the kind of friends we once were. But I can feel myself start to melt. I wrote back that I was looking forward to seeing her.

And that was it for the texts.

Gary Bowen is still making music with his band. The video Amber made has gotten over 300,000 hits on YouTube. And there are rumors of a CD in the works. Some scouts have expressed interest. He has a new girlfriend whom everybody says he's cheating on.

The butterflies.

The air is moist and very warm and green-smelling in the big glass greenhouse in Bowring Park. Kyle opens the glass door and I duck under his arm and step inside. It smells of flowers and earth and algae growing in the rock pools. There's a tinkling fountain in the center of the greenhouse and a few crying, terrified toddlers.

There's one little girl with pale blonde hair the color of a peeled banana, and her cheeks are flushed as if she's just woken from a nap. A butterfly lands on her nose. She screams in terror and tears squeeze out the corners of her eyes and roll down her rosy cheeks.

Butterflies everywhere.

They bat their wings in the soupy air in a slow/fast way, as if they have all the time in the world.

There's a glass case full of chrysalises. Tiny papery-looking sacs, each carefully pinned to a wooden slat.

One papery sac has a hole punched in the bottom. I watch a wing unfold. It's black and white with a strip of fluorescent pink.

It unfolds in the way all unfolding things unfold: pup-tents, origami cranes, inflatable rubber dinghies, the rest of your life. Popping out, unbuckling, flinging itself into being, already knowing what it will become. Unable to stop itself and not knowing but thoughtful about each unfolding pucker and un-dinted, undented, smooth and trembling wing and yes, yes. This is it.

Kyle Keating holds his fist under my nose. There's a brown butterfly on the back of his hand. It's a big butterfly and its brown wings are closed and it has subtle, dull markings. It looks like tree bark.

After a long moment the butterfly on Kyle's hand opens. It's as though it has decided to open. It's had a think. The wings of the dull brown butterfly are iridescent green on the inside.

It is unexpected. I look up into Kyle's eyes, and I see he thinks it's unexpected too.

I would like to say that Kyle Keating gets the idea, during that unexpected moment of awe, to kiss me.

But what happens in that startling moment with the butterfly is something much more inexplicable. You know the phrase "weak in the knees," or "turned to jelly," or "lost control" or "overcome with rapture"?

Never mind those silly phrases. Banish them from your mind.

I will tell you what happens in the moist, sun-beaten heat of the condensation-swathed glass house while we are awed, Kyle Keating and me, in a flickering halo of butterflies. What happens is I stand up on my tiptoes and kiss Kyle Keating right on the mouth.

Some part of me has decided. And there it is. I kiss him.

Acknowledgments

I am deeply indebted to Sheila Barry, Melanie Little, Cindy Ma, Sarah MacLachlan, Laura Meyer and Shelley Tanaka. Everybody at Groundwood and Anansi. Thank you a gazillion times for finding the best editors in the universe. And thank you for everything else that it takes to bring a book into the world, including lots of faith.

Many thanks to my magnificent friends and advisors: Bridget Canning, Eva Crocker, Steve Crocker, Theo Crocker, Holly Hogan, Mary Lewis, Nan Love, Sally Mathews, Larry Mathews, Elizabeth Moore, Lynn Moore, Rachel Moore and Claire Wilkshire. You guys with your eagle eyes and hammering hearts, you are golden.